HOKEE WOLF II

SATANIC RITUALS

CLARK VIEHWEG

Black Rose Writing | Texas

ISBN: 978-1-68433-864-1
PUBLISHED BY BLACK ROSE WRITING
www.blackrosewriting.com

Printed in the United States of America
Suggested Retail Price (SRP) $20.95

Hokee Wolf II: Satanic Rituals is printed in Garamond Pro

*As a planet-friendly publisher, Black Rose Writing does its best to eliminate unnecessary waste to reduce paper usage and energy costs, while never compromising the reading experience. As a result, the final word count vs. page count may not meet common expectations.

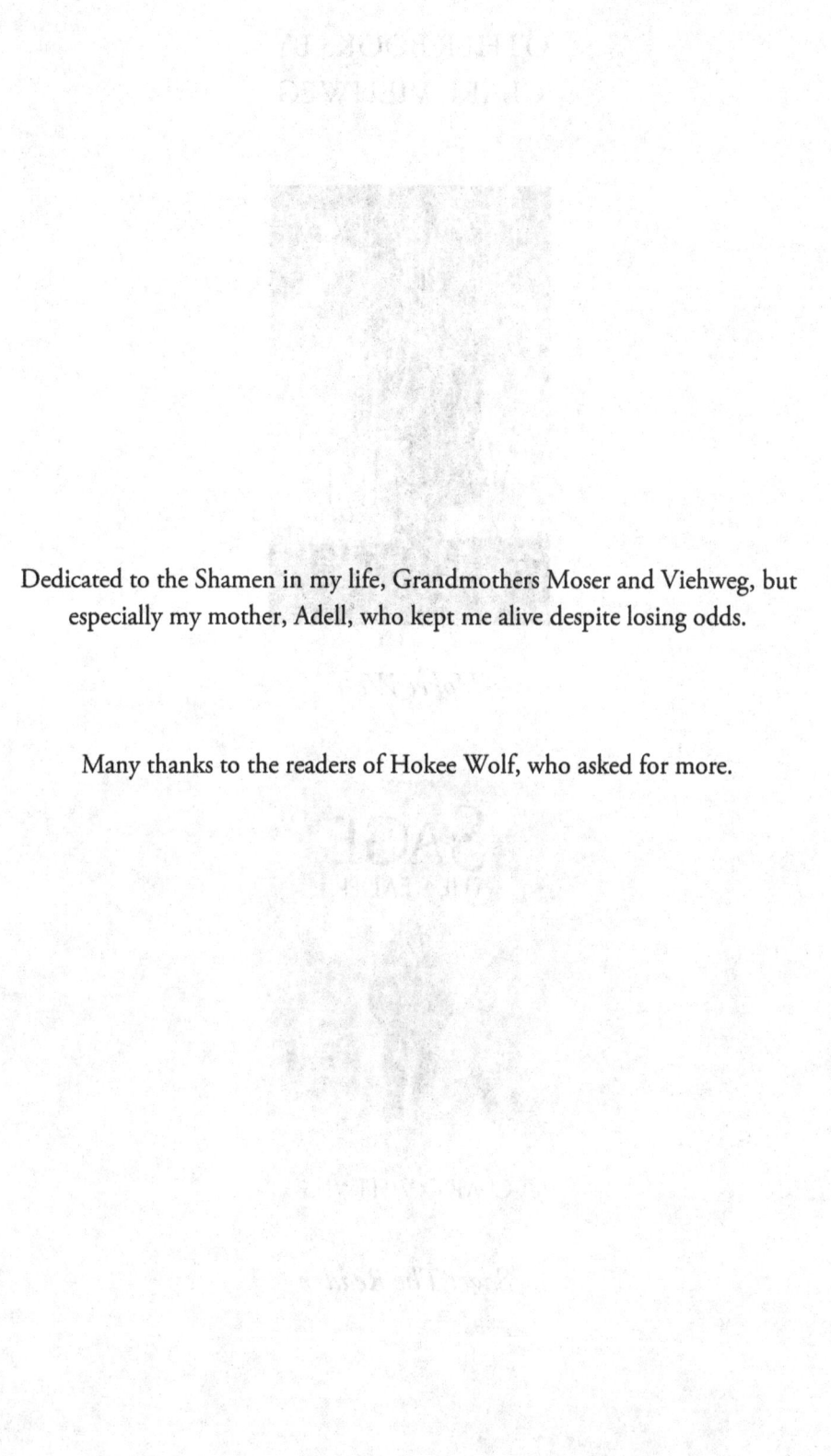

Dedicated to the Shamen in my life, Grandmothers Moser and Viehweg, but especially my mother, Adell, who kept me alive despite losing odds.

Many thanks to the readers of Hokee Wolf, who asked for more.

Hokee Wolf

Sage: The Reader

HOKEE WOLF II
SATANIC RITUALS

PRELUDE

Laura

Laura Taylor's life was about to change in a way she and her parents never expected. A farm girl from Malad, Idaho, with stunning beauty, Laura enrolled as a freshman at Idaho State University in Pocatello, Idaho to study physics. Pocatello is only about sixty miles from Malad, so Laura could easily go home to visit for the holidays.

The school year is fully underway in early October, with the university campus aspens a brilliant yellow in the late afternoon sun. The aspen groves are mixed with tall blue spruce and silver pine, giving the campus a wonderland forest atmosphere. An afternoon sun felt warm on the skin. The warm fall air is what the locals call Indian summer. Laura wore a black tank-top over knee-length white shorts, showing off a perfect body with beautifully sculpted legs.

She meandered down a gentle, leaf-strewn path towards a parking lot below the campus where she had parked her 2005 Honda Civic. Laura had naturally blond hair tied back in a ponytail that swished around a perfectly shaped oval face as she walked. And for the first time, she felt comfortable since entering the university. Being away from home and getting into university life's rhythm had been a challenge, but now, a month later, the student felt at ease. She loved her professors and found the classes interesting. Maybe this university life would not be so bad. Warm sun, beautiful day, spectacular setting, life felt good.

"Look what we have here!"

The voice sounded close behind, kind of guttural in tone, giving the voice a chilling effect. Laura turned to see who did the talking, swishing her blond ponytail as she turned. Two burly young men in their early twenties were wearing Idaho State sweatshirts and blue jeans. Both had long dark hair covered with black ball caps. Even in the shadow of their hats, their eyes glistened with delight. They were only five feet away, with the thrill of conquest coloring their lascivious grins. The men looked and acted like feral dogs who had just found dinner.

Laura noticed that the path she walked on appeared deserted except for the two threatening men. The flight or fight synapses fired in the lizard part of her brain, frightening her into sprinting ahead, hoping to leave the threat behind. The path curved around one of the many stately blue spruce pine trees hugging the trail. Laura rounded the corner and ran straight into the arms of another two grinning young men, looking much like the two she had left behind. They were hunting in a pack. One of the muscle-bound men with red hair quickly grabbed her head, clamping a gigantic hand over her mouth, stifling the screams heard only by the trees. He held his hand over her nose and mouth until she fell unconscious. No one saw the four big men carry the beautiful, young unconscious blond girl through the trees and lay her in the back of a waiting SUV in the parking lot below.

CHAPTER ONE

Hokee Wolf

The modern instrument of torture, the telephone, ruined an otherwise perfect day. Hokee sat drinking a cold Mickey's big mouth for the first time in weeks while sitting in one of his handmade wooden chairs in the shade on his big wide porch. With his long legs stretched on a leather-covered footstool, he was enjoying the day off, hoping to hear from Glory, when his cell phone began ringing inside the house. Unfortunately, he didn't know that Glory was already on her way to pay him a surprise visit.

Cursing himself for forgetting to bring the blasted phone with him when he went outside to watch the sun climb up the side of Caribou Mountain, he hurried inside to catch the phone before it stopped ringing. He made it just in time to catch the call before it disconnected. Disappointment quickly turned into curiosity. It wasn't Glory; his partner turned lover, but Grant Olson, the man whose daughter he saved and who subsequently insisted on paying Hokee a ridiculous sum of money in gratitude. Based in Nampa, Idaho, Olson Construction Company is one of the world's five most prominent builders in the world. They build massive bridges, large dams, municipal airports, and any significant development requiring millions of dollars' worth of equipment and years of experience.

Over the past two years, they lost out on three major projects, each worth over a billion dollars. To bid on these monumental projects, the construction company must spend several million dollars of their own money. In addition, the project evaluation and preparation often take several months or even a year or more, using two or three hundred personnel—everybody from civil engineers, accountants, project managers, plus personnel from dozens of other specialties.

Grant didn't expect to win every job, but to lose out on three major proposals within a short span to the same Egyptian company was mathematically almost impossible. Grant suspected someone in his organization of leaking his bid to the Egyptian company, but he could not identify any suspects. Hence the call to Hokee, his favorite detective.

Although disappointed the caller wasn't Gloria, Hokee was pleased that Grant thought to call him for help and promised to leave for Nampa as soon as he could arrange his personal life. Grant was eager for Hokee to begin his investigation, and Hokee pledged to do his best as always.

Because Olson based his company in Nampa, over 250 miles northwest of Pocatello, Hokee would have to stay on site for several days, possibly a week or more. It was too far away to commute daily, which meant he had to find someone to check on Shilah, his pet wolf. Why-ay-looh (Silver Fox), a Blackfoot shaman and Hokes's mentor, gave him Shilah after Hokee graduated from college and decided to become a detective.

Shila lived with Hokee in Hokee's cave-like house in the middle of a vast open lava rock plain. The wolf has the freedom to roam the lava flats and find his own dinner, which his master sometimes supplemented with rabbits purchased from a local farmer.

There was no way the wolf could accompany Hokee to Nampa and live cooped up in a motel room. While Shila was self-sufficient, he occasionally needed the supplement Hokee kept in an outdoor fridge for his Wolf brother. Shila means brother in Navajo, half of Hokee's mixed bloodline.

Hokee often left Shila, his pet wolf, alone when he went away, but this time he wasn't sure how long it would take to solve Grant's problem. Concerned that he might be absent for an extended period, he called Hilda, his secretary and girl Friday, to see if she would be available to come by his place in a couple of days to check on Shila. Hilda had never been to Hokee's home, and it took a while to give her directions. He hated asking her for the favor, as he knew she carried a crush on him, and he didn't want to give her any reason to hope for something in return. Hokee hired Hilda after some killers hunting Hokee murdered her husband. After confirming her availability, Hokee called Grant back with a promise to leave immediately.

Nampa sits just north of the Snake River Birds of Prey National Conservation area, approximately 250 miles from Pocatello, about a three-hour and thirty-minute drive in Hokee's new black Ford Explorer. In southeastern Idaho, Nampa is south and west of the Bitterroot Mountain Range in a broad valley known as Idaho's banana belt. With moderate snowfall and fertile soil, profitable farming attracted thousands of adventuresome people to move here, turning this part of the state into an industrial juggernaut.

Grant Olson met his wife in high school, and while fooling around, she got pregnant. When a boy got a girl pregnant in America's past, they expected him to marry the girl. After getting the girl pregnant, Grant soon to be a husband and father, never completed his schooling. He worked as a laborer for a cement contractor until the contractor went bankrupt. The bank repossessed all the contractor's cement equipment. With a wife and a new baby boy, Grant needed a job. Grant hobbled on a pair of crutches into the bank with his broken leg in a cast at seventeen years of age, asking to see the manager. His pitch to the bank was simple; you own the equipment, let me have it to see if I can make the payments. If I can make it pay, you get the money for the equipment. The equipment isn't doing the bank any good sitting in a field getting old. If I can't make payments, you get the equipment back.

It was a ballsy, desperate plea for help, especially since he never graduated from high school, but the bank let him have the equipment. Today, Grant is a multibillionaire with over a thousand employees and hundreds of millions of dollar's worth of heavy-duty construction equipment located around the world. He wasn't used to losing, and losing three significant contracts in two years to the same Egyptian contractor rankled. Not only did he not get any of the jobs, but he was out of almost a hundred million dollars, which it cost to prepare the three bids. Something wasn't right, hence the call for Hokee.

CHAPTER TWO

Hassan + The Church

Ahmad Hassan is one of the ten wealthiest men in the world. He is the sole owner of Hassan Construction Limited, which he started in 1970. Given his enormous wealth and influential contacts around the globe, Hassan considers himself a world man. A short man, only five foot eight inches in height, he also has a Napoléon complex, a need to prove himself better than all other men.

Hassan Construction Limited began as a house builder on the Mediterranean Sea coast for Alexandria's wealthy citizens. Ahmad is ruthless in his business dealings, using bribes, extortion, blackmail, and even murder to win contracts and remove competition. Before long, he began building apartment houses, housing tracts, and hospitals. Over time, his company morphed into massive building projects such as airports, extensive canals, and river dams.

Hassan has six wives and several additional concubines. In addition, he supplements his harem every two or three years by adding a new younger woman to his stable. To house his extensive family, Hassan built an elaborate villa on the Nile River bank near Luxor, with enough space to accommodate his ever-growing family. He now has sixteen children, Adio is the oldest, and Chenzira, at three, is the youngest. Out of his ten boys and six girls, Hassan is exceptionally fond of Rashida, a haughty twenty-one-year-old beauty with flashing dark eyes and a figure to drive men wild.

The family is Muslim in name only. Hassan loves the part where he can have all the wives he desires, but he gives lip service to the rest of the doctrine. Such as not requiring his girls to wear the burka.

As his family grew and his sons became adults, Hassan brought them into his construction business, having his boys help prepare bids and manage various projects. He sends all of his children who express a desire to experience the world to Durham University in Durham, England, for their advanced education. Durham University gave Hassan one of his first major building projects, a giant industrial arts complex with five buildings. Since then, he has supported the university with many grants, ensuring access to the school for any of his children wishing to attend.

His favorite child and most beautiful daughter, Rashida, meaning the righteous one, attended Durham, but someone offered her a job ending her formal education early. Intelligent and beautiful, she continued learning on her own with frequent trips back to Luxor to visit with her father.

In October, Muslims celebrate The Prophet's Birthday on the twenty-ninth. Even though the Hassan clan does not adhere strictly to the Muslim teachings, they still honor The Prophet and celebrate his birthday with their neighbors. Rashida is always in attendance, not only to please her father, but to connect with her siblings. Given her international travel schedule and personal desires, it is sometimes difficult to arrange these domestic visits, but she has somehow managed until this year. Unfortunately, recent romantic entanglements surfaced, causing her to cancel this year's visit. Because she has been such a tremendous asset to the Hassan Construction empire, Ahmad let her skip this year's appearance.

*****

Laura felt her body sway as the vehicle she was lying in turned a corner. She opened her eyes only to see the gray carpet under her head before realizing they bound her arms behind her back. Panicked, she struggled to get free, only to find they had also bound her feet. As consciousness returned, so did her memory, and Laura saw all four of the captors' faces in her mind.

"Hey, Zack. Sleeping beauty is awake. Want me to put her back in la-la land."

The voice sounded harsh, and to Laura, it seemed to be filled with triumph. Triumph over what, she wondered.

"Nah, let er squirm, Harold. We'll be back to the church in about five." A fresh voice, probably Zack. He sounded like a hick with meager education.

"My God, but she's beautiful." *What? Who?* Laura didn't know who they were talking about. She couldn't see anything. "And look at those tits. I can't wait to get those clothes off her."

These comments from another strange voice, and this one sent chills up and down Laura's spine.

"Better be careful with your thoughts, Arlo. Neter doesn't want his sacrifices spoiled by brutes like you and me." That sounded like Zack. He must have some authority over the other three thugs.

Laura could not believe what was happening to her. This was southeastern Idaho. Girls got kidnapped in New York and Mexico, not Pocatello, Idaho. *What in the hell was going on?*

"Neter is going to love this one," an unfamiliar voice said in what almost sounded like reverence. "She not only has a beautiful face, but look at that body."

"Yeah, Earl, and we all get to fuck her before she goes in the hole." This was the voice of Arlo, the one that initially sent chills throughout her body. She was now terrified beyond paralysis.

"Keep it up, my man, and you won't get any of her blood." Zack's voice again, and if Laura was terrified before, now her emotions went into overdrive. Pure fear. Mind-numbing, nerve-freezing fear. Who captured her, and what did they mean. Drink her blood and go in the hole?

Before she processed the sparse information any further, the vehicle she was in came to an abrupt stop.

"We're at your new temporary home, darling." This was Harold's voice again. She heard doors opening, and someone grabbed her legs, pulling Laura out of the vehicle. Several powerful arms caught her body before she hit the ground, carrying her into an old, restored Elizabethan house. They took her downstairs into a basement. The room was large, with no windows. There was a fireplace at one end, and in front of a burning fire stood a finely carved pulpit.

They had placed a white linen-draped cot in front of the podium, and her captors laid the struggling Laura on the cot.

Looking around the room, Laura saw a giant hand-painted mural in blood-red lettering.

The Nine Satanic Statements
Satan represents indulgence instead of abstinence.
Satan represents vital existence instead of spiritual pipe dreams.
Satan represents undefiled wisdom instead of hypocritical self-deceit.

As Laura studied the writing on the wall, her fears became nearly catatonic. Unable to process what was happening to her, Laura started becoming dizzy. As she read the statements, her mind was in overdrive, trying to process all the information she was receiving.

Satan represents kindness to those who deserve it
instead of love wasted on ingrates.
Satan represents vengeance instead of turning the other cheek.
Satan represents undefiled wisdom instead of hypocritical self-deceit.

She remembered hearing, *"won't get any of her blood,"* at some point, and *"going in the hole."*

Satan represents man as just another animal.
Satan represents vital existence instead of spiritual pipe-dreams.
Satan rep...

That was the last thing she read before passing out.

CHAPTER THREE

Glory

Hokee was two hours into his drive when he received a call from Hilda, his secretary. A frantic farmer from Malad, Idaho, called wanting Hokee to look for Laura, his missing daughter. She was not responding to phone calls and had not communicated with her parents for two weeks, which was unusual. Richard Taylor, the father, called the sheriff who had not been encouraging. Unfortunately, the sheriff's department cannot devote full time to this one case, whereas finding missing children was Hokee's main business. One of the sheriff's deputies, Robert "Curly" Belingsford, told Richard to get hold of Hokee Wolf, who he claimed was the best in the business at finding missing persons.

Hokee asked Hilda to make up a folder of the pertinent information regarding the missing girl. He wanted her physical description; a picture would be nice, her habits, friends, hobbies, romantic interests, classes at the university, etcetera. Hokee had committed his time to Grant Olson, so he could not work on the missing Taylor girl until he solved Grant's problem. Meanwhile, Hilda was free to begin some grunt work, including calling the girls' parents. He asked her to find out everything she could learn about the missing girl.

Hokee could do nothing about the Taylor girl for now, so he started putting together in his head everything he learned from Grant about his contract problem.

During the past two years, an Egyptian-based company, Hassan Construction Limited, was awarded three major construction contracts, on which Grant spent millions of his company's dollars preparing bids.

Two years ago, Olson Construction Company prepared a proposal to expand the London Airport by building two additional terminal buildings and one new runway. Grant bid 1.8 billion dollars for the job, expecting to net $250,000,000 in profit.

Last year he bid 2.1 billion dollars to build a dam on the Painganga River in India. He also lost this contract to Hassan Construction Ltd. Then, just this month, he lost a 3.4-billion-dollar job to build another nuclear power plant in Japan. Again, the winning bidder was Hassan's company. In each proposal, Grant had his people study the project to minimize costs. While he doesn't expect to win every job he bids on, losing three consecutive jobs to the same Egyptian company seemed strange.

Grant's secretary booked Hokee into the Best Western Plus Peppertree near the Civic Center. She assured Hokee this was not only Nampa's finest; it was also close to the Olson Construction Company. The hotel receptionist gave Hokee a room on the ground floor across the hallway from the hotel's indoor pool. The receptionist assured him this was their best room convenient to the swimming pool, their exercise room, and the breakfast buffet. Hokee had no desire to soak in chlorine doctored water in which little kids pissed and women menstruated. He also had no attraction for free cafeteria-style breakfasts of low-quality food. Hokee found the room acceptable and was unpacking his small travel bag when his telephone rang.

Not recognizing the number, Hokee answered, "Hello, this is Hokee."

"Hokee, this is Gloria. I'm here in Pocatello, and Hilda tells me you have a job in Nampa."

"Hey, beautiful. Yeah. One of my old clients has a problem, and I'm obligated to help him with his problem. Where are you now?"

"I'm sitting on your porch with Shila. How do I get into your house?"

"Go over to the water fountain and look for a blue rock under the waterfall." Hokee's expansive yard had a fountain in the center of his large circular driveway.

"Okay, give me a second to walk over there. I see it. It's in the back of the falls."

"Yeah. I didn't want to make it obvious or easy. Push in on the rock and watch what happens."

Glory was reluctant to get her arm wet, but what could she do. Seeing nothing handy to use as a tool she could stick in the water to push on the rock, she stuck her arm up to her shoulder. Despite it being a warm day in the shining sun, the water was freezing. The cold water surprised Glory until she remembered the water came from the underground river behind Hokee's bedroom. She pushed on the blue rock, and a brass rod poked out of the fountain's side by her knee. Attached to the rod was a small plastic box holding the key to Hokee's house. As soon as Glory pulled the key out of the box, the mechanism slid back into the fountain, leaving no sign of its existence.

"My God, Hokee, this water is freezing."

"I know, but did you get the key?"

"Yes, it's in my hand. Do you have any alarms set for the house? I don't remember one."

"No. My house is too remote to expect any help if someone breaks the door down. The door is solid, though, and would be hard to break through, and then I have Shila. It's a good thing you made friends."

"Oh, yes. I remember how terrified I was for the first time coming over the rise to your little valley and seeing Shila standing in the driveway. How long will you be gone? Hilda didn't seem to know."

"I'm not sure. I just got here and haven't started my investigation. From what little I know; this job should not take any longer than a week. Possibly not that long."

"Would you like me to join you in Nampa?" Glory asked, hoping for a positive response.

She came west to Pocatello for a few days, many months earlier, at her employer's request in New York City, where she was a highly successful television investigative journalist. Beautiful and intelligent, her parents named her Gloria. But after working as a journalist for a few years, her co-workers started calling her Glory because she always seemed to cover herself with Glory in doing her job. She kind of liked the name, so she started using it both professionally and in her personal life.

When in Pocatello, she met Hokee, who invited her to help him solve a robbery. They became romantically involved, but Glory still had her job in New York. Wanting to find out if their relationship was more than a casual affair, she decided to visit Hokee.

She left New York expecting to spend some time with him. She hoped to renew their romance to see what developed and was disappointed Hokee was not in Pocatello. It never occurred to her he might leave town for another job; otherwise, she would have called ahead to make sure he would be home.

"Not right now," he answered. "I don't know where this job will lead me, as there might be a bit of travel. But, since you are in Pocatello, you could do me a big favor."

"And what might that be, lover? Gather up some wood for your sweat lodge?"

"Cute Glory, but I have something a little more serious. It seems a girl is missing from her dorm at the University of Idaho. Hilda has the details, and I've asked her to begin a folder. Unfortunately, she doesn't have your investigative skills. Could you please begin the investigation in my absence? You already know Curly, the sheriff's deputy, who had the girl's parents call for my help. Go visit him and see what you can learn. You might also visit the campus, see if she has any roommates who can tell you anything. I need not tell you how to investigate, so I'll stop with the advice."

"Sure. I'll be happy to start the investigation. I'll probably finish it before you return."

"That would be great, but I have a bad feeling about the case, Glory. Watch yourself."

"I'll be careful. Wouldn't want to make the world's smartest detective look bad." She chuckled but it was difficult to tell if it was a laugh or a snort. "Want me to do anything special with Shila?"

"He's self-sufficient, but sometimes the hunting is meager. You will know if he is acting hungry, and if that happens, give him a rabbit from the outside refrigerator. The rabbits in the kitchen freezer are ours."

"Oh, God. I remember that stew you served. Maybe you'll make it for me again when you return."

"Be happy to make you rabbit stew, my love. Enjoy the house and Shila. I hope to see you soon. Gotta run now. Duty calls. Bye for now."

"Goodbye, lover; keep safe."

Glory did not know she was the one who needed to worry about keeping safe. Using the key from the fountain, Glory entered Hokee's house. Originally a cave with access to an underground river, Hokee added a front half of his dwelling with a distinctive Spanish flair. The home featured expansive covered porches with arches and red geraniums. He furnished the inside with handmade furniture, along with original artwork by the builder himself. Overall, it was a spectacular beauty of grace and symmetry. Glory always found it hard to reconcile the robust and handsome shaman detective with the sensitivity found inside his home. Yet, it was still a delight to enter his house and relax in the beauty and solitude.

CHAPTER FOUR

The Sacrifice

When Laura regained consciousness for the second time, she was lying on her back. They bound both legs and arms to the cot the four thugs dumped her on after carrying her into the basement. She turned her head to see a pleasant-faced woman sitting on a wooden chair beside her cot. Laura wanted to speak to the woman when she felt a pain in her right arm. Bending her head and looking down at her arm, there was an IV tube with a butterfly needle sticking in a vein, with blood running down the tube into a plastic bag.

"Hello, Laura. I see you're awake." The voice belonged to the pleasant-faced woman sitting by her side. "Now, don't act surprised. We saw your name inside the wallet you carried in the backpack."

Fighting to control her fear, Laura asked, "Who are you, and why am I here? And why are you taking my blood?"

What Laura initially thought was a pleasant face turned into a sneering mask of pleasure. "Oh, I am Raven, and get to be your minder until All Hallows Eve. Our Beloved Prince Neter chose me to be your minder and take charge of your blood. I'm afraid we are going to need almost a gallon. So many saints to please."

Laura strained to remember where she had heard the term 'All Hallows Eve.' It reminded her of Halloween, which was still many days away. Was this All Hallows Eve the same thing? Her fears turned into terror as she tried squirming out of her bonds, but they had secured her too tightly.

"Don't struggle too much, angel. I can't have you tearing out the IV. But, you better get used to this treatment. I'm going to take a half-pint of your blood every day until our celebration."

Taking a few deep breaths to calm herself, Laura spent the next few minutes trying to understand her situation and what she might do to help herself. As a farm girl, she had learned to be self-sufficient and solve problems. After a look around, she understood her situation.

Raven wore a tight black silk pants suit, flattering her voluptuous figure. Her long dark hair hung straight down to the middle of her back. Her makeup looked gothic, and Laura wondered how she could ever have thought Raven had a pleasant face. In studying the woman now, Laura realized it was the eyes. Although dark, almost black, they appeared friendly when the woman liked what she saw. But when her thoughts turned back to Laura and what she represented, the eyes became weapons.

Turning her head, Laura saw The Nine Satanic Statements written on the wall and thought she was the prisoner of a witches' coven. She remembered hearing the name Neter twice, but the name meant nothing, and Laura didn't know the structure of witches' covens, so the mistake was understandable. She remembered hearing Arlo talk about fucking her before she went into the hole and Zack mentioning drinking her blood. So that was what the *vampire*, Laura's name for Raven, was doing. She was collecting the blood for their celebration of All Hallows Eve. Raven said this would take several days, and Laura now had a time frame to work out a plan to free herself. They had kidnapped her on the seventeenth, and Halloween was the 31st. Fourteen days until the celebration. If All Hallows Eve was at the same as Halloween. Perhaps witches celebrated All Hallows Eve while the rest of us all celebrated Halloween.

Laura was regaining her composure and inbred self-confidence until she heard a commotion. Turning her head towards the stairs, she saw a tall man enter the room, followed by several individuals, including the four thugs who had kidnapped her from the college.

They all gathered around Laura's cot, gazing down at her as if appraising a cow you might purchase at an animal auction. Then, a tall man who dressed all in black came to stand next to Raven. He had short black hair, a black Van Dyke beard, midnight black eyes that sunk into his skull, giving his face the illusion of a death mask. Laura remembered seeing the picture of someone she thought of as evil in a book she read in high school. In searching her mind, the name bubbled up to the surface, Mephistopheles, the devil.

Laura's bubbling self-confidence nose-dived into deep despair, surpassed only by her growing terror.

"You've done well, Zack. This girl is the best one yet." Then, looking into Laura's terrified eyes, he said, "I don't suppose we're lucky enough that you're still a virgin?"

Laura was too frightened to speak, and even if she were able, there was no way she would respond to such an intimate question.

"We could check for her cherry," Zack said with an eagerness in his voice.

"We'll wait for the celebration," the tall man responded. "Finding out now won't change anything, and it could be a pleasant surprise for everyone."

Focusing his black eyes back on Laura, the man spoke. His voice was strangely calm, as though telling a children's bedtime story. "I am Neter Amon, Prince of the Church of Lucifer. You have the honor of being our special guest for our biggest annual celebration. Being chosen is a high honor, which I don't expect you to appreciate; however, as our honorary guest, Raven will do everything in her power to make you comfortable." Here he laid an arm on Raven's shoulder, bringing a smile of wonder and deep satisfaction to the vampire's face.

Looking into Raven's upturned face, Neter asked, "how much longer?"

Raven bent down and looked at the plastic bag she was filling with Laura's blood. "It's almost full, maybe another two or three minutes."

"Good. I'll send down Zelda, and Dakarba to help get her ready. The rest of you shoo. We want the sacrifice to be a pleasant surprise for our evening Eucharist.

It seemed to Laura that Neter's crowd had scarcely left when she felt Raven pull the IV needle from her arm, then slap on a bandaid.

"We don't want you leaking any of your precious blood, angel," she said with a smirk and an evil glint in her dark unsmiling eyes.

Two women about Raven's age, which Laura estimated to be about thirty, came down the stairs wearing black leotards and black tee shirts. They came over to the cot and stood looking down at Laura while Raven took the bag of blood out of the room through a door Laura had failed to notice. The two women stood staring down at Laura, saying nothing until Raven returned.

Looking down at the girl still in shorts and a tee-shirt, one lady asked, "do we untie her first or just cut em off?" This question was from a woman who had dishwater blond hair and long thin legs. The one they called Zelda. Both women were the same height, but the blond had long legs and a short bodice, and the other woman had short legs and a long bodice. Unless you were observant, you would miss this physiology, but Laura was a farm girl used to observing and judging livestock. Noticing a person's build was just part of her background.

"We better just cut everything off before we untie her, Zelda. She looks like she wants to give us a fight. Besides, she won't be needing those clothes again."

While she spoke, Laura felt a chill, like someone ran an ice cube down her spine.

"I brought the scissors just in case," said the other woman, who Laura assumed must be Dakarba. Leaning down, she began cutting away Laura's clothing, starting with her shorts. She didn't stop until she cut away every piece of clothing on Laura's body, leaving her naked.

Laura was not shy, but when three strange girls stand gawking at you while you're lying helpless, the feelings of vulnerability can overwhelm you. Then all three women began feeling her breasts. They combed their fingers through her pubic hair and stroked her vagina. While massaging her breasts and rubbing their hands all over her body, Laura couldn't help but think of the men examining a horse they might bid on at a livestock auction. The women exploring Laura clucked and murmured about what luck to have such a beautiful sacrifice. Laura could do nothing but endure.

As horrible and degrading as it was, it would only get much worse.

CHAPTER FIVE

The Job

Nampa, Idaho grew up as an agricultural community that slowly developed into an industrial center vying for attention and resources with its big sister city, Boise, the state capital only eighteen miles in the distance. Nearby is the Frank Church-River of No Return Wilderness Area, the largest wilderness area in America outside of Alaska. At two and a half million acres, this national treasure attracts visitors worldwide. These visitors often fall in love with the Gem State's beauty and lifestyle and, looking around, settle in Idaho's banana belt surrounding Nampa. Olson Construction Company is the primary builder of new homes in the area. With Nampa being the company's world headquarters, they are one of the state's largest employers.

Hokee checked into the Best Western Hotel, surprised to find a fresh fruit basket and a champagne bottle sitting in a bucket of ice. Of course, it doesn't hurt to have the largest contractor in the state make your reservations. Grant volunteered to send a private plane to pick up Hokee and fly him to Boise, but Hokee wanted time to think, and he figured it wouldn't take that much longer to drive as he would avoid the airport hassle and car parking problems.

It was nine p.m. when Hokee called Grant as he agreed to inform him of his arrival. Grant wanted to meet despite the late hour, assuring Hokee he was waiting to eat a late dinner. They agreed to eat at the Peppertree restaurant in the hotel, saving Hokee the need to drive around in a strange town.

Grant arrived wearing blue jeans, a western belt with a silver buckle the size of Texas, cowboy boots, and a custom-made orange Lou Taubert shirt. Standing six two with a full head of gray hair, he made heads turn when he entered the room. Hokee wore his traditional dark pants and a black shirt, and his Tony Llamas cowboy boots. With his long shoulder-length black hair held back with a blue leather headband, Hokee did his own share of head-turning. Both were tall, handsome men, and with Hokee's shoulder-length dark hair, the two men made a striking picture.

"Howdy Hokee, welcome to Nampa." Grant's welcome came with a magnificent smile.

"Hi Grant, it's good to see you again." As the two men shook hands, Hokee continued. "And thanks for the welcome gift in my room," referring to the fruit basket and champagne.

As the two men slid into a booth, Grant said, "Aw hell, that's Charlene, my girl Friday. I think she has a crush on you. You ain't married yet, are ya?"

"Nope. Not yet, anyway. Met this unbelievable woman on a job last summer, so we'll see."

"That was the big mail truck robbery we heard so much about?"

"Yeah. That's the one. Thank God we put that one to bed. Damn near killed me." Hokee shook his head as if he still couldn't believe he was alive.

Curious, Grant asked, "What happened?"

Hokee shook his head, almost as if embarrassed. "Damned doppelganger. Almost got me. Guess I'm getting slow in my old age." He said this with a brief smile, like he couldn't believe he was even talking about such a thing.

"Doppelganger? Never heard of such a thing."

"I'll tell you the story over a drink sometime. It gets complicated. Let's eat and talk about your little problem."

As if on cue, the uniformed server appeared, a slim redhead named Cara with big eyes and lots of mascara. "Care for a drink, gentlemen?" She had an Irish girl smile and couldn't keep her eyes off Hokee.

Grant had a whisky sour, and Hokee ordered his usual Johnny Walker red over ice with a splash of water.

After Cara left, Hokee began, "So Grant, you think you have a spy in your company?"

"Goddammit, Hokee, I know I have a fucking spy. Excuse the language, but when you're out nearly a hundred million dollars with no hope of recovery, I get a little pissed."

"You don't have to watch your language around me, Grant. And before we get all emotional and angry with the world, tell me about Wanda. How's she doing? Fully recovered?"

"Oh hell, Hokee, where are my manners? She's made a full recovery, thanks to you. We both owe you a big thanks."

"Come on, Grant. You more than paid me back. I'll never live long enough to spend it all. And besides, just getting her back was worth more than you've probably got socked away." Hokee said this last line with a gigantic grin.

"Well, Hokee, you've got that right. I would have gladly parted with all I have to get her back." Then, after a moment's pause, Grant continued with a small deprecating smile, "well, maybe not gladly, but I'd do it just the same."

The server returned with the drinks, and they elected to wait for a few minutes before ordering dinner.

Hokee took a sip of his scotch before responding. "I'm glad it all worked out and happy to hear that Wanda is doing so well."

Grant took a swallow of his whisky sour before returning to his problem. "I've bid on three different contracts, all worth over a billion dollars, and lost all three to the same Egyptian contractor. That isn't possible in today's world."

"Do you know how many other bidders there were for these projects?" Hokee's question caused Grant's eyebrows to furrow in concentration as he thought about the problem.

"Well, there are only about a half dozen contractors in the world with the resources to consider the three jobs I'm talking about, but I don't think they all bid on every one of the jobs. Each contract had at least three bidders, but I'm pretty sure the only contractors to bid on all three jobs were Hassan Construction and myself."

"When you told me the problem on the phone, I thought about the situation and must agree; it looks like a leak in your organization."

Grant took a big gulp of his drink as the server appeared to see if they wanted to order dinner. Grant ordered the prime rib with baked potato and garden salad with bleu cheese dressing. Hokee had the same spuds and salad but opted for the coconut-covered shrimp.

Grant picked up the conversation where they left off. "I wanted that Japanese nuclear construction job. Using every trick in the book, I ran the numbers like you wouldn't believe. On every major job like this, we figure the cost to the best of our ability. The goal for every contract is to make a twenty percent profit.

There is always a host of unknowns in every contract, especially when dealing with foreign countries and their quirky labor forces and unions. Our practice is to add fifteen percent of the contract's cost for contingencies to the ultimate price. We eliminated this contingency for this job and reduced our profit margin to fifteen percent, figuring we could use our profit to cover these incidental costs. We still lost the contract. Hassan either plans on using inferior materials or somehow screwing the customer. You cannot do this job for less than we bid and count on making a profit."

"Grant," Hokee had a severe expression on his face, "I don't know for sure why you didn't win any of those contracts, but if you have a spy, I can promise you we'll find that person."

"I know you will Hokee, that's why I'm buying dinner." Grant delivered the line with a gigantic smile.

They chatted about light-hearted things such as the rising communist threat to America, the decline of morality, and the lack of decent modern music during dinner. Both men considered any talk outside of their work light-hearted.

After finishing dinner, the men shook hands, agreeing on an early morning meeting at the Olson Construction Company headquarters where Hokee would begin his investigation.

CHAPTER SIX

The Olson Family

Fumiko Martial Arts is owned by Hiroshi Takahashi, who teaches classes in Kung Fu, Judo, Kendo, and Taekwondo. His Dojo is in downtown Nampa near Hokee's hotel. Hokee met Hiroshi during his last job with Grant Olson, and the two men became fast friends. Unable to use his sweat lodge back home, Hokee found the sauna in Fumiko's locker room a satisfactory substitute. Knowing he would be away from home for a few days, Hokee called Hiroshi on his drive to Nampa and planned for an early visit to the Dojo. Hokee had his sauna, eaten breakfast, and still made it to the Olson Construction headquarters building before eight a.m.

Olson Construction Company owns a city block one-half mile from the city courthouse. The building is a six-story steel and glass building covering half of the block, landscaping, and parking accounting for the remaining space. The building is unusual because it incorporates many angles with tinted glass, giving it a faceted appearance. When the sun is at the correct angle, the building looks like a giant diamond with an emerald cut. Locals in the know call this structure the Gem State's real gem.

Hokee parked in one of the reserved visitor's slots. The receptionist greeted him as though he were a visiting prince, ushering him to the private elevator with access only to the sixth floor reserved for Grant and his staff. The big man himself, alerted by the receptionist, met Hokee as the elevator opened, giving him a warm welcome. Grant's humongous corner office had floor-to-ceiling glass walls, providing a panoramic view of Nampa and much of the surrounding country.

A hand-carved teak desk sat against a wall covered with pictures of past projects. There is no trophy wall of photos with the President or movie stars, but only photos showing a premiere contractor's accomplishments. A major dam located in some place in Asia, maybe Thailand. An airport in Scotland and a four-lane highway going through some mountains Hokee didn't recognize. Grant could sit at his desk, look out over the city, view many of his completed projects, or spin his chair around to see distant past successes.

Charlene entered carrying a tray loaded with a coffee urn, two ceramic mugs with Olson Company logos, and various Danish rolls and doughnuts. She gave Hokee a shy glance while saying, "here's to a good meeting and something to put a little meat on your bone." She meant to say bones, and the Freudian gaff nearly caused her to drop the tray. Instead, Charlene blushed a deep red, quickly setting the tray on a corner table, then making a hasty retreat without glancing at either man.

Hokee was quick on the response, acting as though he never heard the Freudian slip. "They look more like fat pills, Charlene, but thanks anyway. And thanks for the champagne last night. That was very thoughtful."

Charlene left the room, too embarrassed to acknowledge the thanks.

Grant poured them both a mug full of coffee before settling onto a tan leather couch, sitting kitty-corner opposite his desk between a glass wall and the door. Then, putting his size twelve black cowboy boots on a coffee table in front of the sofa, Grant motioned for Hokee to join him.

"Well, Hokee. Where do you want to begin?"

Hokee sat on the opposite end of the couch and took a sip of the coffee before beginning. "Man, this is excellent coffee, Grant. You may not want to let Seattle know about this, or you'll lose your source. Do you grow your own beans?"

"Hah! Thank Charlene for that. Better wait until she gains her composure, though," he added with a grin.

"Okay, Grant. Tell me about the bidding process. I want to know all the people who take part in preparing your proposals."

"My God, Hokee. On any major proposal, there may be two hundred people on the proposal team. However, few knew the final quote. When we decide to bid on a project, I assign a proposal manager. I have four senior managers who have been with me since I began pouring concrete for road gutters. They usually manage one of our major construction jobs, and since we never have over three such projects simultaneously, I always have someone with experience around to back me up if I get stuck. Unfortunately, there are not enough seasoned men or resources to do more. So, I choose whoever is available to manage our proposal team."

"I assume this proposal manager knows the bid quote?" Hokee asked, although he was sure of the answer.

"Oh sure, and maybe a half dozen other people whom I'll mention. It was never the same group of people for each bid, although several individuals worked on all three jobs."

"I don't need to know all the components that go into your bid. I just need to know only those responsible for the final preparation."

In thinking about a major construction project, Hokee could imagine all the disciplines necessary to complete such an undertaking. First, someone must schedule every aspect of the job. What are the critical paths, those aspects of the job that must be completed before starting the next phase? Then they must make sure all the materials and equipment are available at the correct time. And what about all the various engineering disciplines the job requires?

"Well, let me see," Grant replied, thinking aloud about Hokee's comment. "On every proposal, I have my brother Bill; he's a Ph.D. economy professor at Brigham Young University in Provo, Utah. He moonlights here, helping me manage costs. Another brother, Edward, with a Ph.D. in Civil Engineering, helps me keep a handle on each job's engineering aspects."

"You have two brothers, both doctors?" Hokee's previous experience with Grant's family was only with his wife, Penny, and their daughter Wanda. He didn't know any of Grant's siblings or children other than the daughter Wanda he rescued from her kidnappers.

"Don't look so surprised, Hokee," Grant said with a smile. "Just because I never finished high school doesn't mean I came from a family of idiots."

Hokee was momentarily chagrined until realizing there was no need to be embarrassed. He had never met all of Grant's family and had made no value judgments about him or his family. Plus, he knew none of Grant's background or educational achievements.

"Given your success, Grant, you didn't come from a family of morons. I seriously envy your family connections. You're lucky to have that kind of family support in your business."

"Oh, you bet I know it. And I'm damned grateful. Besides my brothers, there is my son Gene, whom I'm grooming to take over the business. I believe Gene is the brightest one of the entire family, including me."

Grant leaned forward and took a sip of coffee before settling back against the cushions. He had a faint gleam of satisfaction in his eyes, remembering his son.

"So," Hokee interrupted Grant's reverie, "there are you and your two brothers and son who view the final proposal. Anybody else?"

Grant had to think for a minute while Hokee sipped his coffee. Neither man seemed interested in the sweets resting on the tray, laying on the corner table.

"Well, Charlene. She usually types the final proposal, so she knows the numbers. Then there's the proposal manager. He puts together the final bid. I had a different manager for each bid, so no one manager knew the proposal price for all three of the jobs we're talking about."

"Do your managers all fraternize together? Go out for drinks and that sort of thing?" Hokee asked.

"Maybe when they are all in town," Grant answered. "Although that rarely happens. They manage jobs worldwide and usually live on site for the duration of the project."

"Let me make sure I understand this, Grant. Only five people knew the bid price for all three projects from what you just told me: you, your two brothers, your son, and Charlene."

"Yeah, Hokee. That's it. A real tight group. So you can understand my frustration."

Hokee sat in disbelief for a few moments, letting Grant's summation settle in both of their minds.

"It's hard to believe any of those would leak your bid price to Hassan Construction," Hokee began. "I agree, there has to be a leak someplace, but it may be some procedural thing rather than a betrayal. First, I want to review the final process you go through for each proposal, then talk to each of the individuals involved."

"Okay, let me see who's available," Grant said, getting up and going over to his desk. He was about to page Charlene when her voice came over the intercom,

"I'm sorry, Mr. Olson, but Gene is here with Opal. He wanted to say goodbye before leaving for New York."

"Oh sure, Char, send them in."

To Hokee, he added, "Opal is a fashion model living in New York, but she models all over the planet. She just came back from doing a wine commercial in Japan. Gene is eager to spend some time with her."

One of the most beautiful, breathtaking couples in the world came into the office. Gene was tall, six foot six, with dark curly hair and a Burt Reynolds' face. Opal wasn't short, but at only five foot nine, she looked tiny next to Gene. Opal had gleaming, waist-length black hair and a Monroe figure with long runway model legs. Her figure and Eurasian face made a picture both men and women could look at forever. Hokee looked at the pair in amazement, enjoying the view.

Grant introduced the pair to Hokee, who stood up and shook hands with Gene.

"Did I hear Charlene tell us you were heading to New York, Gene?" Hokee asked.

"Yes, we were about to leave for the airport. Opal has a job next week in the Big Apple. We haven't been together for a few days, and we aren't too busy, so my dad gave me a few days off." Gene looked at his dad while saying this as though seeking confirmation.

"And Opal," Hokee said, looking at the stunning beauty. "Is that an engagement ring on your finger? I didn't know the two of you were betrothed."

Before Opal could answer, Grant butted in, "That's my fault, Hokee. I should have introduced Opal as Gene's fiancée. Opal seems like she's already family, and I forget not everybody knows about these two. If you ever see the celebrity pages from a New York City newspaper, it seems there are pictures of them in every issue."

"That's okay, Papa," Opal said with a grin. "I feel like I'm family already. But we have to go. There is a plane we need to catch."

"Go, go." Grant snorted. "Don't let me hold you up. Oh, wait. Gene, Hokee wants to sit with you and talk about your part in preparing our bids. When are you planning on returning?"

"I planned on spending a week in New York, Dad. If that's okay?" Gene had a comfortable relationship with his father, and Hokee could detect no sign of tension or worry about discussing his family business role.

"What do you think, Hokee? You need to talk with Gene before then?" Then, looking at his son, Grant continued, "you knew I was getting Hokee to look into why we keep getting outbid by the Hassan group."

No one noticed, as there was a slightly involuntary cringe from Opal.

"Oh, yeah. I forgot. Sorry, Dad. Seeing Opal again, I forgot all about Hokee's visit." For the first time, Hokee could sense a little uncertainty in Gene's demeanor. If Hokee needs me, I can fly back tomorrow.

Hokee looked at Gene before answering Grant's question. "I have some other people to talk with besides you, Gene. Let's see how it goes. Maybe I can talk with you on the telephone, although I wouldn't say I like to conduct business that way. You never know who is listening. Let's chat in a day or two. Maybe I'll fly to New York. You can show me the big city. You know us country boys, we always dream of making it to Broadway. If only for a visit."

Hokee had a smile on his face, but it never reached his eyes. He wanted Gene to understand that for him, this was serious business.

Gene was quick and caught the undertone in Hokee's comments. "Sure, okay, Mr. Wolf. If you need me, I'll be happy to return whenever you say." Gene looked at Opal then said, "but I would hate to leave you, darling."

The couple said their goodbyes and left. Grant looked at Hokee and asked, "What do you think, Hokee?"

"A great-looking couple. Let me rephrase, a fantastic couple. I can see why the gossip pages like to splash their photos around. She looks like she belongs in the family. Gene is one handsome man. They go well together. Let's see who's available to talk with today."

CHAPTER SEVEN

The Church

A fireplace in the basement provided the only light as several dozen men and women entered the room carrying a burning candle. Demonic sconces hung on the walls surrounding the room with creative cutouts for holding the candles. The sconces had ruby glass eyes that glowed red once the candles were in place. After everyone was in the room with the glowing sconces, Neter entered, carrying a human skull with an opening on the top. The crown was full of Laura's blood.

Neter, who wore a black, floor-length robe, stood behind the pulpit before resting the skull on a flat spot at the front of the pulpit. As he did so, he mumbled some Latin phrases, after which everyone echoed his statements. With this brief ceremony completed, the room had an eerie, unworldly feel to Laura. The demonic sconces with their burning candles and the fireplace provided all the light in the room. It was only then that Laura, naked and tied to a cross fixed to the wall behind Neter, saw that all the participants were wearing black robes with black masks. It almost looked like Halloween, and it terrified Laura.

"Children of Lucifer, behold our offering to the noble spirit who rules over this world."

Neter's voice sounded enhanced as it boomed around the basement. While speaking, he stepped aside so everyone could get an unobstructed view of Laura as she sagged upon the cross. They roped her arms to the upper crossbar, then spread her legs apart, tying them to a crossbar at the bottom.

"Please help yourselves to a close examination of our sacrifice. Go on and touch her silky skin, observe her perfect body but no pinching or squeezing, and see the purity of her soul. It is with great pleasure we can offer this virgin to our God."

Laura passed out earlier when they tied her to the cross. Sometime later, it occurred to her they may have given her a drug when she asked for water, so she was unsure if Neter knew she was still a virgin or was guessing. It didn't matter; she was far too terrified to care, and she would have willingly surrendered her precious virginity to escape this horror.

Beyond shame and caring, Laura could only stare into each masked face with loathing and hatred as they, one by one, slowly marched past her naked body, touching her breasts, feeling her vagina, and sometimes stroking her face as though caressing a lover. Finally, after everyone examined their guest, they all sat on the floor, and Neter returned to the pulpit.

Holding the skull in the air as though offering a gift to the Gods, Neter spoke again, muttering in Latin. When finished with his offering, he took a small sip of Laura's blood, after which he addressed the crowd in English.

"My dear brothers and sisters, in service to our sacred God Lucifer, it is with great pleasure I offer you this first tiny sip of the blood of the virgin. As you experience this sacrifice on your tongue, feel the life of the virgin renewing your own sacred life."

Neter stepped around the pulpit and handed the skull to Raven, the minder, careful not to spill any of the blood. Raven took a small sip, then, running her tongue around her lips as though relishing a divine treat, handed the skull to Dakarba. As the head and blood made their way through the crowd, they began chanting, "Lucifer, Lucifer, Lucifer."

Tied helplessly to the cross, a naked Laura could only weep in sorrow and fear. It was too easy to imagine her fate. She didn't know how long they intended to keep her alive or how they would end her life.

*****

Glory got in touch with Laura's parents and made the one-hour drive to Malad. The Taylors lived on a ranch in the sagebrush-covered foothills just to the west of the town. Too small to be considered a city, and too big to be a village, everyone in the area called it town, as in *'hey son, run down to* town *and buy us some potatoes for dinner.'*

Their farmhouse was typical for the area, a large two-story clapboard structure with a wide wrap-around porch for sitting in the early evening watching the sunset.

Mr. Taylor was a small weather-beaten man with skin darkened from years of working in the hot summer sunlight. Yet, although short in stature, he possessed remarkable strength. Glory watched as he tossed hundred pounds sacks of oats from the back of his blue Ford 250 pickup onto a raised platform where another man was operating a grain roller producing rolled oats.

Laura's mother was a petite woman with long gray hair pulled back in a ponytail. She was outside working in a garden digging up potatoes with a shovel when Glory drove into their yard.

The Taylors were expecting Glory as she had called before making the trip, so both parents stopped what they were doing and headed towards her car when they saw her drive into their yard. Glory took her time exiting the vehicle, so both parents were almost to her car door before she got out to meet the grief-stricken parents. Both were eager for word about their daughter.

After brief introductions, the Taylors invited Glory to sit with them on their magnificent porch while they talked. Mrs. Taylor offered Glory a glass of iced tea, which she was happy to accept. Although early October, it was unseasonably warm, and the drink sounded good. Glory agreed to wait for Mrs. Taylor's return before resuming their discussion.

The visit to Taylor's ranch proved disappointing, although the iced tea was delicious, and Glory found ranch life interesting. She learned Laura lived on campus in a dorm with three other girls whose names were unknown to the Taylors. Besides knowing that Laura kept in touch with her parents and had grown accustomed to life on the campus, Glory learned little of value.

While driving back to Pocatello and Hokee's house, Glory received a phone call. At first, she thought it was Hokee, even though she was not expecting him to call. Instead, it was Curly, the sheriff's deputy who Glory met during her first visit to Idaho.

"Glory, I called to talk with Hokee but got Hilda instead. She tells me that Hokee is out of town, and you are staying at his place with Shila. She gave me your phone number. Hilda tells me you are helping with the missing Taylor girl investigation. I had Laura Taylor's parents get in touch with Hokee since he is so good at finding missing people, and we have too much going on here in the sheriff's office to search full time for the missing girl."

"Oh, hi Curly. Yes, I just got back into town yesterday. I talked with Hokee last evening and had you on my list of people to call. I went to see the Taylors in Malad today. They are distraught but could offer no real help other than giving me a picture of Laura graduating from high school. Hokee wanted me to help Hilda put together a folder for the missing girl, and I wanted to come by and pick your brains. Of course, that is assuming you have any left after your last embarrassing failure."

"Now be nice, Glory, or I won't give you the news I was calling about."

"Aw, come on, Curly. Somebody has to help you keep that big ego in check."

"There you go again. Why do you come to visit our lovely city and cast aspersions on one of its leading citizens?"

"Oh, my God. And he even speaks the King's English using ten-dollar words. Okay, wise guy. Why did you call?"

"After all those insults and demeaning slanders against my sterling character, I'm not sure you're the right person to confide in by telling you my secrets."

"Come on, Curly, don't make me beg. It just isn't seemly."

"Seemly for you or seemly for me to keep you guessing?"

"My Lord. Would you just come out with it already?"

"Okay, sorry Glory. Your beauty confounds me, and I lose my train of thought. Okay, okay. I can tell you're about to scream. It turns out that we have two other missing girls under very similar circumstances. Last year, and the year before, right about now, the beginning of October, both girls went missing. Both of the girls were beautiful, much like Laura, if you saw her picture. They were young, and like Laura, a freshman at the university."

"Did you find the other two girls?" Glory held her breath, afraid of the answer.

"Sadly, Glory, the answer is no. I'm not sure why no one called Hokee to help in the other two cases. We may not have recommended his services to the parents. Also, the parents may not have been aware of Hokee's reputation for finding missing students."

"Curly, may I come by and look at the files for those girls? It may help us solve this case."

"Sure Glory, you are more than welcome. When do you want to come?"

"I'm about thirty minutes away from your penthouse," Glory's joke for the sheriff's office. "Are you in, and can I come by now?"

"I don't know Glory. It's kind of messy around here. Today is the maid's day off, and the palace is a mess. But if you don't mind a little cow shit on the penthouse carpet, drop on by."

"See ya in a few, Curly. Maybe you should open the windows and light an incense."

CHAPTER EIGHT

The Job

Ahmad lay soaking in a magnificent Egyptian blue marble pool in his Luxor palace, being attended to by three of his most beautiful concubines. Ahmad promised them that if they were creative in finding fresh ways to excite him, he might make one of them his next wife. All three were slave girls; one a Chinese girl from Hong Kong, another was Korean, and the third girl a Caucasian from Canada who spoke only French. Not one of the three practiced the Muslim religion, and Ahmad had no intention of marrying any of them. Still, the ignorant girls were trying everything they knew to please their master.

"Master! Master!"

The messenger boy's shrill call disturbed Ahmad just as he was about to climax. Knowing that he would get no satisfaction until dealing with this latest crisis, Ahmad bade the girls cease their administrations while dealing with business. He feared a principal manager on one of the major contracts he stole from Olson Construction found out he was cheating. To undercut the Olson Construction bid price, Ahmad reduced his bid price on all three contracts. Unfortunately, his firm could not operate with the same efficiency as Olson's, and he found it impossible to meet all the contract provisions and still make a profit. For example, Hassan Construction Ltd. used inferior steel rebar grade 33, whereas the contract called for grade 60; he also used low-quality cement, plus unlicensed and unskilled workers.

With relief, he discovered his worries were unfounded. The problem had to do with his daughter Rashida, and while she was by far his favorite child, she was still a girl, and he disapproved of her lifestyle. He didn't demand his wives and concubines wear the burka; however, he disapproved of them showing too much skin. Rashida's beauty brought much welcome attention to his house, as many wealthy suitors lined up, offering their hand in marriage.

He had to be careful about how he handled the girl. While she loved her father with almost the same passion as he loved her, if such passion/devotion can pass as love, she was headstrong and did everything her way, regardless of his warnings. His daughter was an asset not only to his family but his business, and he didn't want to push her away by being too strict. Yet, the girl had to know her limits and how far she could try her father. Rashida knew full well that while her father loved her above everyone else in the family, he would have her killed in a second if she caused him undue stress. Ahmad had done his best to instill this fear in his daughter while pampering her every wish.

Women in Ahmad's household, as in all the enormous palaces, were all big gossips. There is not much else to entertain them, and he needed privacy to hear his messenger's urgent news. So it was with reluctance that he left his marble pool and lovely harem to listen to the latest.

*****

Grant provided Hokee with a book-lined library to meet with Owen Miller, one of his project managers who led the London airport bid proposal. Owen was a strapping five-foot-eleven built like an NFL linebacker. With shoulders the size of most doorframes and a small waist, he looked capable of bench pressing four-hundred pounds. Owen had a cheerful, pleasant, farm boy face, all freckles and bushy eyebrows topped with a cowlick in his dusty blond hair. It would be easy to dismiss Owen as another stupid jock, except for his bright, intelligent brown eyes.

After their introductions, Hokee asked Owen to review step by step what the completed proposal went through before being sent to London.

"There are six thick volumes to the proposal, Hokee," Owen began. "And only five of us knew the numbers in the price volume."

"Six volumes? My God. I knew it was a big job, but I did not understand it was such a major undertaking." While Hokee knew the bid was over a billion dollars, he did not know the job's complexity.

"Oh, Hokee, you and almost everyone else don't have even the slightest concept of the work it takes to put together a major proposal of this magnitude."

"Okay. I guess I always knew it wasn't something you scratched on the back of an envelope, but six volumes. Wow!"

"Yeah, it takes a while to wrap your head around the whole thing. But let me give you the digest version. You probably are not interested in any of the technical details and what goes into each volume, except for volume six, the project cost, and our bid amount."

"You're right, Owen. Spare me the details, but I would appreciate an overview."

"Sure. We start with the basic architecture. The airport authorities provide a general concept with pretty pictures and a general description. After that, it's up to us to hire the architects and provide the detailed drawings, without which it would be impossible to either bid on the job or build the airport."

"You mean you had to design the airport before bidding on the blasted thing?" Hokee was shaking his head in disbelief.

"Yes, that is exactly what I mean. That's another reason it costs so much money to prepare the bid."

"All right. I understand. No wonder Grant got so ticked off when he lost all three proposals." Hokee shook his head in amazement. Before today, he did not know what it took to prepare a significant proposal.

"After we hire the architects and get a decent set of drawings, we can begin putting together the construction plan. These plans comprise another large volume detailing the construction organization and cover everything from traffic flow to the building sequence."

"Okay, I can see where that could be a lot of work."

"Yes, it is, and a mistake here could cost the contractor his entire profit."

"Wow. It sounds scary. I'm happy to be a simple gumshoe."

"After the building plan is underway, we work on the schedule. These two activities kind of go hand in hand."

"Alright. I got it. Go on."

"Materials. This is an entire volume, including everything from the heavy equipment, the number of cranes and earthmovers we would need, and everything else down to lighting fixtures and light bulbs. And don't forget the toilets." Owen had a brief smile when he added that last line about the toilets, but the comment was only semi facetious.

Owen continued while Hokee paid attention. "Next is the subcontractor's volume. Getting and training the labor force can be both time-consuming and profit-draining. Therefore, it is essential to have the required number of skilled employees and grunts available."

"I understand now why the proposal has six volumes." Hokee sat almost in shock as the magnitude of the project slowly took place in his head.

"Oh yeah. I had a manager for each volume who had a staff of about a dozen people managing a workforce of several hundred people. Of course, each manager handled the prices in their volume, but naturally, we all pitched in and helped whenever necessary."

"I believe this takes us to the pricing or cost volume." Hokee sounded relieved that his agony was about to end.

"It sounds simple on the surface. But here, we spell out all the contingencies, payment schedules, and assumptions. It isn't unusual for the principal to change his mind about some aspects of the design. They may be unhappy with the toilet, or the lighting, or the floor coverings. Whatever it might be, changes to the system affect the work schedule and many other aspects of the job. We must cover these changes in the pricing volume, so neither the principal nor the contractor gets screwed."

"And you put together this last volume?" Hokee asked.

"With a lot of help. But only five or six of us see the summary page with the final pricing."

"Let's go have some lunch, Owen," Hokee said, "then, you can fill me in on this last vital step when I can think straight."

CHAPTER NINE

The Hole

In McCammon, Idaho, a place known as 'The Hole' is an image used by parents in the early pioneer days to frighten their children into behaving. Some parents used a fictional character, such as the 'boogeyman,' to keep their offspring from misbehaving. In a broad area surrounding McCammon, '*The Hole*' was the parent's boogeyman. "If you don't behave, I'm going to throw you into the Hole." It was a threat guaranteed to place fear into the heart of every child.

Thirty thousand years ago, the ancient massive Lake Bonneville covered half of Utah and Nevada and a little bit of Idaho. Around fifteen thousand years ago, the lake breached a natural dam at Red Rock Pass in Idaho, creating a massive channel into the Snake River and many of its deep gorges. The runoff's huge trough this breach made lies between Pocatello and McCammon, fifteen miles to the southeast. During the past five thousand years, Idaho's volcanic activity laid tremendous lava and ash fields over much of this same area, creating the McCammon hole.

'Old-timers' in the areas will tell you stories if you can get them to talk. They speak of the pioneers who settled the place a hundred and fifty years ago. Local Indians living in the area claimed to throw misbehaving wives into the hole they called 'the bottomless pit.' The 'bottomless pit' became 'the Hole,' and these old-timers claim the pioneers would throw their sick and dead children into this hole. There is also the story about a stagecoach robbery that went bad, and when the posse was about to catch the robbers, they dumped the stolen property into 'the hole.' Of course, in the legend, the robbers stole a chest full of gold.

Whatever truths lay in these past tales, the stories reached Neter Amon, who found a local cowboy happy to reveal the hole's location. Located several miles from McCammon in an undulating field of broken and folded lava is a hole in the lava about eight feet in diameter. Rocks dropped into the hole make no noise as they would if they hit bottom. This rock-dropping business led the pioneers to call it the 'bottomless pit' before becoming known as 'The Hole.'

Neter could not have been more pleased. The nearest ranch house is five miles from the hole and is not visible, and sound in the area does not travel that far. From that spot, there are no visible signs of civilization. It was to this lonely place that Zack brought his three kidnap helpers. They each carried an armload of firewood as they had to park their pickup a mile and a half from the hole. On previous trips, they had brought in sawhorses and planks for the sacrament table. In past years, the Church of Satan's followers had carried in buckets of sand to fill gaps in the lava, making a flat surface for the table and the surrounding fire pits. They created a smooth path around the hole for 'the march.' Using their hands, they cleaned out a place in the rocks to stand the cross. Satisfied that the celebration site was nearing completion, the boys left unafraid that someone would vandalize their work. Area residents had stopped visiting the hole decades in the past. Jackrabbit hunters found easier terrain in which to trek. Nobody ever came here anymore, except Satan's little helpers.

*****

Returning from visiting Laura's distraught parents, Glory stopped at the Bannock County Sheriff's office to see Curly. As Glory drove up to the front door of the sheriff's red rock-faced building, the sun's rays reflecting off the smooth surface were nearly blinding. Glory's eyes were still adjusting to the changing light as she squinted her way inside, only to be squeezed in a gigantic bear hug.

"Hi, Glory. My God, but you are a sight for sore eyes. That Hokee is one lucky detective." As he released his victim, the smile on his face almost made up for her discomfort.

"Hello Curly. Thanks for not crushing my ribs." Glory's smile was not as welcoming.

"Aw hell, you know me Glory," Curly recognized the wintry smile and tried recovering, "This is cowboy country along with the farmers, sheepherders and the ah,,, other miscreants that populate our beautiful Gem state. Out here, we're used to manhandling our fillies."

"You know, Curly; if I didn't want to see your folders, I'd kick you in the balls so hard you'd sing soprano the rest of your life."

"Now Glory. Please don't go all citified on me. I'm just trying to be friendly."

"We could be friends, Curly, if you stopped *manhandling* me and never, ever, call me a *filly* again, or you'll be needing a visit to the dentist."

"Okay, Glory. My God, I received the message. It's just that I am so damned glad to see you back." The scolding seemed to have made an impression as Curly appeared sorry for his rude behavior and wild talk. "Let's go over to my desk. The folders you want to see are over there."

Two folders were lying on his desk. Both had red borders. "What's the meaning of the red folders, Curly?"

"We organize our files by name. So we know who these girls were, but the cases are both unsolved. That's what the red borders signify." While giving this explanation, Curly showed Glory to a seat on the other side of his desk while handing her both folders.

"The folder on the top is the file for Vicky North," Curly started giving Glory a summary of the case. "Vicky was also a freshman at Idaho State two years ago when she vanished. She was from Sweden, enrolled as an international student. She met this boy; I think his name was Victor. He was some kid from Soda Springs vacationing in Europe before beginning school. She fell in love, followed him here, and disappeared a few weeks later."

Glory laid down the second folder on Curly's desk, opening the one for Vicky. Skimming the scarce information on the five pages of interviews, she couldn't help but ask. "I assume you cleared the boy, Victor?"

"Yeah, it devastated the poor kid. Their names drew them together, sounding so much alike. According to Victor, they started out making a joke out of the similarity, then fell in love. Her parents also loved the boy. They came over here from Sweden to put a fire under our department to search harder for the girl, but we couldn't turn up a clue. They left here disappointed and feeling like we let their daughter get kidnapped. Of course, we don't know positively that any of the girls were abducted, as there has never been a ransom note."

Glory studied the folder for a minute or two before remarking, "It says here her roommates reported her missing to the campus police on October 8th."

"Yes. I thought I made that clear on the telephone earlier. All three girls went missing in early October." Curly leaned back in his chair, then stood up by his desk. "Want some coffee, Glory? It ain't much good, but Hokee always has a cup." But, of course, that was a lie as years ago, Hokee accepted a cup of the sheriff's coffee and abstained ever since.

"No, I don't think sheriff's coffee sounds appealing, but thanks. Say, Curly, have you noticed that all three of the girls have different colored hair? First, Vicky was dark brown, this second girl, let's see, JoAnn has red hair and Laura is blond. What do you make of that?"

"Not much. The missing girls have three things in common; one, they were all beautiful young girls. Two, they were all freshmen at Idaho State. Three, they all disappeared in early October. So, we assume that someone abducted them."

Glory read some more, then closed the folders, handing them back to Curly.

"October sounds a little like Halloween," Glory commented, "but early October is a little too soon for the covens to collect sacrifices, isn't it?"

"The sheriff's department has no official listing for covens in the area. Every year, there are always a few calls where somebody accuses their neighbor or some other acquaintance of being a witch. Nothing ever comes of it, and let's be frank Glory, nobody believes in witches, do they?"

"I don't know, Curly. You know I'm from New York, and when you crowd eight million people on a small island, you learn some strange things. What do you have here in Idaho, the entire state, maybe one and a half million? Weird stuff happens in the Big Apple. There are people from every shithole on the planet. If you wanted to find a witch in New York, I could practically guarantee your success."

"Okay, Glory," Curly threw his hands in the air, "But as you said, this ain't New York, and I have never knowingly seen a real live witch. I don't think we have any covens in the area."

"Now, don't get all offended, Curly. I never said you have any witches or covens in your Gem state. I was eliminating possibilities for our missing girls. No witches, so who?"

"Well, if we knew that, the girls wouldn't be missing. What is weird is there have been no rumors about the girl's disappearance, nor has any trace of the girls ever surfaced?"

"Wow! It's enough to make your head ache. This missing girl thing is a case for Hokee." Glory had a look of disappointment on her face. And maybe some sadness.

"That's what I thought, Glory. That's why I had the Taylors call him."

CHAPTER TEN

Elimination

Hokee and Owen ate in the company cafeteria. Five hundred people worked in the Nampa Olson Construction Company building, so the company ran a restaurant to keep employees in the building as much as possible. Someone decorated the restaurant with their idea of a San Francisco Bistro. The dark paneled walls had pictures of a black man playing the saxophone and somebody else with a clarinet, but you couldn't see any details about the man.

In the dining room, four chairs accompanied each wooden table covered with blue and white checkerboard tablecloths. Discrete lights shined down on each table, creating shadows between tables, giving the restaurant a feeling of intimacy. They designed the interior to help employees relax and forget about work for a few minutes while eating lunch. Soft jazz played in the background. Hokee kept hoping to hear a little John Coltrane or Duke Ellington, but they never played them. The music was pleasant, soothing, and tasteful for a company cafeteria.

Back at work, Hokee continued with his questions. "After you put together the last pages for the pricing manual, who sees these numbers?"

"I sit down with Grant, maybe one or more of his brothers and son Gene. We may spend two or three days working the numbers, often calling in team members from some other volumes to clarify certain aspects of the bid. But, ultimately, it's just Grant and me. Next, we have Charlene type up the last pages. Then Grant takes the entire bid home overnight to give everything one last review.

I know Gene and his fiancée went home with Grant for the final review. Grant compares our proposal to the RFP; that's the request for proposal," he added, seeing the confusion on Hokee's face. "He has Gene check his work, then it gets boxed up and curried to the principal."

"What about your London office? I see you mention them in the proposal summary." Hokee was still trying to get his head around an operation the size of Olson Construction Company and the complications involved in preparing a bid of this magnitude.

"We had to have a London presence before they would allow us to take part in the bidding. So, Grant opened an office close to the airport, staffing it with other senior people who could answer any question the customer might have. Of course, we prepared Grant to fly over if it became necessary."

"Did the London office see your proposal?" Hokee asked, hoping this might be the source of their leak.

"They might, since it was their responsibility to present our proposal to the Airport Bidding Committee. But Hokee, these people had no access to the other two contracts we didn't win."

Hokee had to think for a few seconds. Something was bugging him, and he couldn't get his head around the problem. "Did any of the London people present the other proposals you lost?"

"By God Hokee, there might have been some of the same people involved. We must ask Grant. After our proposal bid failed, I got reassigned, and I never worked on either of the other submissions…"

After pausing for a second, Owen continued, "understand; when you put in the work necessary for a major proposal of this magnitude, you give it everything you have to be successful, and that takes a toll. I've been in recovery for the past two years, doing light office work, regaining my killer instinct. I'm just now getting to where I could direct another significant proposal."

"Okay, Owen, I think we're through with you. Let's go see Grant and plan for my next meeting."

*****

Wearing one of his royal blue silk robes, Ahmad led the messenger into his private office off limits to wives, concubines, and all palace staff, unless he accompanied them. Once inside, Ahmad went to his desk with the door closed and picked up a black handset, much like a mobile phone, except this unit did not make calls. Instead, it was an electronic scanner to make sure the messenger was not carrying any electronic equipment of his own, such as a listening device or recorder. Then, satisfied that his messenger was clean, Ahmad said, "well, what is it. What's the big message."

"It's your daughter, Master. Rashida. She may be in big trouble."

"What kind of trouble. She doesn't need more money, does she? I understand she is making big money on her own."

"No, I don't think it is money, Master. My brother in New York called to tell me he is worried for her. He found out the Olsons are trying to find out who tampered with their bids. This could be bad news for your daughter. My brother doesn't know any details, but she skipped a business appointment for the first time in many months. That isn't like her, and since you went to visit her last spring, she has been working very hard. Perhaps she needs a break."

"Does your brother know who might be after her? Who wants her head?"

"No, Master. But he worries about her safety. He asked me to talk to you. Perhaps you might call her." The messenger was going out on a limb with this statement. No one tells the Master what to do. Suggesting that he make a phone call was pushing it to the extreme.

"What's your name, boy?" Ahmad almost barked the statement, making it more of a command than a question.

Trembling in fear, the messenger stuttered his name, "J... Ja... Jamal, Master."

"Who else knows about this, Jamal?" This question also came out like the bark of an angry dog.

"Why, no one, Master. I only just told you." The messenger's dark eyes were the size of a small hen's eggs and full of terror.

"Okay, then Jamal. You may go. But speak to no one else about this, or I will have you killed." Ahmad threw his hands towards the door with this statement, as if sweeping the boy from his office.

Ahmad followed the shaking lad to the office door, making sure it was closed and locked before going to his ornate African Black Wood desk trimmed in sterling silver with insets made of gold. An old-fashioned telephone, like one made by AT&T in the 1950s, was the only object on top of the desk. He had stripped the phone of all original equipment and replaced it with the most modern satellite telephone electronics with state-of-the-art encryption. Ahmad liked how the old Bakelite instrument felt in his hands, much more comfortable than those shoeboxes he sees everybody else uses.

He placed a call to a cousin living in New York, whose sole occupation was to monitor his beautiful, headstrong daughter. But, unfortunately, Muhammad failed to pick up the call at his end. Cursing, Ahmad slammed the receiver back into its cradle. Then, without meaning to, he spoke the words out loud, "wait until I get my hand on that lazy bastard."

CHAPTER ELEVEN

The Prison

They locked Laura in a dark, windowless room with poor air circulation. The room smelled of disinfectants, human waste, and dust. She was still naked, but covered by a blanket. Trying to move her hands to scratch her face, Laura found her arms bound to the sides of a cot. She could not tell whether it was the original cot she was lying on in their so-called temple or a different one. She had also lost track of the days. They seemed to feed her at odd hours and with no watch and no window; it was impossible to know night from day.

The only person she saw regularly was Raven. Raven would unlock the room's door, turn on the light and bring in a tray of food. Raven would place the tray on her stomach, then put two pillows under the back of her head, raising it so that Laura could eat. They left just enough freedom in her arms that with a spoon she could feed herself, although with difficulty. At other times Raven came in to draw more blood.

The room appeared tiny with the light on, like it might have been a janitorial closet which would account for the smell. There was a drain in one corner of the room, and whenever Raven appeared, she would invite Laura to use the drain. This was always an awkward affair. Raven had to untie one of Laura's hands so she could get off the bed. Raven always put the bed between herself and Laura in case Laura tried to fight.

The bed covering always came off, and Laura had to squat by the drain and hope for the best. They forced her to smash the solid matter into the drain with a small board provided for that purpose. She then washed the complete mess down the drain by splashing in a bucket of disinfectant-laced water. Some mess always splashed on Laura's legs. Raven came equipped with a towel for just this purpose. As if there was some shortage of cleaning supplies, Raven only brought a dry towel, never one that was damp to help wash off some of the grit.

Every third day Raven brought three other girls from the temple to help with Laura's shower. Neter wanted the sacrifice always to look and smell clean. He didn't want any unpleasant odor associated with their gift to Satan. After untying Laura, with two girls holding each of her arms, they led her out of the stink hole prison and down a short hall to the shower. While Laura was a farm girl in decent shape, she was no match for the four girls sent to shower her. The shower comprised a showerhead with no walls placed near another floor drain. Laura would stand under the showerhead while one girl turned on the water from a nearby wall handle. The water was chilly, and the soap bar they gave her was difficult to lather, but Laura appreciated a chance to clean herself, although she knew they were not doing it for her benefit.

Every day Raven would bring in an IV kit and take half a pint of Laura's blood. With no sense of the passing days, Laura guessed drinking her blood was a weekly ritual as they repeated the blood-drinking ceremony in their 'temple.'

The girls would tie Laura to the same cross every time, and after drinking her blood, they would all pass by, touching, clucking, and snickering while they all had their turn. Laura quickly learned that fighting was futile, only earning stiff jabs in her ribs and stomach. Of course, they didn't want to damage the sacrifice.

It was with great difficulty that Laura kept up her spirits. Her parents were Mormons but didn't take part in regular attendance at any church function. Still, Laura picked up enough religion to help her stay sane. In addition, she had a firm belief in Jesus that helped provide some hope for a rescue.

Jesus loved her and would not let her perish at the hands of these Satan worshipers. During one of her infrequent Sunday school classes, the teacher recited Daniel's story in the Lion's den. If God would protect Daniel, surely he would not let these sinners take her life. This feeble hope was all that kept Laura from losing her sanity.

*****

Glory relaxed in Hokee's hand-carved chair on his porch with Shila lying a few feet away. Frustrated at her lack of progress on the missing Taylor girl case and missing Hokee, she sipped on a gin and tonic, wondering if she should stay here in Pocatello or return to New York. With no idea when Hokee would return and nothing to do, there wasn't much going on in the area to keep her interest. She was ready to pack her bag and head for the airport when Curly called.

"Hey Glory. I thought you might like to come with me to visit one of Laura's roommates. A girl named Diann. She might have a lead on Laura's disappearance."

Glory's malaise disappeared in a heartbeat. There is nothing like a clue to fire up a lonely investigator's synapse—something to stimulate her mind and body to resume functioning. "Oh my God, Curly. I almost forgive you for squeezing the life out of me. But, hell yes, I want to talk with Diann. You won't believe how close I was to packing up my slender suitcase and heading back to New York."

"Aw, you don't want to do that. Think of poor Hokee. I couldn't stand to see him stand around moaning if you leave. Anyway, I thought he was only going to be gone for a few days."

"Yeah, but sitting here with nothing to do is hard on a city girl. I'm used to non-stop action, and here, it seems like you have to wait an eternity for some action to happen. I understand now how kids can become fascinated watching road tar set."

"Now Glory. No need to get testy. Go with me to see this roommate; then, if you still need some exciting action, I'll take you to dinner."

"Okay, but no rattlesnake. I'm not ready to try that yet."

"Damn, and I had the perfect restaurant in mind. Oh well, I guess roadkill will have to satisfy."

"That's real cute, Curly. Are you picking me up or meeting me in town?"

"Do you know how to get to the motel you stayed in during your last visit to town?"

"Oh, sure. I can find it easily." At least she hoped she could remember the way.

"Great. I'll pick you up there if that's alright with you? It's on the way to the girl's dorm. It will help save us some time. Say thirty minutes?"

"Sure. Okay. Plenty of time. I'll see you there."

Glory was eager to talk with the girl, but uneasy about dinner with Curly. Sure, he was supposed to be Hokee's friend, but was he, really? And was the dinner invitation just two friends getting together for dinner, or did he have something more in mind? Oh, Lord. Here a few minutes ago, she was practically ready to slit her wrists, and now the world was full of complications. She would have it no other way.

Diann's dorm was a modern three-story yellow brick building with many enormous windows sided by black wrought iron shutters adding a pleasing decorative touch. Ancient juniper trees flanked the building, and curving walkways led from the visitor's parking lot to the front entrance.

The ground-floor lobby for the dormitory covered nearly the entire first floor. Someone tastefully arranged Naugahyde couches and comfortable chairs in various pastel colors in conversational groupings. Interspersed with each collection were end tables with lamps and oversized coffee tables full of magazines, papers, and backpacks. A bored student wearing her black hair in dreadlocks sat on a stool behind a counter at one end of the room, watching classmates engaged in lively conversations. Curly led Glory over to the bored girl to ask about visiting with Diann.

"Are you looking for me?"

A timid girl in black tights and an orange sweatshirt came up and asked Curly as he stood in front of the counter, with Glory waiting for the bored student behind the desk to respond to his question.

"If you are Diann, then yes. You called the sheriff's office, correct?"

Nodding her head affirmatively, as though afraid to speak, the girl offered a timid smile. "I'm Diann. And yes, I called the sheriff's office. We're all worried about Laura." The girl spoke hesitatingly, as though afraid someone might take offense at her voice.

Glory studied the girl for a few seconds. She was a chubby little thing, only five foot two and maybe 140 pounds, but she moved with athletic grace, light on her feet.

Now it was Glory's turn to act in her investigative mode. Did the girl appear credible? Was she looking for attention, or was she sincere in her concern for Laura's disappearance?

Diann looked at Glory as though reading her mind. "Look, Laura was my roommate. Four of us share a unit. There are two bedrooms and a bath in each unit. Laura and I shared a bedroom. I have not seen her for several days, and the three of us are concerned that something terrible might have happened."

Curly glanced at the two women and asked Diann, "Is there someplace we can sit down and talk with you for a few minutes?"

"Oh, sure. Follow me." Saying this, the girl took off in a fast-paced walk people with short legs adopt while trying to keep up with their long-legged friends.

Diann led them to one of many nooks surrounding the primary room that provided a more intimate setting. Most of these surrounding rooms were empty, and their guide chose the first one they encountered. Motioning to nearby chairs, Diann waited for Curly and Glory to sit before taking a chair on the opposite side.

"Okay, Diann, I'm Curly, and this is Gloria," he introduced himself, then Glory. "I'm with the sheriff's office, as you can guess from my uniform, and this lady is investigating the disappearance of your roommate."

"Hi, Diann. I'm happy to meet you and so terribly sorry about your roommate." Glory started out attempting to set a comfortable, engaging atmosphere. "What can you tell us about her and her disappearance?" The New Yorker was in her complete investigative reporter persona. She was empathetic and understanding, making it easy for people to talk with her and share their stories.

"Well, I didn't know her well. We've only been roomies for a little over a month. She seemed very sweet and kind of shy. I don't think life in Malad prepared her for a big university's fast and varied experience. However, she has seemed a lot happier lately, and she is super intelligent. I believe she was getting comfortable."

"Diann, was she dating anyone, seeing anyone special?" This question from Curly.

"No. I don't believe she had any dates. We were both traumatized by the new university experience. There is so much variety, and we were much too busy getting our classes organized and finding our way around the campus to have a social life. And look at me. I know I'm not Miss America material, but Laura was. Boys were hitting on her like crazy, but she just shrugged them off."

Diann seemed to handle the questions confidently, but worry for her roommate kept the furrows in her forehead. Moving on, Glory asked the following question.

"Was there any boy that seemed persistent? Someone who didn't want to take no for an answer?"

"No. Not one that she talked about. We shared almost everything about our lives. But that's why I called the sheriff's office. I saw this one large boy with dark hair staring at her the day before she disappeared."

Diann seemed about to cry with the remembrance. Something about the event had her spooked.

"Tell us what you saw, Diann."

Curly's tone was abrupt and way too intense, causing the girl to flinch away.

In a more soothing voice and speaking in an unhurried manner, Glory resumed the questioning.

"Please relax, Diann. Curly gets a little excited sometimes, and I have to beat him with my fists." Glory smiled her award-winning television reporter's smile, which was rewarded with a brief, timid smile.

After Diann took a couple of breaths, Glory continued, "what can you tell us about this boy you saw, Diann? What were the circumstances?"

"Well, it was the day before she disappeared. We passed each other on the Quad, going in different directions. She headed towards English 101, and I was going to my algebra class. When I got to the building, I turned around to wave and saw this big boy; he looked like a bully."

"This is the boy with the dark hair you mentioned earlier?" Glory was trying to nail down the specifics.

"Yes, he was across the Quad from me, so the distance hindered specifics about his face, but something about him seemed off. Most students between classes are too busy to stand around gawking. But this boy stood partially hidden by the shrubbery blocking the view of those going into the English building, and he was watching Laura as she crossed the Quad and entered the building. His interest in her seemed beyond that of a boy looking for a date. He was way too intense. He stayed there for a couple of minutes after she entered the building, then he stalked off in the opposite direction."

"Did you ever see this boy again?" Glory asked. Curly seemed to have taken a clue from Glory's earlier scolding and was letting her do the questioning.

"Yes, and that is why I think something is wrong. The next day, the day Laura disappeared, I saw this same boy with three others hanging around the student's lounge. They were all very muscular. I thought they might be football players at first, but these guys didn't seem to fit in on the campus. They looked too old to be students, and none of them were carrying books or backpacks. And everybody you see on campus has one or the other, and some carry both."

"And that's the last time you saw the boy with the dark hair?" Curly couldn't help himself. He couldn't let Glory have all the fun.

"Yes. I never saw the man again or any of the other men with him at the lounge. I know this isn't much to go on, but I believe those four men abducted Laura. She is quite exquisite." Diann was about to cry again, so Glory jumped in to ease her pain.

"Thank you, Diann. This information has been beneficial. You did well calling this in, and it gives us a starting spot. Hopefully, we'll have your roommate back soon."

As Curly and Glory walked back to his vehicle, he asked, "are we on for dinner?"

"As long as you understand, this is just a dinner." There was no smile in her words.

"Not to worry, Glory. If I make an inappropriate move or suggestion, Hokee will nail me to the barn door with rusty nails and use me for target practice."

"In that case, Curly, take this girl to dinner. I'm famished."

CHAPTER TWELVE

Another Elimination

Grant had Charlene page Art Waytown, the Nampa proposal manager for the dam on India's Penganga River. Bryce Holliday, the principal proposal manager, lived in India, supervising the local Olson Construction office. Art worked for Bryce, interfacing with the people in Nampa.

Hokee was waiting in the conference room Grant had given him when Art poked his head in the door, "Are you Hokee Wolf? Charlene told me to meet you here."

"Yes, hi Art. Come on in. Grant told me he would have you sit down with me for a brief chat. I wanted to ask you about the India dam bid."

Art was a middle-aged man with a full head of dark hair and white sidewalls. He had a nice build, someone who kept his body by eating right and getting plenty of exercise. So if it surprised him to see a native American Indian-looking man with long black hair built like an atlas, he kept it to himself.

Seating himself in a comfortable chair opposite Hokee, Art began with no prompting. "I don't know what to tell you, Mr. Wolf. I've gone over everything with Grant."

"That's fine, Art. And please call me Hokee. I have just a couple of simple questions about the final procedure in assembling the bid. First, how much of the process did you handle?"

"Well, gee. Pretty much everything." Art scratched his day-old beard. "I ran the Nampa part of the proposal, and Bryce did the on-site part in India."

Hokee could see he would have trouble communicating with the engineer, Art's primary profession, before getting into management. He was an old-time civil engineer who still carried five different pens in the pocket protector in his blue denim long-sleeved shirt pocket. Hokee had only seen pocket protectors in pictures before running into Art.

"So, you never saw the final quote sent to the principal?" Hokee was getting right to the point.

"Well, yes, and no. We do almost all the engineering and materials part of the bidding here in Nampa. Of course, I helped Grant work up the final numbers together for that part of the bid. Over in India, or is it down in India? Heck, I never could keep that right in my head. Anyway, we get the package from Bryce in India with all the labor and subcontracting costs and schedule. Grant and I put it all together after reworking some numbers regarding the schedule. Then Gene took the whole mess back to India. Bryce had to do some slight modifications on the labor part with Gene, after which they took the package to the Indian government."

"Are you telling me that Gene flew to India to help Bryce put the final proposal together?"

"Yeah, isn't that what I just said?" Art seemed a little peeved at the question, as though he didn't speak clearly.

"Yes, Art. You were very clear. I guess I'm surprised that Grant sent Gene instead of going over himself."

"Oh, hell, the old man has been grooming Gene to take over the business for years. By now, Gene probably knows almost as much about contracting as Grant. Well, not really, but the kid is good."

It seemed a little odd to hear Art refer to Grant as the old man and Gene as the kid. Art seemed older than Grant, although Hokee guessed they were probably about the same age.

"Okay, Art. I think we're through here. Thanks for dropping by."

"Nah, happy to help. I only hope you can figger out how we keep losing these big contracts."

After Art left, Hokee went in search of Grant, who was still in his office.

"Grant, I'm ready to look at the Japanese bid now. Who do I talk with?"

"I'm afraid you have to go to Japan to do that, Hokee. Roger Krammer, our Japanese office manager, put together our bid on the nuclear power plant almost single-handedly. Of course, we supported him with our staff here cranking out numbers, but Roger put it all together. Gene went over for the final number crunching, and of course, I saw the final numbers, but Roger and Gene took our bid over to the Japanese government office building. Do you want to talk with Roger?"

"Grant, I need to speak with everyone who had anything to do with putting together the final packages for all three contracts. To discover the leaker, I have to understand the process and talk with everyone involved."

"I'll have my pilot take you anywhere you need to go, Hokee. I offered to have our plane pick you up in Pocatello."

"I know Grant, and I appreciate the offer. It isn't a long drive, and it gave me time to think. I want to visit Bryce in India, then Roger in Japan. Is that possible?"

"Oh, sure. When do you want to leave?"

"I'm through here in Nampa. I just need to grab my bag from the hotel. How soon can the plane be ready?"

"I'll have Charlene call the pilot to get the plane ready. Then, she'll have the caterer stock the plane with food and booze and new bedding. It's a fast plane, but you are headed to the other side of the planet. It's a long flight. The plane should be ready within an hour—time for you to grab your bag and head on over to the airport. I'll have someone drive you so your Explorer can stay here in our parking lot. It's fenced and guarded so no one can break in while you are away."

Grant's plane was a G650 with a plush gold velour interior divided into a working area with a table, oversized lounge chairs, and a couch, plus a minibar stocked with all the major high-end brands. Towards the rear was a bedroom and bathroom with a shower. A discrete sign suggested showers last no longer than two minutes.

Besides two pilots, the crew included a hostess to serve meals and drinks and keep the passengers happy. On this flight, Hokee was the only passenger. With a flight time of approximately fifteen hours, two pilots shared the cockpit, taking turns. Having a hostess freed up the pilots to concentrate on flying, as they had someone else to care for their passenger.

Joan wore a white pantsuit that fit her slender figure perfectly. She fussed over Hokee until he was ready to find a place where he could disappear. As Hokee was the only passenger, Joan had nothing to do except keep him happy, which she seemed pleased to do continually. Finally, Hokee asked Joan if she ever drank alcohol? When she answered yes, he insisted she makes herself a drink and join him before he went crazy. Joan seemed more than willing to accept his offer.

While Joan was making herself a drink, Hokee called Glory.

"Hey, stranger. I thought you would never call."

"Hey yourself. Thought I'd let you know I'm on my way to India."

"India? I thought you were on your way home."

"Sorry, sweetheart. Duty calls. It turns out they only completed one final bid in Nampa. Olson's local offices on-site delivered the other two proposals. So the only way to find out what happened is to visit both places. How are you doing? Missing me?"

"Not hardly. Curly is sitting here with me eating dinner at the Himalayan Flavor; it's an Indian restaurant."

"What on earth are you doing with Curly, and how's the missing girl's case going?"

"That's why I'm with Curly. Jealous? I wouldn't blame you. He's mighty handsome for an Idaho deputy sheriff." Glory looked over at a surprised Curly and gave him a wink; like, *don't take it seriously, pal.*

"You ain't getting me on that one, Glory. And you are the only person on the planet who finds Curly handsome. And there ain't no correct answer to your question. Besides which, what does a New York City girl know about Idaho deputy sheriffs? Handsome or otherwise? Hell, you only know one, or am I missing something?"

"Okay, Hokee, you got me. Maybe too much Taj Mahal. My God, these are enormous bottles. And I'm not really a beer drinker. Anyway, Curly received a call from Laura's roommate. Laura is the missing girl in case you forgot. We believe she was stalked and grabbed by four muscular young men. It looks like they specifically targeted her."

"That's excellent work, Glory. You're going to have that case all wrapped up before I get back."

"Don't I wish. But, Hokee, two other girls went missing the past two years under very similar circumstances, including the time of year."

"What, the beginning of October? Halloween isn't for several days yet. What have you guys concluded from this?"

"Nothing yet. Curly doesn't know of any witches' covens in the area, and anyway, they don't kidnap someone for sacrifices, do they?"

"I don't believe they do or ever did. It looks like you guys have a puzzle. I wish I were there to help. Maybe a good sweat would clear things up a bit. Have a go at it if you find the prospect appealing."

"No, thanks. I'd probably burn the place down. So we'll keep working and waiting on the master. How much longer will you be gone?"

"It looks like two or maybe three days. I'm getting some ideas, but they have to be checked out before I can say anything."

"Okay. Good luck with that. I'm going to start folders on the other two missing girls. Maybe something will pop out to help with the search."

"Thanks, Glory. It's kind of you to pitch in like that. I appreciate it a great deal. Hopefully, we'll find the girl soon. It's too bad you don't have a deal with your New York television buddies to investigate the missing girls. It could make a great expose. Let me know if you need anything. I love you, Glory girl. Goodbye for now."

"I love you too, Hokee Wolf. Come home soon. Bye now."

Glory couldn't believe it when four strapping young men came into their restaurant. Her alarms all went off. She just knew with every instinct in her head that these were the guys who kidnapped Laura.

Now, what was it that made her think that? It wasn't the way they dressed or their general appearance. It was the way they moved, with a kind of swagger, like bullies on a playground. They acted like they owned the world.

She wanted Curly to get a glimpse of the boys, but they turned and left before he had a chance for a good look. Glory tried to get him to heed her suspicions, but he wouldn't listen. He considered it highly unlikely that anyone had that kind of psychic ability. As she sat there fuming, Glory wondered how anyone who was friends with Hokee could be so dense?

CHAPTER THIRTEEN

Gene's Travails

Gene Olson always found New York fascinating. Of course, Nampa, Idaho, isn't a hick town, at least these days. Still, whenever Gene went to the Big Apple with Opal, it always felt like visiting a foreign country where, fortunately, nearly everyone could almost speak English. Although to be fair, Gene wondered how anyone could mangle the language so thoroughly. Opal's New York friends said Gene had an accent, but Gene thought they were the ones who spoke in a strange tongue.

Opal was one of the most sought-after models in the world. WonderList ranked her number four on the top ten highest-paid models, with an annual income of over ten million dollars. Photographers loved her dark silky soft skin, perfect without flaws. She had a classic face and jawline that could be any of a hundred different nationalities by the creative use of shadows and makeup. She looked slightly Eurasian and could pass for nearly anyone she wanted. Today she had a gig with Jaques, a photographer in a studio over on Newark Avenue by Fourth Street somewhere in *The Village*. For this shoot, she modeled swimsuits while Gene was bumming around the historic district, looking at old buildings.

Without a guidebook, Gene was relying on his memory of the city to keep him oriented. He loved exploring, having visited Korea Town and the meatpacking district on previous visits. After wandering around for a couple of hours, Gene was bored, and without realizing how, found himself in Washington Square Park. Somewhere he took a wrong turn. It turned out to be a horrible mistake.

At first, the park seemed appealing with its monuments and metal sculptures. Gene loved standing in the large divided circle in the park's center, looking down 5th Avenue through the Washington Square Arch. Although relatively small, the park contains dozens of trees, including the Hangman's Elm, referred to by the locals as 'The Hanging Tree.' Records show it is over 300 years old. The English Elm is the most prevalent species in the park, but plenty of Hawthorn trees and eastern redbuds added to the variety. Paved paths meander through the trees, providing pockets of isolation where you are invisible to other park visitors.

It was in one of these blind pockets that two dark-skinned men grabbed Gene from behind. One man held his head with one hand while pushing a rag over Gene's nose and mouth with the other, muffling any cry Gene might make. The other person jabbed a needle containing a powerful drug into Gene's thigh, which almost instantly put him to sleep. They were near W 4th St, running down one leg of the park. The two men quickly carried the unconscious Gene across Washington 4th to Laguardia, a side street where their white Toyota SUV waited. A fisherman discovered Gene's body on Pier 34 in the Hudson River. The abductors had slashed his throat and left him for dead. Fortunately, since the weather was chilly, Gene wore a thick tan turtleneck shirt with a heavy collar. They cut deep in their hurried execution, but Gene's heavy turtle neck shirt and heavy collar absorbed most of the knife thrust, and they failed to hit his jugular. Although nearly dead from the loss of blood, Gene survived. Some suggest that since he was unconscious when they slit his throat, it was easy for his assailants to assume that Gene would die from a loss of blood. For many days, the police searched but never located a witness to the abduction and assault.

*****

Hokee was several hours into his fifteen-hour flight when he received the call from Grant on his way to New York. The only information Grant had regarding the assault was that it wasn't a robbery. Gene's wallet and Rolex watch were still on his body. It seemed like a targeted hit, but for what reason, neither man could find an answer. After Grant's call, Hokee sat for a long time meditating. Deep, slow breaths while visualizing a still mountain lake surrounded by quiet mountains. After reaching his zen state, Hokee let his mind loose to seek answers. If you search for an answer, you may find it, maybe not, or perhaps you didn't recognize it when it came. But if you allow your mind to seek the solution for you, Hokee found it rarely failed.

After a few minutes, Hokee sat up, rubbing his eyes. It now seemed too coincidental in Hokee's mind that Gene's assault occurred soon after he started looking at the bidding irregularities. What better way to deflect suspicion than to commit the crime in New York? Just another street mugging. Except this time, they made a mistake. The muggers didn't rob the body. And Hokee had an uncanny way of finding the bad guys.

In Hokee's experience, all countries have a unique scent, India included. As soon as Hokee stepped off Grant's plane in New Delhi, it was the heat, the humidity, and the smell that assaulted his senses in that order.

The heat was in the low 90s, but the humidity made it seem like a hundred.

We know India for its incense and spices, yet Hokee was unprepared for the assault on his nostrils. Jasmine, paprika, turmeric, and nutmeg from vendors set up right outside the airport mingled with moped exhaust, foul city air, and human waste. It wasn't uncommon to see individuals taking a leak or defecating on the side of the road. Hokee didn't know what to expect, but it wasn't this.

Melissa Bryce, Holliday's secretary, waited outside the airport, standing under a vendor's umbrella, trying to stay cool. She wore a sleeveless white blouse and tan skirt with sensible black flat-soled shoes. Her long black hair, smoky dark skin, and brown eyes bore the look of a native. She was a classic Indian beauty. The girl was holding a copier photograph of Hokee, probably sent by Charlene.

"Mr. Wolf, oh Mr. wolf." Waving the picture and grinning as though she had just won the lottery, the girl made a beeline for Hokee.

Hokee waited for the girl to come up to him, as he didn't know which way she would take them. When she arrived, he was instantly aware of her beauty, while noticing a subtle sheen of moisture on her upper lip and below her eyes. It had not been as cool under the umbrella as she would have liked. Melissa would have killed for a soft cloth to pat the moisture she assumed took away from her looks.

"Oh, Mr. Wolf. I'm so glad you are here. Standing around in this heat is not fit for a beautiful young lady such as myself." She wore a smile more expansive than the Mississippi, and you could see the girl felt delighted with her success in catching the man they had sent her to fetch.

The girl talked faster than a bankruptcy sales auctioneer, and Hokee was still figuring how best to answer the whirlwind at his side when she erupted again.

"Oh, where are my manners? I'm Melissa, Mr. Holliday's secretary. He sent me to fetch you. I even got to drive his Mercedes."

Hokee had to grin despite his tired, aching body. The flight was just too damn long. "Well, Melissa, why don't you take me to your car and let's get out of the heat and stench."

"Oh, sorry about that." As though it was all her fault. "It always stinks around the airport. They put none of those portable toilets here for the vendors, and many people have to walk here from town. It's a long walk. It will smell a lot better when we get to the office. Living here, you kind of get used to the smell."

"Is it a long way?" Hokee asked. Then, seeing her confusion, he continued asking, "to the office?"

"It's about a three-hour drive unless we get stuck behind a water buffalo hauling cow pies. India has over 90 million of those smelly creatures, and people use the manure to build houses until the monsoon washes them away. They can tie up traffic for an hour or more. I mean, the water buffalo can tie up traffic, not the monsoon."

Hokee didn't know quite how to respond to this, so he said nothing.

After what seemed like a long uncomfortable pause, Hokee asked, "how long have you worked for Mr. Holliday?"

This question seemed to put the sparkle back in Melissa's eyes. "It will be three years next month. November 15th."

"Let's see, then. So, you would have been here when Olson Construction bid on the big dam project?"

"Oh yes. It was quite exciting. It was a lot of work and many long hours. And we were ever so sure we were going to win that job."

Cutting right to the chase, Hokee asked, "did you help prepare the final bid before shipping it off to the government?"

Disappointment on her pretty face. "No. Mr. Holliday typed the final few pages himself. He didn't want another London job fiasco." The girl looked frightened, like she had just said something wrong and was about to be punished.

"It's okay, Melissa. That's why I'm here. Grant wants to find out what went wrong. I know about the London job."

"Please don't tell Mr. Holliday I said anything. We're not supposed to talk about it with strangers. Oh, I guess they didn't mean you."

"Don't worry, Melissa. Your secret's safe with me. So, it was just Mr. Holliday finishing up the proposal all by himself?"

"Well, until the very end. Then, that handsome Gene Olson showed up with this glamourous girl on his arm. Oh, my God. Was she ever beautiful! I guess she was his fiancée." Hokee looked over in time to see the wistful expression on Melissa's face. A look that said, *'if that girl hadn't been there, I might have had a chance.'*

"So, Melissa, let me get this straight. Bryce, Mr. Holliday, put the final number for the proposal together with the help of Gene. Is that right?"

"I guess so. Mr. Holliday sent all the office staff home so he could work on the proposal alone. It wasn't until the next day that I saw Gene and his fiancée as they were getting ready to drive back to the airport. That is when Mr. Holliday introduced us to Gene and the woman."

Hokee assumed the girl was getting weary of saying fiancée, as if not saying the word would make it go away.

"Did he say anything else? About having Gene's help with the proposal, and who else might have been there?"

Melissa furrowed her eyebrows in concentration before replying. "No, I don't think so. Mr. Holliday might have said they came over to help him with the proposal, but maybe I just assumed that to be the situation. They all left together. Not in the same car. Gene and the woman drove his rental back to the airport, and Mr. Holliday left in this car to deliver the proposal to the government."

It was looking like any answers to be found in India would have to be at the Olson Construction headquarters with Bryce.

CHAPTER FOURTEEN

Laura's Dream

A pretty little girl in a blue and white gingham dress ran barefoot across the lawn, laughing and having a good time playing chase with a black Labrador. The lab had a white streak across his forehead that accounted for his name, Blaze. The pair had almost reached the apricot tree standing at the edge of the lawn when the girl tripped and fell. While falling, something grabbed her arms, keeping her from hitting the ground. Laura woke with a jerk, finding her arms tied to the cot. It wasn't the first time she had dreamed of falling, but the other times she woke up startled but safe in her own bed. Realizing her predicament anew, Laura almost cried. She found her spirits sinking and her hope for rescue waning.

Falling into despair, the only thing that kept her going was a firm belief in God. Somehow, she just knew that God would send her some help. She focused on Danial in the lion's den and how frightened he must have been until he found his faith in God. While not religious, Laura had a deep spirituality that even this ordeal could not quench. She knew God had a plan even if she perished, and somehow, everything would be alright.

The door to the janitor's closet opened, admitting Raven and three other girls, all beaming with smiles of delight. They untied Laura, allowing her to stand and stretch. Laura had learned it was futile to fight the four girls who together could manhandle her with ease. Although a farm girl, her parents did not expect Laura to do manual labor at home. She helped with the chores and housekeeping, but her primary forms of exercise were biking and climbing. But these chores did not build big muscles.

She had climbed to the top of Mt. Oxford ten miles away several times over the years, admiring the view. On a clear day, you could see Salt Lake City, a hundred miles south.

Laura had to pee, which she accomplished without a hint of embarrassment. After the first half dozen times, the routine became tiresome, and the four minders had grown weary of making fun of their captive. You can only belittle someone so many times before it loses its flavor.

Tonight, the four guards led the naked girl back to the main hall, where a blazing fire was already sending sparks spiraling into the large chimney opening.

They allowed Laura to walk without restraint as she had learned there was no escape and peacefully accepting the inevitable led to much less pain. Laura walked over to the cross and turned around. She stood with the cross to her back, holding out her arms, which the girls tied to the wooden cross. They no longer bound her legs.

Within minutes after they had secured Laura to the cross, the room began filling with members of Satan's church. Zack entered with his three goons, making a big fuss over the naked girl as they strolled past her nude body, reaching out and stroking her breasts and pubic hair. They gloated at their conquest, bragging about how much fun they would have on the feast day. Laura trembled, not knowing if they meant eating her for the feast or sampling her body in other ways. Neither idea had much appeal and watching them drink her blood, smacking their thick lips like they were eating honey, Laura could all too easily see them chowing down on an arm or leg.

*****

Ahmad was in his private Boeing 747, flying to Japan when he got the call. His daughter was safe; they had eliminated the threat. But, relieved that she was safe from whatever had threatened her safety, the news did not dispel his fear for her ultimate safety. Not her physical security, the safety of her soul.

Ahmad was not a spiritual or religious man, but he had grown up in a strict Muslim family and believed in the prophet Mohammed. He believed in Allah and the mandate of keeping the women in his life covered in burkas. That Rashida was disrespecting not only the Hassan name but the very laws of Mohammed were troublesome. Flaunting her body in front of the infidels was more than a frustrated father should have to bear. True, her body was exquisite.

He had seen some of the more graphic photos of his daughter and, as a man, could appreciate her stunning beauty. His anger arose just because he admired her beauty. This vision of loveliness was something that only her father and husband should ever experience, not all the jackals in the world.

As a father, he should have had her dragged back to Egypt, where the town's inhabitants would stone her to death. However, Ahmad could not bring himself to exert this punishment. He loved his daughter and did not appreciate her actions. But the vision of her beauty being marred by stones would not take a seat in his soul. He knew he should do something, but what could a father do short of locking her in his castle. Then there was the benefit to his business. Clients who knew about his daughter fought for the right to benefit the contractor. Many wanted to take her for a wife, but many others wanted to exploit her body in ways the prophet would never condone.

Hassan's big nuclear reactor project in Japan would take up his time for the next couple of weeks, and then he would take care of the problem. Ahmad could not allow her to disrespect the prophet any longer. He knew he was a hypocrite flaunting the prophet's laws all the time by his drinking and cheating on contracts, but he did this in private, not in full view of the entire world. No, he might be a sinner, but by Allah's holy laws, he would not allow his daughter to bring down the family name.

CHAPTER FIFTEEN

Strike Three

Olson's India construction office is in Gandhinagar. The city of Gandhinagar is the capital of Gujarat, and to Hokee, it appeared to be quite wealthy. They intersperse a mixture of ornate temples and modern skyscrapers with beautiful green gardens and stone-lined waterways. Gandhinagar looks like a modern city with centuries of growth and splendid monuments to the past, but like most of India, there are modern buildings next to cardboard shacks and water buffalo dung dwellings. Most women wear bright, colorful blouses and skirts, even the beggars who seemed as thick as the tourists.

The reign of various kings defines India's architecture. The Pallavas kings are famous for stone-built structures rather than hand-carved from the rock. And the Chulas kings built exquisite temples such as the highly ornate Shiva temple. Then, for pure beauty, the Hoysalas are recognized for their incredibly intricate detail and the Nayaks for thousands of pillars. Throughout Gandhinagar, it is possible to visit examples of almost every early period of India's history.

Melissa drove Hokee to an ornate stone building near the modern railroad station and a 5-star hotel next to Karnavati University in a small industrial park. Within the park, there are several three-story flat-roofed buildings made of orange stone. Olson Construction leased one entire building, housing over 200 workers. Although Olson did not win the contract for a new dam, they had over a dozen other major projects throughout India, making Bryce Holliday a busy and popular man.

When he met Hokee in the reception area, Bryce was wearing tan cargo shorts and a blue Pacific Legend's Aloha shirt with palm trees and turtles painted down the right side. Bryce was a big man, six-six, and 240 pounds of Hollywood hunk. Dark curly hair topped a face reminiscent of Dean Martin, causing women to palpitate wherever he went. He carried himself well and kept his body working out in a home gym and running a half-hour every day. His morning run before the daytime heat built up was his favorite time of day. The route he ran varied daily, taking him to exciting temples and markets no matter where he ran. Blessed with good looks, he had heads turning everywhere his runs took him.

Hokee was curious about how Bryce knew he would be in the lobby, but everything happened so fast, and there was so much to take in; it felt like his head was on a swivel he never got the chance to ask the question.

"Is this your first time in India, Hokee?"

"What gave me away?" Hokee asked with a smile. "Was it my tongue hanging out or just the bulging eyes?"

Sensing his visitor's awe, Bryce continued, "India has some pretty fantastic sculptures, monuments, and interesting sights to go along with a history older than most other cultures on earth."

"I can see that, Bryce, but it's difficult for someone like me to appreciate such magnificence next to the squalor and poverty."

"Unfortunately, Hokee," Bryce continued, "it takes a stranger to notice the disparity. Living here for any length of time, you get used to the stench and unsightly underbelly and take it for granted. I suppose the natives have lived with and endured it for so many centuries; they no longer even notice it."

"I wonder if the caste system that Gandhi tried to eliminate, or at the least change, has anything to do with this dichotomy?" Hokee's question caused Bryce to raise his eyebrows, but he smiled as though it was so clear as to be hardly worth mentioning.

"Any civilization this old must have a lot of secrets," Bryce said in explanation. "After a certain period, this all becomes the status quo. Shall we go on up to my office? Can Melissa get you some refreshments? This office specializes in making world-famous iced Chai?"

"I'll follow, and I would be crazy not to try your world-famous Chai."

Bryce had an office on the third floor, but the building had no elevator, so they walked up wide rose-colored granite stairs with hand-carved railings and impressive sculptured balusters. Bryce's office occupied nearly one-half of the top floor. There was a bamboo desk in front of an ergonomic chair with two facing padded leather chairs for guests. Next to a window overlooking the industrial park was a bright red Naugahyde couch and a coffee table. He had a small round table in the center for more intimate working meetings, and they devoted the rest of the room to a large drafting table and two large flat filing cabinets for drawings.

"Let's sit on the couch, Hokee, and you can tell me what brings you to our home, half a world away from our real home."

Bryce acted like it was just a casual comment, but Hokee thought he detected just a hint of annoyance in the invitation. Like, why in the hell did Nampa send me this guy? Are they checking up on me?

"I thought perhaps Grant would have told you about the reason for my visit," Hokee responded.

"Why, no. I got a call from Charlene, who told me to meet your plane and that you would explain the purpose of your visit when you got here. She said it was essential to Grant."

"I guess I understand that, Bryce. However, the nature of my visit has to do with some sensitive information, which I suppose is best dealt with in person."

"What are we talking about, Hokee? What kind of sensitive information? Grant has an encrypted satellite phone." His demeanor made it apparent that Bryce was concerned and unhappy about the intrusion into his private kingdom. There still appeared to be a fear that Hokee was some kind of hitman sent by Grant to deliver bad news.

Hokee picked up on Bryce's concern and was quick to explain.

"Grant is concerned that Olson Construction is out some hundred million dollars in proposal costs over the past two years, and losing three significant contracts in a row to the same Egyptian contractor has him concerned that there may be a leak in the organization. So he asked me to look into this for him, to see if someone is helping the competition."

"Oh, I remember now. I didn't register the name at first. So you are that detective guy who rescued his daughter, Wanda. Grant doesn't suspect me, does he?" Here Bryce couldn't help but offer a self-conscious chuckle. Like, of course, it couldn't be me.

"No, Grant thinks highly of you. Bryce. I'm checking out all three sites where the bidding originated. You were not privy to the other two bids, so naturally, your name was never on the suspect list. Some people saw the production of all three quotes, and somewhere there may be a traitor. We don't know for a fact that it wasn't a coincidence, but neither Grant nor myself believe this is the case. I'm just checking out all the loose ends."

"Whew. There for a minute, you had me worried." Bryce had a wry grin that said, *like, not really; I was just kidding.*

God, as if being movie-star handsome wasn't enough, the guy has to have perfect dimples. This thought ran through Hokee's mind.

"What I would like is for you to run me through the final proposal preparation. Who helped put it together, and who saw the final quote you gave to the Indian government?"

"Well, Hokee. That's a pretty short list. Of course, there's Melissa and me. She helped put the whole proposal together. Hell, there must have been three thousand pages, I believe; six volumes. Then, just before we submitted, Gene and his fiancée, oh, what's her name, Opal, yeah Opal. They came over for the last couple of days with some numbers from Nampa. Together we massaged the proposed quote, and then the four of us wrapped it up. That's all the people who saw the final numbers. Just the four of us."

"Thanks, Bryce. That's what I thought I might learn here, but the only way to know for sure was to come and find out. Please don't let my visit concern you, and I know for a fact that Grant values your contribution beyond what you might believe. He is always singing your praises."

"Thank you, Hokee. I wish you success in finding the leak. Is there anything else we can do here in India to make your stay comfortable? The City Club next door is a 5-star hotel; we could put you into a company suite if you would like."

"Thanks, but no. If you would have Melissa call me a taxi and then alert my pilot. I want to go on to Japan and finish this trip."

"Certainly. However, it seems a shame to come all this way and not take in some of our famous sites and excellent food. Are you sure we can't persuade you to stay over, at least for one night?"

Hokee stood, letting Bryce know their interview was over. Bryce asked Melissa to drive Hokee back to his airplane. He wouldn't hear of a taxi. As they were walking out, Hokee thanked Melissa for the Chai.

"You were right, Bryce; it was world-class Chai. At least it sure beats that stuff they call Chai in Pocatello."

That last statement of Hokee's was not the most polite comment to make about someone's hospitality, but by the time he realized his lack of manners, it was too late to change, and besides, Japan was waiting.

CHAPTER SIXTEEN

Glory's Hunt

Glory had Curly drop her back at the car she had left in the hotel's parking lot. She could tell Curly didn't want to let her out of the car; he wanted to have a drink with her at the lounge inside the hotel, but a little of Curly goes a long way; and besides, Shila waited for her back at Hokee's. She didn't need an excuse to avoid having a drink with the man, but feeding Shila sounded plausible, and Curly didn't push the invitation. Neither of them wanted to get on Hokee's yellow list. They both knew about his penchant for writing things he didn't like on a sheet of yellow paper.

Back at Hokee's cave-like house, Glory wanted to sit outside on the wide veranda, but the October chill had her reconsider. A fire already laid in the living room fireplace seemed too good an invitation to pass up, so Glory started the fire before curling up on one of Hokee's handmade couches with a notepad and pen. As the fire warmed up the room, Glory made notes about the three missing girls.

They were all abducted or went missing about the first of October. The only exciting thing about this month, in Glory's opinion, was Halloween, and that wasn't for a few more days. If someone wanted a Halloween ceremony with a pretty girl, it seemed strange to take the girl at the beginning of the month.

And then there were the four thuggish-looking men Glory saw at the restaurant. There was no doubt in Glory's mind these were the men Diann saw in the student's lounge. But who were they, and why did they enter the restaurant and turn and leave so suddenly? When she saw them come into the restaurant, she thought it was to be seated and have a meal, but they barely came inside before leaving. What caused them to leave so suddenly?

The more she thought about it, the stranger the incident became in her memory. Glory tried playing the scene back in her mind. As an investigative reporter, she trained herself to notice details and recall them at will. Sitting now in Hokee's living room, warming up to a crackling fire, she closed her eyes and, in her mind, watched the four men enter the room.

The biggest, a tough-looking square-faced man with a blond buzzcut wearing a blue Idaho State University sweatshirt with the sleeves cut short, was the first to enter. A tattoo decorated his upper arm. Glory focused her mind on seeing the image. It appeared for only a microsecond, barely time for a glimpse.

She strained, but couldn't get a sense of the tattoo. Then, remembering one of Hokee's exercises for memory recall, she laid down and began breathing. First, a long breath in and then slowly letting the breath out while focusing on relaxing. Then repeat a second time. There is an exercise he taught her where you go through your entire body, relaxing one small part at a time, starting with your left foot. The practice can easily take up to thirty minutes, but you can get 90 percent of the effect in five or ten minutes with a bit of practice. Glory didn't want to spend that much time at present. If it seemed something that would be beneficial, she could always do it later.

After getting the body relaxed, Glory focused her full attention on the breathing process: steady slow inhalations and the same controlled slow exhalation. By focusing all of her attention on the breathing process, her mind became silent. According to Hokee, this exercise put you into the present, the moment of now.

Glory focused her attention on getting the tattoo's image from the blond man's arm with an empty mind. Once she gave this command to her subconscious mind, Glory relaxed and opened her eyes. Now all she could do was wait. The trick is not to think about it. Instead, let it come to you. It almost invariably works, and Glory had barely settled back down when she saw the man's arm flash by in her mind. Either it went by too quickly for a good look, or the man's arm didn't rotate sufficiently to expose the entire design; all she could grasp of the image was a twisted face of some weird *being*, done in red and black ink.

She focused her mind on the other three men who entered the restaurant with the blond man. They all wore the same blue ISU sweatshirt, but with sleeves still attached. They all had brutish looks—dark penetrating unsmiling eyes above sneering smiles and weightlifter postures. Legs slightly spread apart with arms hanging out twenty degrees from the body. She didn't see any other tattoos, but three of the men never entered the room as far as the first man.

The big question in Glory's mind was this: *what did these four men want with Laura?* And hard on the back of this thought was another: *what did they do with her?* They looked old enough to have been responsible for the other two missing girls, but why only once a year in October?

Going back to her list, Glory continued, noting that they never heard from the first two girls again, nor were their bodies discovered. Were the girls eaten? Were they taken to someplace remote and repeatedly raped, then killed, and the bodies buried? Lord knows, she thought, there were enough sinkholes in the lava fields to bury thousands who would never be discovered unless by someone like Hokee on a vision quest.

Glory's looked at her list.

Three missing girls.

Early October.

Once each in the past two years-plus the present.

All very attractive.

All freshmen at ISU.

No contact with anyone after the disappearance.

No bodies ever discovered.

Four male suspects, no names-only suspects for now.

The girls all disappeared during the daytime.

All three Caucasian girls.

All from good families.

Laura, Vicky, Joann.

Laura's roommate thinks Laura was a virgin (a factor?)

Were the other two girls virgins?

This list provided little to go on. Then, Glory remembered visiting Hokee's office and being shown a scrapbook by Hilda containing letters from dozens of parents thanking Hokee for rescuing their child. How does he do it? Looking at the information she had collected, Glory guessed Hokee had only this when he started his searches. Yet he found the missing girls and boys. Then she remembered.

Hokee was a shaman and used the sweat lodge to visit other realms of consciousness. He could see other realities at will. She had even been a participant. Hokee invited her to take a sweat, didn't he? She suspected that this was the only way to collect the information they needed to find and possibly rescue Laura, but she was afraid. Hokee had warned her about how easy it was to get lost in that space and having had her mind stolen before; Glory didn't want to take that chance again without Hokee to be a guide.

She had a sudden inspiration. Perhaps one or more of those brutes she saw in the restaurant also went to ISU. If they did, she might spot their picture in the university yearbook. So tomorrow, she would call Diann to find out if it would be possible to see the school's yearbooks.

CHAPTER SEVENTEEN

Gene's Recovery

When Opal reached her New York apartment after the photo shoot and couldn't find Gene, she almost lost her mind. At first, she assumed he got lost and would soon either call or show up, looking chagrined. After a half-hour passed and still no word, she got anxious. He may not have called earlier because he never wanted to interrupt her work. However, either he would also know she would be home by now, or she would have called him to let him know she would be late. Therefore, if he got lost, he would certainly call her for help. She dialed his number.

Opal heard the phone ring six times before someone said, "Allo."

"Who is this? I am calling Gene."

"Franko. Found phone. I keep it."

"Mr. Franko, where did you get the phone? You can keep it. Just, please tell me where you got the phone and if you know what happened to the man who owned the phone."

"I do no nobody. Found phone on peah,,, by rivah."

"Please, do you know what happened to him?"

"Nah. Saw amblance. Do no nuten."

"Can you hel..," but there was nobody there. The man had disconnected the call.

At that moment, Gene was in the recovery room on the 5th floor of the Metropolitan Hospital Center on 1st Avenue. They put fifteen stitches in his neck, and although he nearly bled to death, they expected the tall man to make a full recovery, with a scar to help him remember his trip to the Big Apple.

Frantic after the phone call, Opal began calling hospitals. First, she called the Columbia Presbyterian Hospital because she once did a photoshoot inside the hospital, and besides, it was the only hospital she recognized. Then it was Mount Sinai, and then Opal started calling police precincts. On the third try, she got lucky and found the precinct that handles the Village area's peers. They told her they found someone on Pier 34 with his throat slashed. They had taken the victim to the Metropolitan Hospital Center on 1st Avenue.

Opal called for a taxi and had them rush her to the hospital. When she ultimately found the emergency personnel who had treated Gene, they directed her to a recovery room. Unhappy with the hospital's appearance, Opal called Grant to see what he wanted her to do with his son. She thought the hospital was too busy and short-staffed to monitor Gene properly, and Grant put her on hold for a few minutes. When he got back on the line, he informed Opal he planned to have Gene taken over to the New York Presbyterian. According to his sources, this was one of the finest hospitals in Manhattan.

The New York Presbyterian doesn't smell like a hospital, nor does it resemble one on the inside. The silence stuns most first-time visitors. It almost feels like a mortuary, except it looks more like a classy hotel. There isn't the antiseptic sick smell associated with most hospitals, and the extra-wide carpeted hallways look more like an upscale hotel than the usual linoleum and tile. They painted the halls in a pastel rose, matching the restaurant-style carpet's floral design. The tightly woven rug helps deaden the sound while making it easier to wheel beds and stretchers. They also had indirect lighting, and most of the hospital personnel dressed more like office workers than the white lab-coat look favored by the less expensive hospitals.

The rooms are all soundproofed, and with the door closed, it is impossible to hear sounds from adjoining rooms. Opal found the Presbyterian much more to her liking and rarely left Gene's room except to grab a cup of coffee or a snack. As she returned to the room after one such trip, she saw two large men in civilian clothes walking down the hall, opening the doors, and looking into each of the rooms at the patients. The hospital discretely numbers the doors to each room, so it is difficult to tell which room you are looking for without someone to show you where to look. The men were both large, tall, and big-boned, and both radiated menacing vibrations. She passed them and entered Gene's room a few seconds before the men reached the door she had just entered. The two men stopped at the entrance to Gene's room, gazing at the patient. They looked hostile, frowning at Opal like she was a nuisance.

The men whispered back and forth for a few seconds before moving away, and she lost sight of them as they passed the door to Gene's room. A few seconds later, they walked back past the doorway, going the way they had come. This time they barely glanced into the room, but in their faces, Opal saw looks of malice. Not understanding why these men should have such feelings towards a man they didn't know, Opal went over and shut the door. The nurses said Gene could leave the hospital tomorrow if the doctors consented, and Opal vowed to take the two of them away from the city. To hell with the modeling job. She was in high demand and could get more work anytime she desired. That the men had some beef with Gene, Opal was sure; she just didn't know what or why, but she wouldn't make it easy for them to find him again.

*****

Boeing stopped servicing the old 747s, forcing Ahmad to hire his own maintenance crew. The men were all well trained, but the 747 is much like a big city in that the air conditioning is a complex mixture of electronics, refrigeration, and filtration systems. Several elevators service all three main floors, and the galley is much like a commercial kitchen. Also, Ahmad had installed a jacuzzi, a small gym, and a steam room. Besides all of that, his state-of-the-art entertainment system, including the latest Hollywood movies and several pornographic entries, entertained both him and his bodyguards. He also traveled with no less than six concubines to keep him occupied while in the air. None of these comfort systems had anything to do with the airplane's primary operational controls.

While his money bought a competent maintenance crew, it would take an army to keep everything functioning correctly. He was enjoying three of his mistresses in an enormous round bed when the lights went out. Shortly after that, the air conditioning stopped working. Emergency lighting came on, allowing Ahmad to call the pilots to see what had happened.

Captain Abbas informed Ahmad that a circuit breaker had popped, possibly from an overload. A trained engineer was on board for just such an emergency, and he was already hard at work fixing the problem. Meanwhile, the airplane cooled down, forcing Ahmad to climb under the covers of his massive bed with the three ladies keeping him company. The combined body heat helped keep him comfortable when one of his aides entered the room, holding a satellite phone.

When a person has the power and money associated with men like Ahmad, they are not used to suffering the *little people's* setbacks. While many men in that situation roll with the pummeling, that was not Ahmad's disposition. On the contrary, he was a spoiled bully used to having everything his way, and when faced with a setback, he felt inclined to destroy. Cursing the airplane, his engineer, and the pilots who had nothing to do with the plane's malfunctions, he finished by excoriating the poor maid who interrupted his tirade with a phone call.

One of his cousins in New York called to tell him about their failure to kill the man threatening his daughter. On top of being cold and without proper lights, this call was more than his overwrought nerves could handle. Screaming obscenities, he let his relative know that failure was not an option. Unless they killed the person threatening his daughter, he would have them eliminated.

Hassan Construction Limited had problems with all three of the major contracts they had stolen from Olson. Inferior materials and workmanship quality caused issues with the airport and dam projects. They were already behind on the nuclear power plant's schedule in Japan, and the work had barely started. Ahmad needed to spend time at each of the projects to soothe the principal's concerns, but he needed the damn plane functioning. He couldn't very well kill the airplane, but by damn, he could kill some people who worked for him unless they did a better job of keeping his plane functioning.

CHAPTER EIGHTEEN

Neter

A blazing fire in the fireplace cast flickering light throughout the basement temple. Only adherents to the Church of Satan would call the place a temple, but tonight, all the wall sconces around the room held burning candles, some for the first time, providing a mood that could almost be festive, nearly temple-like. Hanging from the cross, an already badly dispirited Laura saw the murals hiding in shadows.

The overall effect was chilling, even frightening. If possible, an already sickened Laura became even more dispirited. It took everything in her power to hold it all together.

Some were pictures of grotesque beasts having sex with women. There was a collection of some of the evilest faces imaginable. Humanoid faces and bodies had red, yellow, and green eyes with horribly disfigured noses, ears, cheeks, and chins. They had tilted mouths that would go ear to ear, except the ears were not on the same level. Some heads had horns and most bodies had red skin.

There were plenty of pitchforks, arrowhead-shaped tails, and hot coals. It looked like hell to Laura, but the *creatures* seemed to be frolicking, fucking, and having a ball. Creatures were the only thought that came to her mind. While looking vaguely humanoid, they also didn't resemble any creature she had ever seen or wanted to see. It was registering somewhere in the bottom of her consciousness that perhaps the beasts in the room for the '*TEMPLE SERVICE*' were also the creatures painted on the wall.

Neter Amon stood behind his podium, stationed in front of the girl on the cross. Tonight she wasn't naked but draped in seductive folds of white silk panels stressed by bold red silk ribbons around her breasts and vagina. Not a real Virgin Mary pose, considering the cross and all, but in Neter's mind, it was the image of a virgin he wanted in the minds of his followers. He was reasonably sure the girl was a virgin, and it was this virgin he intended to offer his suppliants.

Neter Amon was not his real name, of course. A prostitute in Winnemucca, Nevada, in one of the city's many brothels named him Harold Anderson. No one knew her actual name. In the business, she went by Crystal. No one knew who the father was or why she chose Harold Anderson to put on his birth certificate; she never said. Perhaps it was a family friend, or maybe a relative. Crystal nursed the brat for six weeks before giving him to the madam. What the madam did with the boy she never said, nor did Crystal ever ask.

A rancher with a cold, barren wife frequented the brothel and became friendly with the madam. Knowing his wife had always wanted a baby and thinking having a boy around to help do the chores may not be all bad, he paid the madam five hundred dollars to cover medical expenses and took the boy home. The mother's medical costs were never explained as no doctor ever visited except to treat one of the girls.

No one anywhere ever treated a slave worse. The rancher called him Howie and had him do chores when he was four years old. By the age of six, Howie was feeding the hogs and cows, and by seven was working in the fields mending fences. Located around the ranch were watering troughs for the animals, but the water had to be pumped using an old-fashioned hand pump. It was Howie's job to make sure there was always plenty of water in the animals' troughs. This was hard work for a young boy, and in Nevada's summer heat, it was often beyond his capability to keep all the troughs full. The rancher's answer was to beat the boy with his belt. He would remove his belt and lash the boy across his back and buttocks until Howie could not sit down.

At ten, Harold ran away to live on San Francisco's streets, where he fell in love for the first and only time. His passion was the Church of Satan in the 'Black House' at 6114 California Street, founded by Anton Szandor LaVey. Szandor allowed Harold to live in the basement of the Black House, and over time, he introduced young Harold to every depravity imaginable of sick human minds. Harold might have lived in the Black House his entire life, except for the incident with the police chief's daughter, Beth.

The Church of Satan was and is a big attraction to the sick and depraved and bored in our society. Maybe all three symptoms describe the same being. Ordinary citizens curious about the strange church find their way inside to check out what happens during a satanic worship session, as it is not just those who live in a world alien to most of humanity. Over time, many Hollywood celebrities and other famous people such as Jayne Mansfield, Diane Hegarty, and Marilyn Manson were church members. It was only natural that the SF police chief's daughter should be curious and investigate this unusual church. Unfortunately, Howie was on duty when Beth visited the Black House wearing a thin red sheath with spaghetti straps. Beth was voluptuous with size D cups, and the overall effect on young Harold, then only 23, with raging hormones, was to take the girl upstairs to his room and rape her repeatedly. LaVey had no choice but to drive Howard out of the church and out of the Black House.

Before leaving San Francisco, Harold legally changed his name to Neter Amon. He chose Neter because it was a Jewish surname and in his twisted mind, since Jesus was a Jew, using a Jewish name made him a brother to God. Not that Neter ever believed in any God other than Satan.

Neter chose Amon as his surname because it sounded like Amen, usually taught to mean So-Be-It. The ending of The Lord's Prayer. Neter intended to move to Boise, except the car he was driving died in Pocatello, and without the funds to replace his ride, Pocatello became his new home. It didn't take him long to establish himself as the leader of a new Church of Satan.

Standing at the pulpit, Neter raised his arms in supplication to his idol, praising Lucifer for being brave and standing up to a dictatorial God. In Satanism, there are no sins and no sinners. Man is merely an animal, with indulgence being encouraged rather than abstinence. As the most vicious animal of all, Neter enables his followers to satisfy their most animalistic urges.

Turning to the girl hanging from the cross, he blasphemes her purity while providing detailed descriptions of the delights they will all share with the virgin on the upcoming celebration. Next, he invited the entire congregation to pass by their sacrifice to Lucifer, admiring her voluptuousness. No one appreciated this aspect of Laura more than Neter, and he couldn't wait to ravish this latest offering. His arousal and desires were contagious, infecting everyone present. They could hardly wait for the time when they could rip off the girl's sheets and begin devouring her in every way imaginable. In the meantime, once they all passed by and inspected the goodies, they stood raising their goblets and drank her blood.

CHAPTER NINETEEN

Japan

In the air again, Hokee called Glory. It was late evening where he was but early morning in Pocatello.

"Hello, darling. Good morning." Glory was excited to hear from Hokee, even if it was early morning, and eager for him to return. She hoped he was calling from the airport for a ride home, forgetting he had driven to Nampa.

"Hi Glory. Good morning to you, but it's evening in my part of the world."

"Damn! Where are you? I hoped you were back home."

"I wish I were there with you also, but to answer your question, I'm in the air someplace out of India heading for Japan. So hopefully, this will be my last stop."

"Are you making any progress, and when do you believe you'll be back?"

"Geez, lady, give the man a break. Where's the foreplay with all the sweet talk before we settle down to business?"

"Okay, I love you. Is that enough sweet talk? Now when in the hell are you going to come home?"

"All right, already. I love you, Glory, and will return as soon as I can. Japan should be my last stop before heading home. I don't expect to be there for more than a day. Probably less. Tell me, how are you doing on the missing girl case?"

"Curly and I met with Diann, Laura's roommate. Laura is the missing girl. Diann believes she saw the four men who grabbed Laura, and I think I saw the same men in the restaurant when I was with Curly. But, unfortunately, they left before Curly got a look at them."

"What makes you think it was the four men the girl saw? And what made the roommate think the men she saw were the men who took her roommate?"

"Diann saw this man she described as a thug, a brute. He appeared to be stalking Laura. Diann later saw the same man with three others who looked just like him. She said they gave off bad vibes. I guess that's new age talk."

"I know the next part," Hokee exclaimed. "You also felt the bad vibes in the restaurant."

"It's so freaking weird, Hokee. But in the instant I saw them, I knew those were the men who abducted Laura. I know it. But I can't explain it."

"You're doing great, sweetheart. You need not understand it. Understanding in life is the booby prize. I can explain it to you sometime if you're interested."

They were both silent for a few seconds, thinking over Glory's revelations.

"Hokee, I believe I can identify the men if I could see their pictures. They appear to be familiar with the university grounds. Someone took all three girls from someplace on campus. I wonder if they went to school there and perhaps had their pictures in a yearbook?"

"That's a great thought. Maybe Hilda can help you run them down."

"I thought I'd call Diann this morning to see if she can get me into the student union and show me where I can find the books. If not, I'll give Hilda a call."

A few minutes later, they ended the call. Hokee wanted to take a nap, and Glory was eager to do investigative work. Hell, she thought, if we can find out what is happening to those girls, there might be a story in there for television. If not New York, maybe local?

Olson's Japanese office building sits in Sapporo, on Hokkaido, Japan's second-largest island. A thirty-three-mile-long tunnel connects Hokkaido to the Japanese mainland facilitating transportation. Hokkaido is Japan's more northern prefecture, lying just south of the Russian Island of Sakhalin. Sakhalin was in dispute between Russia and Japan for centuries until after WW II and the oil discovery. Russia now controls the sparsely populated island, keeping a close watch on what happens on Hokkaido. The new Japanese atomic energy plant being built in Noboribetsu on the Pacific Ocean's coast has the Russian's attention. Japan would dearly love to have Sakhalin and its oil back as part of Japan, but losing a world war has its costs.

Hokkaido is a large island four hundred miles wide and over 700 miles at its longest. The island is mountainous, with extensive forests and lakes. It also has many cities and airports. Olson Construction has contracts to build two new airports in different cities, coordinating everything from its offices to Sapporo. It surprised Hokee to discover the town surrounded the entire Sapporo airport. Hokee assumed the city grew up around the airport. The airport appeared modern, as did the whole city. This airport is a busy place with two large terminals, although Hokee did not see inside of the terminals as his plane taxied to the business lounge.

Walking down the steps of Olson's jet and seeing so many tall modern skyscrapers, Hokee was struck by wonder, amazed at the development since the war ended. What a contrast to the airport in India.

Next came the scents. Jet fuel, of course, and engine exhaust fumes, but kitchens in the nearby terminal were also venting out delicious odors of cooked rice and soy sauce. Highways ringed the airport producing a cacophony of sounds adding to the screaming jets taking off and landing. Although mid October, the air was pleasant, around 65 degrees Fahrenheit, although Sapporo is in the north and has snow festivals. While comfortable, Hokee could feel winter in the air.

A pretty Japanese girl named Akito met Hokee at the stairs' foot, introducing herself as his hostess and driver. She had shining black hair cut in a pageboy style, curling around her oval face stressing a natural beauty. Bold brown eyes with thick lashes sparkled with excitement. Akito ensconced a perfect ten figure in a pale blue jumpsuit with a gold chain belt. Her Harley Davidson-style short boots added to her slender height. Hokee couldn't help but think, *'those Olson folks sure know how to find beauties.'*

"Akito, you are a vision to behold. The Olson's are lucky to have such a beautiful employee."

"Why, arigatou gozaimasu Mr. Wolf." *Thank you very much.*

"Let's stick with Hokee, if you don't mind Akito. How far is it to Olson's building?"

"About ten minutes. It's only three kilometers Hokee." When saying Hokee, Akito ducked her head, but Hokee still saw the grin on her face.

The Olson Construction Company building was a standalone single-story building with a flat roof. A green flat stone shale siding with black trim gave the structure a look of permanence, like maybe the building had been standing there for five hundred years. In a small business park alongside the Ishikari River, the location was scenic and relatively quiet. Akito drove into the company's private parking lot, parking in the slot reserved for visitors.

She escorted Hokee through a fantastic lobby with a small koi pond, a bubbling fountain, and a small brook with a Japanese bridge connecting the entrance to the hallway and Roger Krammer's office.

Roger was a small man with elfin-like features. He had little blue bead-like eyes and bushy brows that sat over a longish nose with a mere slit for a mouth and hardly any lips at all. Still, when Roger saw Akito with Hokee, his eyes lit up in pleasure radiating throughout his face. Getting up from a desk the size of an aircraft carrier, he rushed around the monster holding out his hand.

"Konnichiwa watashi no shin'ainaru yu jin, Mr. Wolf. Or greetings and welcome to Japan."

"Well, hell, after a greeting like that, the best I can do is howdy, and I'm happy to meet you." Hokee had a big grin on his face while he shook hands. "And it's just Hokee if you don't mind."

"Hokee, it is, and it's good to see someone from the home fort, even if it is to check my honesty." Roger also had a grin spreading the slit of his mouth almost from ear to ear.

Hokee half expected to see Snow White dancing with butterflies after watching the facial expression of his host. Although after glancing back at Akito standing in the doorway, he thought, *'who the hell needs Snow White anyway when we have this beauty.'* He had the thought but wisely kept it to himself.

"No one I know believes for one second there is anything wrong with you or the conduct of your business. However, someone within the Olson Construction Company has been providing our bid prices to Hassan Construction, and we know it isn't you, Roger. So my visit is to ask for your help in trying to figure out who is leaking our prices."

"Yes, I'm sorry for the slur; it's just that I'm so used to using Japanese with our local business partners that sometimes I'm trying to think in one language while speaking in the other. I'm told that this will disappear as my Japanese improves, but I'm looking to be back to Idaho before that happens."

"I can't speak for Grant, but I know he appreciates your skills and wants all of his employees to be happy. I'm sure if you are eager to get back to God's country, Grant will make it happen."

"Thanks, Hokee, but I've already talked about this with the boss, and he plans on bringing in another manager in about three months after we finish our Category II reviews on one of our contracts."

Seeing the look of confusion on Hokee's face, Roger was quick to explain. "Category II reviews occur after reaching a major milestone. It's when the customer and contractor sit down and evaluate the progress and performance to date. This review is a significant event, and a successful review is necessary to release a substantial contract payment."

"Oh, thanks, Roger. I wondered what you were talking about," Hokee responded.

"Before we talk business Hokee," Roger continued, "is there anything Akito can get you to drink? We always have a fresh pot of tea ready to drink and, of course, anything else you might want. I have some fantastic sake warming in the heater."

"I'm good, Roger. Maybe a little of that sake later."

Looking at Akito, Roger gave her a dismissive wave. "I'll buzz you if we need something, Akito. Thanks, and would you shut the door?"

Pointing towards a couch in front of a glass wall looking into a peaceful Zen garden, Grant suggested, "Let's get to it, Hokee. Okay, if we sit on the couch?"

Hokee stood for a few seconds in awe of the graceful garden and the peaceful feeling he experienced just looking at its beauty.

"I'll be happy to sit there, Roger, but honestly, I don't know how you ever take your eyes off the garden to do any work. Your garden is superb."

"Thanks Hokee. I find it helps me think clearly."

Hokee and Roger sat as Hokee began asking the same questions posed to Art and Bryce, managers of the other two significant proposals.

CHAPTER TWENTY

Finding Opal

Glory parked in the administrator's parking lot next to the student union building. She drove a rental and didn't worry about getting a parking ticket if they issued such a thing on the campus. Diann met her at the building entrance and escorted her to the basement where they had a computer room with access to the internet. What Glory saw looked both striking and impressive. There must have been fifty computer stations and students occupied almost every station. Glory attended NYU back in the day, and while they had computers, her university never provided this kind of facility.

Diann explained they discontinued making the old-fashioned printed yearbooks. The photographic books became too thick and heavy. Instead, they stored all student photos digitally and available online for easy access. Diann used her student ID to open up one of the spare computer stations and showed Glory how to use the system. Both women agreed that the men who abducted Laura were in their mid-twenties, and if they attended Idaho State University as their sweatshirts proclaimed, it would have been three to five years ago limiting their search.

Diann stayed with Glory for almost an hour and a half before leaving for class. Before she left, Glory went to the cafeteria around the corner and got herself a cup of coffee. The search proved slow going. There are sixteen thousand students at the university, and in the pictures, they all looked so young. It took almost three hours before getting her first hit. Zack Carpenter attended the school for two years, leaving three years ago. His yearbook picture for both years showed a snarling face looking angry. Even looking at the picture, Glory felt a shiver run down her spine. It was possible to see the evil in his eyes, but perhaps that was a projection of her thoughts. She already felt in her bones that Zack was one of the kidnappers. Finding Zack would be enough for today. Her butt ached from sitting on the hard chair, and she had exhausted her patience for scanning computer images. She closed down the link and returned to her car. The hunt for Zack Carpenter was about to begin.

Back at Hokee's homestead, Glory settled down in her favorite chair in front of the fireplace with her laptop. She was an experienced investigator used to data and personnel research projects, but nothing she tried proved helpful. Zack Carpenter didn't show up in any database. Glory was pretty sure he had a local address, but nothing showed up either in Pocatello or any of the towns within a twenty-five-mile radius. Further internet searches revealed several Zack Carpenters, but none fitting the description emblazoned in Glory's brain. His yearbook picture described him as coming from Florida, but there were no Carpenter families in Florida with a son named Zack. Something she learned only after several frustrating hours online.

Her research suggested that if Zack lived locally, he lived with someone in a house or apartment under some other name. Using Diann's student ID and password, Glory logged onto the university computer system and the student yearbooks. She wanted to see if she could find someone who knew Zack and where he was living.

The sun went down, and Glory fed another log onto the fire. She wasn't having any luck in nailing down any other information about Zack. Glory was all set to quit when a picture showed up in the activities section of the digital photographs showing Zack on the university's wrestling team. The coach was still at ISU, but it was too late to reach him tonight. Tomorrow. She was damn well going to find that bastard Zack wherever he was hiding.

*****

With their bidding discussions over, Roger and Hokee enjoyed a cup of sake chatting about the Japanese culture. According to Roger, the only four people to see the final bid preparation were Grant and himself, his secretary, Gene, and his fiancé, Opal. The only people to see all three bids were Grant, his secretary,

Gene, and Opal. The proposals' size and weight necessitated a currier, and in each case, Olson people delivered the proposal personally.

The elimination process pointed to Opal, but why would a glamourous internationally famous model bother calling Hassan Construction with Olson's proposal price. Curious, he used Roger's internet service to research Opal Nevada. The name sounded fake, like the names of many old movie stars or strippers. Opal Nevada proved to be a dead end. There were no birth records for an Opal Nevada posted anyplace in the United States. She looked Eurasian, but where in the hell do you start that kind of name search. There was only one thing that made sense, and that was to check out Ahmad Hassan.

Jackpot. Hassan had sixteen children, the oldest female being a girl named Rashida, which was ironic as the name means righteous. The hits kept coming as Roger and Hokee discovered that Hassan's daughter Rashida was an international model using the name Opal Nevada. She chose the name Opal for her professional name because she loved the beautiful stone's brilliant rose colors and thought the name Opal made her sound more precious. She chose Nevada because it gave her character an American twist.

Hokee had a real problem. What was he going to tell Grant and his son Gene who was still recuperating in New York? That Opal had given the final bid prices on Olson's last three primary bids to her father was no longer a question.

What a hell of a mess. He couldn't just go back to Idaho and accuse the girl. He had no actual proof. Gene was smitten with the girl and would not listen to an accusation lightly. If the girl denied making the calls, what could he do?

Over another sake, with a Kirin beer backup, Hokee discussed the problem with Roger. Roger had a facile mind in that elfin body and suggested they meet with Ahmad to discuss their suspicions. Lacking substantive proof, any discussion with their adversary would be meaningless without further ammunition. Once again, Roger came to the rescue.

Roger started calling company contacts in England and India. It didn't take long before discovering that Hassan Construction was in trouble with both major projects. After culling the information available, Roger put in calls to both governments in charge of the projects. He and Grant had talked about Olson's bids on all three projects and knew there was not much room for Hassan's error. Olson believed Hassan was not nearly as efficient in their construction business as he was, and by stealing the jobs, Hassan had to make unauthorized substitutions to make a profit. In both London and India, they caught Hassan using inferior materials and using unskilled, low-quality labor. Roger's calls to both governments confirmed their beliefs. In both countries, Hassan was facing legal problems.

Hokee's next call was to Luxor, Egypt, and the Hassan Construction Company headquarters. After much confusion and stalling, he learned Ahmad was actually in Japan reviewing his company's progress on the nuclear reactor project. They spoke a lot of Japanese on the phone, so Hokee had Roger take over trying to locate Ahmad and make an appointment. Ahmad was proving reluctant to have any meeting with Olson personnel, so Hokee had Roger explain Hokee was a nuclear engineer with extensive knowledge about atomic reactors and wanted a job. He, Hokee, had believed that Olson had the contract, but in learning that it was a Hassan project, had Roger call to set up an appointment. Ahmad didn't need another engineer, but he realized an American nuclear engineer might make a good goat, someone to blame for their problems. With this idea in mind, Ahmad agreed to meet with Hokee the next day.

Ahmad was curious to meet this Wolf guy. He did not understand the trouble he was about to face.

CHAPTER TWENTY-ONE

Gene and Opal

They started drawing blood twice a day but insisted on making Laura drink plenty of liquids. Their congregation continued to grow as All Souls Day neared, and they needed more blood, plus they were saving a little each day for the big event. If Laura refused to drink, someone would hold her nose, making her breathe through her mouth, then one girl, usually Dakarba, dumped drink down her mouth, making her gag. It was that or having them feed it to her through an IV. She ended up drinking the liquid voluntarily. They gave her juices, usually apple or tomato, but sometimes plain water.

A man secured a strong latch outside the door to the room she now called The Cell. They no longer kept her tied down to the cot, but whenever the door opened, there were always four or more ladies to make sure their sacrifice didn't escape. They would not allow clothes, but they gave her a sheet to sleep under whenever she was alone. When they led her from the Cell, she was always naked unless they wanted to dress her up in something seductive for the audience. They still secured her to the cross whenever they brought her into the main chapel.

Laura came from a family of strong-willed individuals. While they kept her naked and humiliated, she kept her sanity, and even more important, her will to live and survive whatever they had planned for her. Laura came from a farm and knew a great deal about how animals reproduced and survived. Laura understood she was being paraded and glorified as a sacrifice to Lucifer. Although it was also clear to Laura that her sacrifice meant being raped by Neter and the men on some alter they talked about, located some place they called '*the hole.*' When they left her alone in The Cell, she exercised by performing isometrics to keep her strength. There was never a time when she didn't dream about escape. If they let their guards down for even a second, she would be ready to react. In her mind, she could see herself running naked down the street, screaming for help. She couldn't believe that God would let them kill her. God would not allow that to happen.

Laura started meditating whenever she was alone. After the first couple of days, it became more manageable. They made it easy, leaving her alone for two or three hours between taking her blood and bringing drinks and food. Something strange started happening during these meditation sessions. Whenever she lost herself in the chanting, and her mind became blank, she saw this strange animal in her mind, and after a while, she recognized it as a wolf. It wasn't frightening, more comforting like the animal wanted to protect her. Laura had never seen a live wolf, and other than the Little Red Riding Hood and the big bad wolf story, she knew little about the animals. But this wolf seemed to have friendly eyes. At least she hoped they were friendly. They looked highly intense. They also made her feel safe. Strange, she thought, to feel safety from a wolf.

*****

Opal and Gene were staying at the Waldorf Astoria back in New York because Opal had always dreamed of spending a few nights in the iconic hotel, and besides, it was on Park Avenue, perhaps one of the most famous streets in the world. The hotel was also protective of its guest's privacy, making it difficult for unwanted pests by using a door attendant to check reservations or room numbers of returning guests.

Gene had fully recovered from his ordeal on the dock, although he wore a silk ascot to hide the scar on his neck. Opal thought the ascot gave him a European look, which she found sexy. Figuring that whoever had attacked Gene would focus on Opal's apartment, the couple felt comfortable roaming the streets and catching a few rays of sun in the park.

Although nearly in the middle of October, the city experienced a minor heatwave turning the park into an attractive spot to relax and make wedding plans. Opal was afraid of her father and what might happen if the Olsons found out she was Rashida Hassan. She told Gene she was an orphan from England but had earned enough money from modeling to pay for a fantastic wedding.

Gene wanted to get married in Nampa with his family in attendance, but he wasn't crazy about a big church wedding. Opal favored getting married in Hawaii by the ocean. With its many beaches, Hawaiian palm trees swaying in the tropical breeze, and an active volcano, it was a favorite fashion photographer's location. Opal had modeled for over a dozen layouts on the various islands and couldn't get enough of the island's hospitality. The sun and water also reminded her of her home in Luxor by the river. She wasn't worried about her father discovering that his famous daughter was married. Since he had coerced her into betraying her fiancée and his father's company, Opal felt she had the leverage to hold off any of his angry outbursts. At least that was her thinking until a few moments later.

They were sitting on a bench in Central Park south by a pond when she saw the two men from the hospital walking down a path not twenty yards away. The men looked like feral animals let loose from the zoo. Drool practically ran down their chins when they spotted the couple huddled on the bench making wedding plans. They had an evil look in their eyes, and there was no mistaking their intentions. How they had discovered Gene's location was a mystery, but how, no longer mattered. There were no police officers within sight and only a few people walking in this part of the park. Would the men kill Gene in public, in full view of four or five people?

Opal carried a can of pepper spray in her purse in case the men attacked. A better plan would be to call the police. Gene fumbled in his pockets for a phone, but indecision gripped him as he was about to dial 911. What would he say? Two men look threatening, so please send help?

Opal studied the men, and the more she looked, the more she was convinced her father sent them. She didn't know why her father would do such a thing. He seemed happy for her success and her forthcoming marriage to an Olson, son of her father's most prominent business rival. The Olson Construction Company was known worldwide as one of the leading construction companies in the world. Being married to an Olson would bring honor to her family, yet her father tried to kill her fiancée.

Gene was not shy when it came to fighting. He had a little martial arts training and was himself a big man, unafraid of a fight. Taking Opal's hand,

Gene pulled her up as he stood. He faced the men unafraid, and when two men saw the look in his eyes, they backed off, deciding to wait for a more appropriate time to execute their master's orders. They would watch and wait. Their time would come.

CHAPTER TWENTY-TWO

Hokee meets Ahmad

Hassan's Japanese Construction headquarters is near the city of Yamaguchi in the Yamaguchi Prefecture, Japan. They were building the atomic reactor near Nagato next to Japan's Sea in the southern part of the Japanese mainland. Hokee had Olson's plane fly him in Hiroshima, the nearest airport to land a jet plane. While in the air, he called Glory to update her on his plans and see how she was coming along on the missing girl case.

"Hello, Glory here." She knew the Idaho area code was 208, but with Hokee in God-only knows-where, she answered the call as though it was local. Perhaps Curly was trying a new gambit to spend more time with her.

"Moshi moshi. Hi honey, everything okay on the home front?" Hokee sounded tired, as well he should. Although spending most of the past three days on an airplane, he was weary of traveling and heartsick over the dilemma posed by Opal. Besides, traveling can be hard on the body. This is if you aren't used to breathing recirculated air and spending hour after hour penned up in an aluminum box.

"Oh, Hokee. I am so happy to hear your voice. Moshi moshi back at ya. When are you coming home?"

"I'm on my way. Although, there will be a slight detour. Still in Japan, but nearing my last stop. Should be back in the air and on my way back to Idaho in a few hours."

"Does this mean you found the leak in Olson's bidding process?"

"Yes, and it's breaking my heart."

"Tell me, lover, what's the problem?"

"I believe it's Opal. Gene's fiancee. It turns out she is the daughter of Ahmad Hassan, the contractor who stole Grant's last three bids. Her given name is Rashida Hassan. Rashida is a beautiful name, meaning righteous. It's too bad there was nothing righteous in her actions."

"Oh, poor Gene. Does he know yet?"

"No, I haven't notified the Olson's about my beliefs or suspicions. I'm on my way to meet with Ahmad. A few ideas are churning around in my head. It will be interesting to see how it comes out. What's new on your end?"

"I found him. Well, at least I believe he's the one who helped kidnap Laura. By found, I mean we know his name but haven't found out where he is living. So my next move is to find a roommate or university professor who knows where he might live."

"Sounds like actual progress, Glory. You keep this up, and you're going to steal all my customers."

"Not happening, and besides, I agree with you, there is a bad feeling about this case, Hokee. I believe it could get gruesome. I'm not sure why. It just feels bad, more like something rotten."

"Hell Glory, it can't be any worse than that monster in the Caribbean."

"Okay, you have a point. But this situation still has a wicked, no, make that an evil sense. It has the feel and stink of evil to it."

"In that case, Glory, wait for me. I'll be home in about twenty-four hours, and we can do it together. Maybe take a sweat and see what it is we're up against."

"I don't plan on tackling the men by myself. Right now, it's just research. So I'll save the heavy lifting for the master."

"Swell, don't get yourself killed. I almost lost you once."

"Don't worry, sweetheart. I'll only poke around in the bushes until you get home to slay all the monsters."

"Sure. You do that, Glory. I can almost, but not quite, see you holding back. I know how you won all of those awards for your investigations, but that's also how you lost your mind by going off by yourself."

"True, but I learned my lesson, Master. I'll be a good girl and wait for my knight in shining armor. Well, at least I'm a girl, and I'll be good for you. Maybe. And anyway, your armor only shines where it ain't all rusty."

"Thanks, honey, keep it up, and you'll be walking home. Oh, that's right, you are home. Oh, gotta go. We're about to land. I'll call you when I'm back in the air."

"Bye, Hokee."

There was no waiting limousine from Hassan, nor even a taxi. A few minutes after landing, a taxi searching for a fare entered the business executive's terminal. Hokee grabbed the cab and sat back, admiring the scenery. On the right was the stunning five-story pagoda Rurikoji temple surrounded by magnificent trees and gardens. It is no wonder they list the hotel as a national treasure. A guidebook left in the taxi showed pictures of the Jyoei-ji Temple, famous for its zen garden and a beautiful pond near a small bamboo grove. Any other time Hokee would have had the driver take him for a tour, as he was sure to find solace in the garden, but duty called. Business before pleasure.

Ahmad spared no resources to satisfy his personal desires; however, the same was not true for his business facilities. Hassan Construction houses its employees in a single-story cinderblock building with three outlier trailers. Taking a chance that Ahmad would be in the larger cinderblock building, Hokee had his driver take him to the parking lot in front. Flipping the driver five hundred dollars, Hokee asked him to wait. If he stayed, Hokee would double the amount. He told him it might be a few hours. Given the prospect of this big reward, the driver promised to wait.

Behind the reception desk sat a huge, dark-skinned man wearing a kaffiyeh. There was a computer terminal on the desk and telephone, but no writing materials. The man wearing a headdress had a heavy pistol strapped to his side. Not sure in which language Hokee should address the man, Hokee said, "Mr. Hassan!"

The man lifted the telephone receiver and spoke Arabic. He didn't smile or attempt any communication with Hokee. He never looked in Hokee's direction after their first brief initial exchange. A few minutes later, a slender Arabic girl entered the lobby introducing herself as Mariam, a name Hokee recognized from the Bible. She was a rather plain girl with a look of fear in her eyes. She tried an introductory smile, but it barely left her lips and certainly didn't reach her eyes. As he searched for something to ease the tension, Hokee realized he felt the same stress from the man at the desk. At first, he wondered if it had anything to do with his visit, but the more he thought about it, that didn't seem right.

Why would an American nuclear construction engineer cause front office personnel to be uncomfortable? It made little sense. Then he got to wondering. Ahmad rarely visited his construction sites, preferring to leave the day-to-day operation to his contractors and project manager. Perhaps Ahmad's visit had something to do with the company's problems, and the local office was uneasy with the big man on site. This felt right, causing a brief spasm of sympathy for the workers, but he didn't have time to think much about it as they were soon standing in the doorway to Ahmad's office.

Sensing company, Ahmad glanced up and saw this tall, large-boned, American Indian standing in his doorway. The man has long black hair held off his face by a white headband featuring a large jade stone set in front, right over the third eye. The man's blazing eyes were dark blue, almost midnight black in the shadows and without a hint of humor. For the first time in a very long time, Ahmad felt a tickle of fear down his spine. Whatever this man was, he was no nuclear engineer.

Ahmad was not large, but his body had gone to fat, giving him a roly-poly appearance, but not the fat fun uncle type you might see at weddings or Christmas parties. There was cruelty and greed written all over his face, from angry dark piercing eyes to his quivering jowls, but Hokee could also see the fear behind his scowl.

"Hello, Ahmad. Excuse me for the deception; I am not a nuclear engineer. I just wanted to see what a world-class thief looks like and to take home some of your money."

"Why, you bastard." Ahmad reached for the telephone to call for help.

"If you pick up that telephone before I ask you to," Hokee spoke firmly and calmly, "I will rip the arms from your fat, bloated body and stuff them up your greedy, lying ass."

The fear Hokee saw lurking behind the mask came out full force. Ahmad was not used to being spoken to in those terms. And never in his buildings. But the look in the dark eyes of his tall, brooding visitor left no room to doubt his intentions, and he clearly could do as he had promised.

"W wh-who the fuck are you? What do you want?" His hands sitting on top of the desk began quivering. Hokee guessed Hassan might have a hidden alarm he could push to summon help.

"I am known as the Wolf man. I came to blow down your flimsy, rotten little empire. So just sit there, Hassan, and do not reach for an alarm, or I'll kill you. I'll tell you what you are going to do. And if that goon with a gun out in your reception desk comes in without an invitation, I will kill you both."

First, I know about your daughter Rashida and how she has been feeding you the proposal costs on Olson's contracts. Second, I know you are in deep shit on every job you stole. You had to undercut Olson's prices, and you aren't nearly the contractor he is and couldn't make a profit at the prices you bid. Third, you are using inferior quality building materials and semiskilled labor. My research has uncovered many contract discrepancies in London, India, and here in Japan. I have a briefcase full of documents proving your malfeasance. And using your daughter against her fiancee's father is unforgivable.

I plan to leave here just as soon as you deliver me one hundred million dollars in United States greenbacks. **Until I get that money**, you will not leave that desk, even to take a piss! Now pick up the phone and call whoever you need to call to get me that money. If I suspect you are playing me for one second, I promise you, Ahmad, you will live but in severe pain the rest of your miserable fucking life. Now make the call. And if I see anyone who looks threatening or if the police show up, I'll kill you where you sit."

Hokee had not bothered to shut the door, and it was more than likely that many people heard his outburst. Ahmad went white and started shaking.

"I..., I can't get that kind of money quickly."

"Ahmad, don't even try going there. If I don't have the money in a briefcase in my hand within two hours, I am going to tear the fingers from your hands and flush them down the loo, or toilet, or crapper, or whatever the hell they call it here. Honey pots? You better start calling."

Hokee leaned against the door in a relaxed pose, but the menace in his eyes brought no comfort to the Egyptian. Ahmad picked up his phone and made a call to somebody. He spoke in Arabic or some other funny dialect Hokee didn't recognize. He made two other calls speaking the same language, but Hokee heard one hundred million U.S. dollars in both calls. Ahmad had sweat running down his jowls and a look of desperation, but the fear was being replaced by hatred.

"It's okay to hate me, Ahmad, but don't fuck me. And if I ever find that you damage the Olson's in the future, I promise to bring down the wrath of Allah on your filthy business, your life, and I'll destroy your home there in Luxor. Like the big bad wolf in the children's story, I'll blow your house down."

Hokee noticed a change in Ahmad. An even greater fear in the man's eyes had replaced the hatred. Turning away from Hokee, Ahmad made another call, this one lasting only a few seconds. Finally, he uttered some command, then hung up the phone. Sweat was now visibly pouring off the man as if he had just taken a shower.

Ahmad sat at his desk, afraid to move, yet found it impossible to sit still. He sat squirming in his chair when the phone rang.

"Moshi moshi."

Ahmad answered the phone. Apparently, they used some Japanese in their work. The call turned out to be from a bank.

Trembling, Ahmad told Hokee they needed to go to the bank.

"Bullshit Ahmad. Bring the bank here. You are not leaving this room until the money is in my hands. You swing the big dick over here, Hassan. Act like it. Get the damn bank to come here with the money. If I see a cop car anywhere near this place, you will never take another breath. I promise."

Ahmad began chattering on the phone, even raising his voice, nearly screaming. Ultimately, he calmed down and replaced the handset.

The only expression Hokee could read on his adversary's face was resignation. They did not speak for forty-five minutes until an armored truck drove into the parking lot. Japanese men dressed like bankers the world around exited a limousine right behind the armored truck. The truck's rear door opened, and a man dressed as a guard with a gun on his hip exited carrying an oversized briefcase. It might even have been a small suitcase. Hokee wasn't sure. The guard met the banker types, and they all headed towards the building.

Hokee went around Ahmad's desk and stood behind his chair.

"If I see anything suspicious, Ahmad, I will break your neck. Are we clear?"

"Yes, yes. Money's here. You see."

Ahmad made to stand, but Hokee placed a hand on his shoulder, keeping him in place.

"Have them place the money on the desk. If the guard with the gun draws his weapon, you are a dead man. Open the case; then they can leave. I want to see the money. I'll count it after they have gone."

Three men entered the room in about two minutes: the two banker-type men and the armed guard. Hokee was skeptical about the bankers. Were they who they were supposed to be, or perhaps special forces personnel hiding in banker's clothes?

Apparently, they were bankers as they started addressing Ahmad, showing him some forms he needed to sign. They chatted in a mixture of English and

Japanese for a minute while Ahmad signed. They paid no attention to Hokee, who stood by Ahmad's side as though he was an advisor. In Japan, principals pay no attention to the help.

Once Hassan signed the papers, which then changed hands, the guard laid the money case on the desk, then opened it for all to see. Seeing all those greenbacks was a lovely sight, but Hokee paid little attention other than one quick glance. He watched the guard and the bankers, but Hassan dismissed them, and they seemed eager to leave. Hokee assumed they could feel the powerful energies in the room, and the feelings were not friendly.

After the men left and returned to their vehicles, Hokee watched to see them drive away. Then, satisfied they were alone, he went to the front of the desk and riffled the stacks of bills. The bills were in ten-thousand dollar denominations. Doing a quick count of the stacks satisfied Hokee there were a hundred million dollars in the case. He closed the case, looked at Ahmad, and said, "I let you off easy today, fat man. You never want to see me again."

Hokee left the building, seeing no one in the lobby. He guessed the employees had all fled the grounds in fear. His taxi was waiting. Well, he could pay for the man's waiting time now. It was time to catch a plane home, thinking he would call Glory on the way.

CHAPTER TWENTY-THREE

Heading Home

Gene and Opal were hurrying along New York's 5th Avenue, past all the famous glitzy stores featured on the world's most famous street. Stores like Louis Vuitton, Bergdorf Goodman, Prada, Trump Tower, and Cartier. They only had a few roads between themselves and their rooms at the Waldorf, yet every time Gene looked back, he saw one or both kaffiyeh's bobbling along following them down the street. Gene wasn't worried about being assaulted on the street in full view of the other pedestrians, but he didn't want to lead the killers to the place they were staying. So they turned left off 5th Avenue onto E 50th, heading towards Park Avenue and their hotel when they passed St. Patrick's Cathedral.

St. Patrick's is one of the most beautiful cathedrals in the world, with massive stained glass windows, huge spires, and intricate gothic style sculptured facades rising over three hundred feet in the sky. Thinking to take a brief rest inside the Cathedral, check out their shadows, they walked up the stairs between the two enormous towers, stopping in front of the tall, heavy bronze doors. Turning around to check on their pursuers, they saw the men a few yards back down the sidewalk when one man reached into his jacket pocket for a telephone. They both watched the man speak for a moment, then turn and look at them. Nudging the other man, they both turned around and started walking back down E 50th. Bewildered but happy to see the men leave, Gene and Opal continued back to their room, wondering why the men disappeared? It looked as though someone relieved the men of their assignment.

Gene decided it was time to return to Nampa, and he would not leave Opal behind. Besides, there was no way she would stay back, regardless. She had doubts about the men's disappearance. The two men in kaffiyehs looked like men from her father's private security force. The more she thought about it, the worse it felt. Would her father have Gene killed? She knew he didn't want her marrying an infidel, but to have him killed to stop her marriage? She would have to have a serious talk with her father. It wouldn't hurt to stay with her fiancee for a few days. She could always return to modeling.

*****

Back on Olson's private G650, Hokee sat in one of the plane's luxurious reclining seats with a tall glass of Johnny Walker Blue fixed by the alluring Joan. She found her only passenger attractive and seeing no wedding ring or hearing him talk about a special woman in his life; she hoped to appeal to his basic animal desires. It was a long flight back home.

Hokee recognized her flirtatious acts for attention, but his mind was on what would happen back in Nampa. How would the Olson's react to his news? Specifically, Gene? Realizing he had eaten little and feeling hungry, he asked the attentive Joan to fix him dinner. While she was busy in the galley, Hokee punched in the number for Glory. She might have news about the missing girl, and he respected her insights, and perhaps she could help with his dilemma.

"Hello lover. It's about time you called." Glory had been trying to locate the coach for Zack's wrestling team without success and felt frustrated.

"Hello yourself, beautiful. Thanks for the warm reception."

"Sorry Hokee, I'm just peeved at my lack of success on this *minor* project you dumped in my lap."

"Don't beat yourself up, Glory. I'll be home soon, and we can tackle it together."

"Speaking of soon, exactly when are you expected back with Shila and me?"

"It looks like tomorrow night. I have to return the plane to Nampa with a little present for Grant. Then I'll drive back to Pocatello. I should be home in time for dinner if you feel like cooking."

This was a joke, as they both knew Glory couldn't boil water without burning up the pot.

"Oh, that's just great, sweetheart. I'll plan on chicken cordon bleu. We'll start with a bottle of chilled Dom Perignon and pickled cucumber wedges."

Hokee had to laugh at the pickled cucumber wedges. He did not get where that pairing originated.

"And here little ole dumb me thought we always had roasted rocky mountain oysters with our champagne."

"What in the hell are rocky mountain oysters and excuse the French. And where do I get them?"

"That wasn't French darling, and if you don't know how to cook rocky mountain oysters, better look it up in Julia Childs." He gave her a second to digest that, then changed the subject.

"So, I guess the search for your kidnapper isn't going well?"

"Oh, Hokee. In all my years of investigative reporting, my most difficult interfaces were with the major learning institutions. I swear to God, there isn't a more obtuse administrative organization on the planet, except, of course, our government. But enough about me. How about your meeting with the Olson's? How are you going to handle that mess?"

"Boy, that's tough. Do you have any suggestions? On top of Opal's snooping for her father and betraying her fiancee, I believe her father tried to have Gene killed. I'm not sure how to present my information?"

"Aren't you the man who preaches there is no substitute for the truth?"

This stumped Hokee for a minute before he answered.

"Glory, there are truths, and there are truths. My teacher once posed a problem for me. They stationed a soldier overseas during the war. While on leave, he partied too much with his comrades, fell over drunk in a gutter, puked, and drowned in his vomit. What does the commanding officer tell his parents? Your son drowned in his puke, or your son died while serving his country? What would you say is the truth?"

Glory didn't hesitate. "They are both the truth, but I get your point. You can shade the truth to make it palatable, or you can be blunt. I guess you need to make your truth to the Olson's palatable."

"Gee, thanks, honey. I appreciate the expert advice."

"Not a problem, big guy. Solutions to messy problems are our forte. Just do your best, then get your butt home. I need you here to help me with my problem."

"Okay. Will do Glory. See you soon. Bye."

"Bye Hokee."

While Hokee relaxed in his seat, Joan set the table for two. Ever hopeful, she thought sharing a dinner of roast beef would be an excellent chance to spend some time alone with her handsome passenger. She could have saved herself the angst of rejection as Hokee internalized his problem with the Olson's and barely noticed the attractive hostess. Offering a brief thanks for the food, Hokee left the half-eaten meal before retiring to the bed in the plane's back cabin. The girl's constant chattering interrupted his thoughts, and he wanted to be ready for his meeting upon landing.

Hokee wouldn't consider Grant a friend. The only friend in Hokee's life at the moment was Glory. He didn't count his mentor Why-ay'-looh as a friend, more like a father. The life Hokee lived didn't lead itself to making friends. Sure, he saved the lives of many grateful people, but friends? Not so much. Not even Curly. Although friendly, Hokee would not consider him a friend. Not someone you would count on in an emergency unless it was convenient for him.

Still, Grant had been extremely generous, and Hokee didn't enjoy bringing him unpleasant news. Hokee had the impression that Grant thought highly of Opal, and of course, Gene was crazy in love. He could only imagine their reaction to her betrayal. Just before the plane landed, Hokee called ahead to have his Explorer standing by when they landed. He wanted to deliver the news and leave quickly, allowing the family to handle their problems alone. It was pleasant news to learn that Gene and Opal had both returned to Nampa. He could confront everybody at the same time. Hokee called ahead to make sure everyone would be available.

Grant had Gene and Opal at home in the big house when Hokee arrived carrying a large briefcase, the kind you often see salespeople use who carry around a bag full of samples to show prospective customers. They were all excited to see Hokee and hear about his successes. At least Gene and Grant seemed excited. Opal appeared eager, but Hokee could see the fear in her eyes.

The scene was almost too perfect for spoiling. Grant relaxed in a big chair in front of a large picture window overlooking a flower garden they had pruned for winter's snow. He was wearing a black warmup suit and had a giant snifter of brandy and a smile wider than the Golden Gate Bridge. Gene and Opal sat on a nearby couch, holding glasses of what appeared to be excellent red wine. Gene wore a white turtleneck sweater, hiding the bandages on his neck. Opal wore a beautifully tailored white jumpsuit that brought out the highlights in her silky black hair.

When Hokee entered the room, all three rose to greet him, although Opal stayed a little behind Gene. Like a child who has displeased her parents hides behind someone or something. Hokee wasted no time. In his experience, the only way to take lousy medicine is all at once.

"Hi folks. Grant here is a little present from Opal's father, Ahmad Hassan. Her name is Rashida Hassan. Rashida means righteous. You can decide if the name is appropriate. There are a hundred million dollars in this case, Grant. A reluctant gift from Ahmad. There is a hundred million here to cover the costs of your proposals and as payment for his crimes." Hokee sat the heavy case down on the floor in front of Grant.

"Also, you will find documents describing Hassan's corruption on all three contracts. What you do with the information is your business. He tried to have Gene killed because he thought Gene was a threat to his daughter. After hearing you hired someone to check out the bidding process, some of Ahmad's relatives monitoring Opal believed Gene to be that threat. They didn't know about me. Ahmad has removed that threat."

All three looked at Hokee with a mixture of horror, grief, and disbelief on their faces. Then, with a final glance around the room, Hokee headed for the door.

"I'm going to leave you now to talk things over by yourselves. This is the reason I wanted you three to be alone. Now you can decide what to tell the world. No one besides me and the folks in Ahmad's world knows the truth. I'm pretty sure he won't be bothering you. He's agreed to leave Opal alone to live her life as she chooses."

Grant and Gene both tried to say something, but the words stuck in their throats. Finally, as Hokee closed the door, he heard Grant croak a weak, "thanks, Hokee."

Back in the Explorer heading home, Hokee called Glory.

"Hey honey, be home in just a few hours. Put on something sexy, and I'll ..., no wait, that came out wrong. Everything you wear is sexy. So, on second thought, just be there."

"Oh, Hokee, you say the sweetest things."

CHAPTER TWENTY-FOUR

Church Service

Neter didn't hold a service every evening. It made no difference for Laura, who was no longer sure if it was daytime or evening. Her room had no window, and whenever they let her out, it was only to go to the place they called their chapel. Both arms were sore from the IV needles they used for the bloodletting, and her body was aching from too much bed. At least they no longer kept her tied to the bed so she could do some isometrics, although her room was barely big enough to do much. The stench from the drain was now probably the worst part of her confinement. Laura found it difficult to breathe, and she asked Raven for some bleach or disinfectant but got no response. At least they gave her plenty of liquids to drink, and the food was alright, but the foul odor made it difficult to eat.

When Raven and the other women brought Laura into the sanctuary this night, the fireplace had a blazing fire, and someone had lit all the candles in the sconces. Each sconce featured a different beast from the underworld. At least that was Laura's belief after seeing the heinous sights they made with candlelight flickering behind evil-looking colored glass eyes.

The other clue that this would be a memorable evening came when the girls spread Laura's legs, tying them to a crossbar fixed to the bottom of the cross. Laura was no longer distressed at her nudity. They had feasted their vision on every pore of her body for days, caressing, feeling, squeezing every inch of her perfect skin with groping hands and lust-filled eyes. Laura didn't know what more they could do to her, but she wasn't frightened anymore. By now, she knew they were keeping her alive for their big celebration, which she had figured was going to be Halloween, the night they alternately called All Hallows Eve.

They had Laura tied to the cross when Neter entered wearing a shiny black robe. On his forefinger was an overly large ring featuring a skull with glowing ruby eyes. The source of light for the ring was not noticeable. Behind Neter came the four thugs, as Laura called them, followed by the rest of the congregation. Glancing at Laura with approval, Neter walked to the podium, sweeping his robe in the manner of a Caesar.

"Fellow Satanists, welcome to our sanctuary and another delightful evening with our beautiful, lovely, glorious bride for Satan. Tonight, we will begin preparing our sacrifice." Neter raised both arms and his voice when he said, "all hail, the true master of the universe."

The entire crowd joined in, "All hail to the true master of the universe."

Neter continued, arms still raised as though he were the Pope addressing a crowd in front of St. Peters in the Vatican. "All hail to our master, our real savior, and our dear brother. Tonight, we prepare the sacrifice for our Lord."

Neter dropped his arms and started reciting the Nine Satanic Statements. The audience joined in the recitation. Shouting out the statements as though they were the only truths in the world.

Satan represents indulgence instead of abstinence!
Satan represents vital existence instead of spiritual pipe dreams!
Satan represents undefiled wisdom instead of hypocritical self-deceit!
Satan represents kindness to those who deserve it instead of love wasted on ingrates.

Sigil of Baphomet

Suspended from the ceiling above Neter's head were all nine of the Satanic Statements and the Sigil of Baphomet, the church's symbol.

Laura zoned out at the monotonous repetition of statements she had heard every time they brought her into the main sanctuary. She was intimately familiar with the first statement. The members indulged themselves in every kind of depravity concerning her body. Both sexes seemed to delight in fondling her breasts and vagina. They played with her hair and stroked her skin, making lascivious and lewd comments about the fun they would have on all soul's night.

After reciting The Nine Satanic Statements, the congregation joined in singing Satan's Hymn, or The Song of Lucifer led by the tall man in black robes with dark eyes and short black hair. The Van Dyke beard gave Neter a Mephistopheles look. Boris Karloff as Dracula never looked so evil.

"Dear brothers and sisters in life. Tonight we are going to prepare our sacrifice to our Lord and Master, Lucifer."

Neter made this statement with a sweeping bow back towards the cross and the naked Laura.

"I have assured you that our sacrifice is a virgin, most pure. Remember this. I do not want to see one drop of her blood. Our preparations begin by removing all of her body hair, leaving only the hair on her head. We will start by shaving under the arms. Then the legs and finally the public hair. Raven will begin by shaving the right armpit. After that, each girl will take turns with the lather and using the razor."

It appeared as though the females became giddy at the prospects of fondling their sacrifice once more and rubbing lather on her skin.

"Remember, no blood. Be extra careful." Neter practically shouted out the command.

Raven felt it necessary to command Laura, "Don't move," although the command was unnecessary. Laura was practically afraid to breathe, let alone move.

Raven started shaving as instructed, then the other keepers followed her. After finishing the armpits, they moved on down to the legs. All the females in the congregation took part in the shaving. While someone was shaving on one of Laura's legs, others stroked her other leg, especially the inner thigh. The men all crowded around wearing the look of a wolf pack surrounding a wounded deer.

"Okay. Now comes the most important part. Since Zack is the one who found our gift to the Master, he gets the honor of shaving her pubic hair. No blood, Zack."

Zack strutted to the front, taking the razor from Raven. The look of his brutish face resembled what you might see on the face of a child on Christmas morning. He had Earl apply the lather.

Laura concentrated on not shaking. She knew they didn't want to hurt her just yet. Other than collecting her blood to drink, of course. She couldn't look at Zack. There was too much anger and hatred in her body towards him to allow any glimpse of his face. She turned her head and shut her eyes until she heard Neter's following words.

"Over on the table beneath the statements are spray bottles of rose water blessed by our High Priestess, Nardramia, who will rejoin us on All Hallows Eve. So everyone, grab a bottle. Now."

There was a general shuffling as people joined in a line to pick up a bottle.

"Okay. I want our virgin washed with rose water. Wash off all the soap and residual hair. I want the ladies to pay attention to her hair. We want her hair to be squeaky clean and smell like roses."

For the next thirty minutes, the congregation took turns spraying rose water all over her body, and as commanded, the ladies took care of her hair. Finally, with the spraying finished, Laura stood spread eagle on the cross with her eyes closed.

She didn't know how. She didn't know when. But Laura was convinced that her God would not abandon her any more than he would leave Daniel to the lions.

And after she got free. The devil better watch out.

CHAPTER TWENTY-FIVE

The Coach

Shila is a full-blooded wolf given to Hokee by his mentor, Way-ay'-looh, an authentic Shaman. Shila never barks. Sometimes he growls when he senses danger or strangers and seldom shows emotions. Until Hokee drove into the yard when returning from Nampa. Then, Shila jumped up and down like a young puppy chasing a ball with a big grin on his face and a tail wagging like a flag in a stiff breeze.

While Shila, standing on his hind legs, was mauling his master, Glory came out of the house and joined in the fun.

"Wow! I'm going to have to go away more often."

Hokee had a grin from ear to ear while being kissed by Glory, with Shila standing on his hind legs with his front legs on Hokee's shoulder next to Glory.

Breaking the embrace as Shila dropped to the ground, Glory gave Hokee a last squeeze. "Welcome home, stranger. It's about time. The wolf and I were about to head off back to New York."

"New York ain't big enough for the two of you," Hokee responded, still grinning. "It's sure good to see the both of you. After India and Japan, this seems like heaven. Even though we're looking at nothing but lava rock and scrub brush."

"Let's go inside, Hokee. Supper's going to get cold. It is supper, isn't it? Not dinner?"

"Honey, if you fixed something to eat, it doesn't matter what you call it. Let's go inside, Shila."

Glory led the way inside, where she had a hot dinner waiting in the oven. It was the best carry out meal offered by Jakers Bar and Grill. One of Pocatello's premier steak houses. She thought about pretending to be the cook, but Hokee knew her too well for that scene to be believable. Jaker's steaks were delicious, even if they had been resting for over an hour. Glory had to guess when Hokee would return. There were plenty of table scraps to make Shila happy.

With full bellies, Hokee and Glory moved onto the couch for a more intimate seating arrangement.

"How's the missing girl investigation going, Glory? Are you making any progress in identifying this Zack Carpenter?"

"No. And it's making me crazy. He must live with someone or possibly under another name. There is no Idaho driver's license for anyone with that name. There are no local or state public records for Zack Carpenter."

"I thought you had a lead on someone who might know him," Hokee responded. Now that he was back home, it was time to join in the hunt.

"Yes, his wrestling coach when he spent some time at the University. I have a meeting with him tomorrow. It's taken me some time to locate him since he retired last year. He lives in Inkom, which is just down the road a few miles. Now that you're back, we can go see him together."

Jimmy Tanner is a wiry five-foot-eight with a full head of snow-white hair and a dazzling smile. He used the smile while professional wrestling to disarm his opponents. You wouldn't think to look at him; he could have been a fighter until you noticed the cauliflower ears and wondered if he was in an accident or something. His secret was an ungodly strength in his arms that belied his stature. His opponents in the wrestling ring looked at this slender little man with the big disarming smile, thinking this must be some mistake. Jimmy capitalized on the smile, luring his opponent into making a mistake, then pinching them on the mat. Afterward, all they could do was shake their heads, wondering how they could have been so wrong.

After retiring from professional wrestling, Jimmy took a job as a wrestling coach for ISU in Pocatello until retiring two years ago to tend to his llama ranch in Inkom. Jimmy enjoyed raising llama's because, like goats, they eat almost everything and are easy to manage. He has a standing contract with a wool distributor in Kellogg, Idaho, who buys fleece for some of the world's most prestigious weavers. Llama fleece is lighter and warmer than sheep's wool and doesn't contain oil, making it very pricy, reflecting customers' prices for llama fleece clothing.

When Hokee drove into the ranch yard with Glory, they saw Jimmy coming out of a shed carrying a bucket of oats. Jimmy looked like the man in Grant Wood's Gothic painting of the farmer with a pitchfork and his wife, except Jimmy had more hair. He wore bib overalls and a broad-brimmed straw hat. They watched as he poured a little of the oats into a manger as he walked along, making small piles in the trough between the sidebars. As Jimmy walked along, dumping out the oats, the llamas came running and jostled each other out of the way, heading for the nearest pile of oats. Finally, he saw the Explorer enter the yard, and his otherwise plain pinched face lit up the yard with his trademark grin. When he finished with the oat bucket, he set it down and headed over to the vehicle.

Gloria exited the vehicle first, looking like the NY fashion model she is, wearing a tight white pantsuit with a blue semi-sheer blouse. Hokee watched Jimmy ogling Glory while he got out wearing his all-black bad-ass look. Black cowboy boots, black straight-legged pants pulled down over the boots, and a black long-sleeved silk shirt topped with a ten-gallon black Stetson. He held his long black hair back with a white headband. Jimmy stopped in his tracks as Hokee got out of the car. Glory was a vision in white, with the striking good looks to make any man pause, but Hokee also made Jimmy pause. He was expecting a woman to visit, but this man was unexpected. Not that Hokee looked menacing in his all-black clothes, but it was the eyes that made Jimmy stop. Hokee had that look in his eyes that nearly everyone found intimidating. For Hokee's part, he wanted answers, and this man had answers to some of his questions. Seeing Jimmy stop and guessing the reason, Hokee put his warmest smile on his face, a smile nearly as charming as Jimmy's.

"Jimmy, I'm Gloria, but everyone calls me Glory," she said, advancing towards the still unmoving man holding out her hand to shake.

"Don't mind my partner. This is Hokee," she said, nodding towards the man in black advancing towards them. "I hope you don't mind if we both talk with you."

Whatever caused Jimmy's paralysis ended, and he stuck his hand out to Glory and then Hokee as he joined the other two.

"Howdy, and happy to make your acquaintance. I'm sorry about that little freeze a minute ago. Hokee looks so much like one of my old wrestling opponents in all those black clothes; it confused me for a moment. This guy, we called The Black Panther, also dressed in black cowboy outfits, and he was the dirtiest fighter in the business. He's the only guy to put me on the mat against my will. I still won the fight, but it cost me both of my ears, as you can see."

"You look like you could still take him out," Hokee said with a smile.

"Only in my dreams, but thanks, Hokee. Okay, if we sit on the porch?" He asked, looking at Glory. "I can get us some coffee or water if you like."

"Sure, let's sit," Glory responded. "And I'm good for drinks. How about you, Hokee?"

"Yeah. I'm good. Let's go sit down."

Jimmy led the way across the yard to a large white clapboard farmhouse with a wrap-around porch. Jimmy sat in a porch swing, showing with his hands the two matching oak wood rockers on each side for Glory and Hokee. The house had a flower garden, which featured only mums at this time of year, but what a beautiful array of colors. Blue and yellow rows with accents of red and occasionally a white mum to make it more enjoyable.

"You have a wonderful place here, Jimmy," Glory said with enthusiasm. "I don't believe I've ever seen a llama before. I mean in the flesh, not the movies."

"Yeah. I don't understand it," Jimmy responded. "They are one of the easiest farm animals to care for and one of the best cash crops a man can have. But hey, I'm not complaining. If everybody grew llamas, I would not get nearly the same price for my wool."

"That reminds me," Hokee said. "A few years ago, it seemed like all the farmers in the area started raising ostriches. Their meat supposedly tasted better than beef, and ostrich burgers became the big thing. I admit to never trying one, and the next thing, nobody raises them anymore."

"Miserable fucking birds, excuse the language," Jimmy said. "And fast. Lordy lord, but those buggers could run fast. A neighbor down the street had them for a couple of years. The damn birds were always getting out, and he continually asked us to help chase them down and get em back in the pasture. Of course, I never ate the meat either."

"Well, if we can get off the farm animals," Glory interjected. "Tell us what you can about Zack Carpenter."

"Another miserable fucking animal. And this time, I won't ask for forgiveness. But, sometimes, ya gotta say it like it is."

"I get the miserable part," Glory said, "and from what little I know, your assessment is accurate, but we need to find him and wonder if you can help?"

"I don't have any idea where you could find the bastard, and frankly, I don't want to know." It was clear from the expressions on Jimmy's face that Zack wasn't one of his favorite students.

"Was there any other student that he was friends with?" Glory was getting desperate. "We haven't been able to come up with an address for Zack, although I'm sure he lives in the area. I was hoping maybe we could find a roommate or someone who knows him."

"He was only in the wrestling program for one semester. He behaved as though rules were made for somebody else. It got so nobody would wrestle with him more than once. After a couple of months, not one person would get in the ring with him. I couldn't get him to follow the most straightforward instruction. He isn't stupid, just mean." Jimmy shook his head as though he was still trying to find some way to reach inside of Zack's head for an answer.

"There wasn't someone he palled around with?" Glory wouldn't give up pushing for something to help her cause.

"Well, now that I think back on it. There was one kid that tagged along with the Carpenter boy. Let's see. I think his name was Earl. Yeah, that's it, Earl." Jimmy seemed so proud of himself; Glory hated to burst his bubble.

Hokee was content to sit in his rocker watching the llamas eat oats across the yard throughout this exchange. You couldn't tell whether he listened to anything being said, for he made no visible response to either the questions or answers. He might not have even been there as far as Glory and Jimmy were concerned, but absolutely nothing escaped his attention.

"Would Earl have a last name?" Glory tried hard to keep the frustration out of her voice.

"Yeah, yeah, yeah. Give me a second. It's stuck in here someplace." Jimmy pulled off his straw hat and started scratching his head like maybe the scratching would loosen up some of his gray cells. "Anderson! Yep, that's it. Anderson. Earl Anderson."

Looking at the satisfied smile on Jimmy's face, one might think he had just won the lottery.

"Okay, Jimmy, the six million dollar question. Or is it the sixty million dollar question? Hell, it doesn't matter. Jimmy, do you have an address for Earl Anderson?"

"Oh, good heavens, no. I never had that information. Maybe you should try the registrar at ISU. They would have had his address while he went to school. He might still be in school for all I know."

You could see the disappointment in Glory's face. Hokee's face revealed nothing.

"Jimmy, can you think of any way we might locate either Zack or Earl?"

Glory asked with all the poise of an experienced investigator, but Hokee could see it was strictly a formality in her eyes. She didn't expect any helpful information, and she wasn't disappointed.

CHAPTER TWENTY-SIX

Planning

ISU was no help in providing an address for either Zack or Earl. Hokee and Glory were sitting on his porch watching Shila track a wandering seagull that seemed to have lost its way. It liked the fountain where it stopped for a drink and bath, carefully monitored by Shila. Then it just soared up into the sky, drifting aimlessly in lazy circles. It reminded Hokee of the progress they were making on the missing girl case. Just aimless drifting.

"Glory, what do you know about infinity?"

"Well, infinity is a long way away."

"That's true. But from where you are sitting, how far does infinity extend, and in which direction?"

You could see the wheels turning behind those big blue eyes before she responded. "I guess it goes in every direction all the way to, well, infinity."

"Great. Now, does that make you the center of the universe?"

You could see Glory struggle as she thought about the question. Glory is not stupid. She is, in fact, extremely bright. Her persuasive interviews as a professional investigator for television proved that, but being hit with problems of this caliber would cause anyone to pause in their answers.

"Well, I guess it does. But that is the same for everybody. Right?"

"Of course. Except that almost no one realizes this truth. Now, since you are the center of your universe, which goes to infinity, what does that make you?"

Glory looked at Hokee like she wanted to kill him, but she was curious to see where this was going.

"How many guesses do I get?" Glory was only half jesting, and half of her wanted to kill Hokee for bringing up such a complicated subject.

"There is only one word. It makes you INFINITE."

"Hokee, I love you. But is there a point to this? I don't enjoy feeling stupid."

"Where we are heading in this conversation is towards consciousness. We need answers, and since our beings extend to infinity, somewhere in that realm dwell our missing subjects, Zack and Earl. So if we expand our consciousness outwards towards infinity, we should run into these two wandering souls somewhere in there. Yes?"

"Okay, smartass, I understand now the basis of your questions about infinity. But how does that help us locate Zack and Earl?"

"We need a sweat lodge session. I can expand my consciousness through meditation, but not to the same extent possible in the lodge. There, we can both expand our consciousness to where it includes both individuals."

Glory had experienced sweat lodges with Hokee in the past and knew those wise men, shamans, spiritual leaders, and mystics throughout history all used plants to expand their consciousness. Ancient peoples made teas or soups for the entire tribe, and the wise men would then lead the people on a journey to explore reality. For example, the American Indians used peace pipes, while people in the northlands used soups. Hokee preferred the sweat lodge, chiefly because that is how he had learned.

"When do you want to do the sweat, Hokee?" Glory still wasn't crazy about getting naked and crawling into a skin-covered bunch of poles on an overheated mound of dirt. Still, she also knew that powerful visions came from this experience, and she knew from experience that these trips of expanded consciousness came at a price. However, the price one pays for the experience in a sweat lodge is small compared to the price one might pay to take other shortcuts.

It is possible to experience expanded consciousness using many types of herbs. Still, the price can be fearful, as Timothy Leary and his partner Richard Alpert (Ram Dass) learned while professors at Harvard. Taking shortcuts to enlightenment can be really hard on the body.

Next to his house and a natural solid lava wall, Hokee built a custom sweat lodge suitable for two people. Ordinarily, he always did his sweats alone, but prudence suggested that he might as well provide for some company, although when he built it, he had no one in mind.

It was a simple structure, cedar poles soaked to make them soft, then curved into a roof resembling an igloo. Antelope hides covered the support poles with a small two-foot opening on one side. Inside the sweat lodge was an eighteen inch deep hole for the hot lava rocks. Five feet away from the sweat lodge was a three-foot circular rock-lined fire pit where Hokee could heat the lava rocks. Once he placed the hot stones inside, Hokee swung an animal skin flap down, covering the opening.

"Let's get a fire going and get ourselves ready. We need to spend some time meditating on our questions and asking for help with our quest." At this point in his life, Hokee was sanguine about the sweat lodge experience. After several hundred sweats over two decades of life, he became accustomed to the uncomfortable expanse of the infinite, but today he was in for a novel experience.

Before long, with Glory's help, they had a pleasant cedarwood fire heating the lava rocks. With this chore accomplished, they sat on Hokee's porch wrapped in blankets as the days had suddenly turned chilly. It was getting later in October, and it is Idaho.

"Glory, what do we wish to learn from our sweat today? What is our aim?"

Looking like a China doll all wrapped in her blanket, Glory answered. "We want to learn how to find Zack and Earl."

"Okay. Is that all?" Hokee wasn't trying to be rude or insensitive. Instead, he was using this time to educate Glory.

"Well," you could see the wheels churning behind those beautiful gorgeous eyes, "we want to find Laura."

"Alright honey, you're doing fantastic. Please keep it going. What else?"

"We know some of the men who grabbed Laura, but not all. And we don't know why or who might be behind this kidnapping." You could see that Glory was proud of herself for putting this all together, and she seemed eager to get started.

"That's excellent, Glory. We need answers to all of those questions. Now, what is our plan for getting this information?"

While Glory thought about the question, Hokee began preparing the herbs and water for their sweat. First, he checked his medicine pouch to make sure there were sufficient herbs inside to make a good sweat. Next, he doctored a small pail of water with a few drops of particular oils he had previously extracted. He found that three parts lavender oil, two parts peppermint oil, two parts of sage oil, and one part eucalyptus tree oil provided the enhancement he preferred.

Hokee also extracted his oils, as opposed to buying essential oils from another. He was never sure of the purity if he used other oils. Hokee used the oils and herbs in the sweat lodge as part of a ceremony. This was as close to religion as Hokee ever ventured.

Watching Hokee, Glory could see the precision and dedication in his movements. Finally she had an answer. "We track down Zack and wring his f-ing neck, making him tell us all." Glory had a grin on her face, but a question in her eyes. "God, Hokee. I don't know. What is our plan?"

"Great question, honey." Hokee had a big grin on his face. "We track down Zack and wring his f-ing neck, making him tell us all."

Shila was lying by Glory's feet, so she nudged him with her foot. "Shila, go take a bite out of your master."

Shila looked back up at Glory like, "what's with you, lady?" Then promptly went back to sleep.

"Seriously, Glory, we need to uncover what is behind this kidnapping? It isn't for ransom. It isn't some personal grudge. I believe the two previous missing girls put those questions to rest. It has to be some sort of ritualistic fetish, and the only festival of sorts coming up, if you can see it as a festival, is Halloween. But that is still a few days away. So why abduct someone almost three weeks before the festival. It seems a lot riskier. Although they never found the other girls, so maybe the risk is less than I think possible."

"So, oh wise master. What is our plan?" Glory couldn't keep the smug grin from her face.

"We need to find a trail inside of consciousness. Those men who kidnapped Laura were operating under someone's instructions. There are always threads of consciousness woven through time. We need to find the time these threads begin and track them back to their source. But, I must tell you; this could be dangerous."

"Worse than having somebody steal my mind?" Glory's pinched face showed fear and having second thoughts about the entire sweat lodge idea.

"No, of course not. And I won't let anybody harm you during our journey. But if we can find them, they can find us. And this business has a dark feel about it I have never encountered before."

"What kind of danger could we be facing, honey?" Glory was seriously worried.

"We don't know who these people are or what they want with Laura. I believe we can safely assume they do not want any interference. When we go into our search mode within the sweat lodge, they will know we are searching and will want to know who we are. Depending on their skill, they could find us before we find them. I'm just saying that after today we have to watch our backs. Carefully."

"I always kind of liked your back, Hokee. It's so big and strong. And I..."

Here is where Hokee grabbed Glory and, pinning her to the cushions, smothered her in kisses.

CHAPTER TWENTY-SEVEN

The Sweat

A naked Hokee sat across the hot rocks from a naked Glory. The only light came from the white-hot glowing stones. Hokee had them both take a few deep breaths of the hot air. It burned the nose and throat, providing the setting for the herbs to follow. After suggesting that Glory breathe and relax, Hokee threw the first of the sage and cedar chips onto the glowing rocks. The pungent odors worked their magic, loosening the cells of the throat and lungs. After taking another deep breath, Hokee threw the first cup of water onto the white-hot coals. The steam flash mixed with the sacred oils sent both voyagers far into space, away from time.

Hokee immediately located Glory in the far distant depths of consciousness and grabbed her with his mind, letting her know she was not alone. Being this far outside of ordinary consciousness can frighten and unsettle novice travelers.

Pleasure-seekers using LSD or magic mushrooms often get lost and scared to the point of jumping out of windows. That this could and did happen was such a risk that the early pioneer in LSD research, Timothy Leary, formulated the three rules for tripping. Set, setting, and dosage. Set is your mindset. If you are frightened, worried, or confused about something, the trip will augment this state of mind. Your mood has to be in alignment with what you are doing. You want pleasant thoughts and a relaxed mind. The setting has to do with the place you are located. You don't want to trip from some place that isn't safe or where you don't feel safe. And of course, the dosage has to do with your size, experience, physical health, and the amount of the drug you are about to ingest. To satisfy all three criteria, you need an experienced guide, such as Hokee.

With Glory in tow, Hokee took them deep into the realm of consciousness. This realm could look like celestial constellations, it could be a field of absolute blackness with pinpoints of light, or it might feel as though you are falling from a high cliff into an endless pit of total black nothingness. Many give up at this point in the trip, afraid of becoming lost, and turn back. Instead, Hokee plowed on with Glory by his side, powering through the darkness.

On the other side of night is a whole new universe of light. It can be so bright it burns your eyes, which, of course, are closed. The light comes from inside of your skull and is confusing. How can the light blind you if your eyes are closed?

Many people who make it this far retreat, seeking the shadows and darkness. The light is too intense for them to tolerate. But, for the experienced shaman, it is here that the hunting begins.

Time in these outer dimensions, the far reaches of consciousness, has no meaning, and the shaman must monitor the situation. Our human bodies have limitations. During this process, our bodies are pouring forth significant quantities of sweat. Most get lost with no reference to time. Sometimes, with inexperienced guides, a traveler may faint and fall onto the hot rocks or fall over unconscious. It is up to the guide to monitor the physical well-being of those on the journey and bring them back before harm occurs. Hokee, with his vast experience, has no concern about his well-being when in a sweat lodge. For him, it is almost like coming back home. But Glory has no such background, and Hokee has to be careful not to let her get too far from her body.

It was in this vast outer universe that they both saw Zack and Earl. Glory recognized them from the restaurant, and she was quick to point them out to Hokee. It isn't like you see their physical bodies or even their souls or spirits. It's like seeing shadows on the wall. The men weren't there, but they had left their footprints. Or perhaps we should say soul prints. Unfortunately, Glory's body needed water, so Hokee reluctantly brought her back into the sweat lodge, where he gave her a bottle of cold water from a cooler just outside the lodge.

"Whew. Boy, I needed that drink." Glory said. "I forgot how much water one needs for this ordeal."

"Yeah, I know. This heat is intense. Do you think you could make another trip, or do you need some time to recover?"

"I'm good, Hokee. Just gimme a minute and another bottle of water, and I'll be ready. How is it I could recognize Zack and Earl without their bodies?"

"An excellent question, Glory. And I'd like to give you an answer, but then I would have to take away your cooking privileges."

Even across the hot coals, you could see the fire in Glory's eyes. "Go to hell, Superman. Answer my question."

"Well, since you can't cook anyway, I guess that wouldn't be an enormous loss on your part." Hokee said this with a big grin on his face, but Glory looked like she was about to throw a water bottle at Hokee, so he quickly amended his statement. "What I was about to say, before being so rudely threatened, is that it's all shadows."

"Shadows?" Glory asked.

"Well, okay. Footprints are a better metaphor. You know from our previous discussions that everything is energy, right?"

"Right." Now Glory looked interested instead of angry.

"And you remember that this energy is all wavelengths. So everything and everybody is simply a vibration."

"I remember. And even our thoughts are vibrations." Glory looked proud of herself for remembering this last bit.

"Correct, and very good, honey. Now, when we have thoughts in our daily lives, these thoughts travel outwards towards infinity. And we know how far that is, right?"

"Right. Infinity is a long, long way away." Glory was getting into the conversation, forgetting her thirst.

"Now, our thoughts do not travel at the speed of light. In fact, science tells us our thoughts travel instantly to the end of infinity. Well, they would travel to the end of infinity if infinity had an end."

"Are you telling me that my thoughts go outwards forever?" Glory didn't quite like this idea.

"The technical term is *for eternity*, not *forever*." Hokee had a grin on his face, although it was a little hard to see with just the glow from the rocks.

"Listen, hotshot, are you going to answer my question or continue to criticize my linguistics?"

"Okay, Glory. All energy has a signature, much like our fingerprints. Just as we all have unique fingerprints, our thoughts all have our signature, so anyone catching our thoughts can instantly tell whose thoughts they are monitoring."

Glory thought about this for a few minutes while Hokee drank some water. "So, way out in space, anybody can catch my thoughts and know they are mine?"

"I know I use the term space, but in reality, we are talking consciousness. Most of us are unaware of what the term 'consciousness' means. Consciousness extends to infinity, of which you are now familiar. When we journey out of our bodies, it feels like we are invading space, but actually, we are experiencing an expanded awareness of our consciousness. It seems strange to think that people can get lost in their consciousness, but I've seen it happen."

"Let me get this straight, Hokee. So here in the sweat lodge, when you do your magic thing with herbs and water, we don't go into space, but into our consciousness?"

"Technically, that is correct; however, there is one minor hitch to your observation."

"Oh my God, Hokee. Is this shit ever going to end? I think I'm getting a handle on this space, consciousness, and infinity crap, and you keep changing the damn rules."

"Sorry, Glory. There is just one more minor change to our thinking. There is only one consciousness. We allow ourselves to expand our limited awareness into the vastness of unlimited and eternal consciousness."

"Are you telling me I don't even have my own consciousness?" Glory was getting upset, and if it weren't already hot in the sweat lodge, she would steam from within. "Of course, we all have our consciousness. What you and I experience and assimilate into our being is our own; it is our individual consciousness in action. Still, when we expand our human consciousness beyond our five senses, we are touching the infinite."

"Let me see if I understand what you have been telling me." Glory had a look of desperation and expectation on her lovely sweat-drenched face. "When we expand our consciousness, we enter an infinite consciousness, which is not our own?"

"That is correct. There is only one infinite consciousness. Some say that this infinite consciousness is the mind of God. So when we enter this consciousness, it is possible to see into the consciousness of anyone in the universe. In infinite consciousness lives the thoughts of everyone. That is how we can see Zack and Earl. Remember, we programmed them into our consciousness before beginning our sweat and focusing on them before our search helped us locate them out of the infinity of thoughts. We caught a hint of them, but not their actual thoughts.

That is why I want to go back if you are game. We barely saw them the first time."

"I get all this infinity crap now," Glory growled with some satisfaction. "How far away is infinity? It's to the God-damned infinite. That's how it can store all those fucking thoughts. No wonder people get lost there. It's fucking infinite."

"By jove, I think she's got it." Hokee had a big grin on his face.

"If it's okay with you, Hokee, I'd like to call it quits and go get a cold shower. I want to think about what you have been teaching me before we try again. Maybe tomorrow?"

"Sure, honey. Infinity will still be here tomorrow."

"Hokee, you know I love you. But if you mention infinity one more time, I'm going to give you a first-hand look at an infinite bruise on your handsome face."

CHAPTER TWENTY-EIGHT

Dealing with Earl

The women watching Laura started getting sloppy after the shaving ceremony. They still locked Laura in the janitor's closet, called the cell, but no one stayed in the room with her anymore. And they stopped tying her down to the bed several days ago. Sidella, Zelda, and Karnilla took turns sitting in a chair outside of the cell to make sure Laura didn't break out and take off. Still, since their prisoner showed no signs of resistance and seemed to have accepted her fate, the girls started getting sloppy. The daytime shift wasn't too awful for the minders, as there were other people around to talk with help pass the time. The early evening watch wasn't too bad either, as there was some activity to help pass the time. But the late-night shift proved to be another story.

The watcher used a padded metal folding chair sitting outside of the cell, and during the first two shifts, there was enough traffic in the area that the women didn't need to sit the entire shift. But the late shift was quite different.

A soft light filtered into the hallway from the principal room, and it was quiet, with no distractions, and the women found it hard to stay awake. After sitting for a few hours, the women's butts got tired. They got up and walked around a little, stretching their legs. As the days and nights went on and their prisoner did not escape, the women became careless, leaving the area for longer and longer periods until they barely checked in at all. Whoever had the late shift would show up, check the lock, go into the primary room, find some blankets, and sack out on the floor.

After applying the lather to Laura's pubic hairs, Earl Anderson had difficulty keeping the girl out of his mind. She had such perfect tits, an absolutely gorgeous ass, and legs any model would kill to gain. Besides that, she was stunningly beautiful. He and two other men helped clean up the mess made with the rose water getting it ready for tomorrow night. They put out all the candles and checked the fire, making sure there was no threat of a log rolling out, creating a problem. The other two men left, but Earl hung back, claiming he had lost his phone and wanted to look around. The others offered to help him look, but Earl said he would only take a minute and suggested they go ahead.

When he was alone, Earl went to Laura's cell only to find the watcher absent. Whoever had the late shift either had not shown up or had wandered off somewhere, perhaps to use the toilet. Earl just wanted to take another look at Laura. An excess of testosterone fueled his lust, driving him crazy. He unlocked the door with no one around to witness his actions and went into the room, shutting the door behind him.

Laura had been lying down on her cot when she heard the lock on the door flip open, and since no one ever came into her room late at night anymore, she became instantly alarmed. By the time Earl entered the room, Laura had a blanket wrapped around her body like a Grecian robe, leaving both hands and arms free.

The women had given her a toothbrush previously, which they started leaving in her room. During the past two nights, Laura had scraped the handle along the floor, honing it into a sharp, pointed, lethal weapon. When Earl entered, she had the toothbrush in her hand like an ice pick, slightly behind her back, so it was not visible. Having watched several prisoner movies growing up, she started calling her weapon the shiv.

After shutting the door, it disappointed Earl to see the girl wrapped in a blanket. In his fantasy, she would lie naked on the bed, waiting for him to have his way. Damn, but she was a great-looking piece of ass. And now it was all covered up. Of course, he couldn't fuck her. Neter would cut off his penis if he molested her before All Hallows Eve. But he should be able to stroke her breasts and maybe play a little with her clitoris. He got a boner remembering when he spread the lather around her clitoris.

"Hey baby, what's with the blanket? It ain't like nobody hasn't seen you naked before."

"What are you doing here, Earl? It is Earl, isn't it?"

"See there. You know my name, so you must have been thinking about me." He had a cocky grin on his beady-eyed face that reminded Laura of a feral dog they had to kill a couple of years ago as it kept chasing their sheep.

"Yeah, Earl. You remind me of the shit I have to smash down this stinking drain every day. You smell the same too."

"Now that's not nice. I just came in to keep you company for a while. I figured you must be lonely in here all by yourself."

"How did you get past my minder outside? Sidella, isn't it?"

"There wasn't anybody there. I guess they figure you ain't a threat to escape anymore. That means I got you all to myself."

"What do you want, Earl? You know you're not supposed to be here." Laura was across the bed from Earl in the corner opposite the drain. She kept the toothbrush hidden but was still nervous. Earl was a big powerful man, and while Laura was a sturdy, healthy young woman, she was no match for a man like Earl. If he attacked her, she only hoped to stick him with the shiv, quick and someplace that would hurt like hell.

"Ah, well. I just wanted to have another look at the mighty fine body you have hidden under that blanket. Maybe squeeze those delicious melons on your chest and scratch your sweet spot. Bring you a little pleasure. What do you say? Wanna drop the blanket?"

"What? My God. You've been ogling me, fingering me, stroking me for a week or more. What more in God's name do you want. You know you can't fuck me."

"Yeah, but I can play with you. Now drop the blanket. I won't ask you again." It frustrated Earl that the girl wasn't naked, lying on the cot as she had been a few days ago. He was not told the women gave her a blanket. He was also surprised that Laura wasn't cowering in fear. He knew he presented a bad image.

"Earl, you need to leave this room. I will not accommodate your wishes, so you may as well go." Had Earl looked into her eyes, he would have seen the resolution and knew he had a fight on his hands if he persisted. Unfortunately for him, he was trying to pretend he had x-ray vision and see her tits under the blanket.

"Listen, little girl. I came here for a private show, and by God, you are going to give me one if I have to tear that blanket off and pin you down on the cot."

He should have been watching her eyes to glimpse her determination. "Like hell, fat man. Just try it, and you'll be one sorry son-of-a-bitch."

"I'm through fucking around, sister. I'm coming for you." Earl kneeled on the side of the bed, grabbing for her blanket with both hands. Kneeling and reaching, he was slightly off balance, or he might have recovered. Just as he came forward to grab the blanket, instead of backing off as he expected, Laura leaned into him, whipping her hand around holding the toothbrush pick, stabbing it into his neck at just the right spot to hit his carotid artery. She wasn't aiming at his artery; it was the unlucky spot the pick entered.

Earl grabbed his neck, but it was too late. Blood spurted out like water from a ruptured fire hose. "Oh, you bitch." At least, that is what he tried to say. Unfortunately, it was hard to speak with a toothbrush stuck in his neck, and it sounded like, "Wraa u sch."

Laura jerked her hand back, still holding onto the toothbrush. She wasn't sure the fight was over, and she didn't want to take any chances, but the neck injury finished Earl. He fell over on the cot, moaning as the blood poured out of his neck. Laura rolled back, horrified, releasing the blanket, which was now partly under Earl. It wasn't the sight of blood that upset her. Back on the farm, she had helped her father harvest many of their animals. They never slaughtered their animals but harvested them. So it was having just killed a human she found upsetting. Laura was uncertain of what to do next. Should she call for help? What would they do to her?

"I told you to leave me alone." Even to her ears, it sounded weak, but she was not sorry.

It took almost two minutes before he stopped struggling. Now that Earl had unlocked the door, she thought about escaping, but Sidella was sitting in the chair when she opened the door with a surprised look on her face. "Hey, the door's supposed to be locked. Now how did you get it open?"

Laura thought about stabbing Sidella, but before she could act, the woman was quickly out of her chair, blocking the hallway.

"Earl unlocked the door earlier. He came in attempting to molest me."

"Why that son-of-a-bitch! Just wait until I get my hands on him." Then Sidella saw the blood dripping off Laura's hand onto the floor. Laura had palmed the shiv, but the blood still dripped. "Did he hurt you? That asshole?"

"No, but I think I hurt him. He's inside on the cot."

To her credit, Sidella didn't scream when she went into the cell. Instead, she looked at Earl, felt for a pulse, then asked, "What the hell happened here?"

Without even considering her actions, Laura slammed the door and turned the lock with Sidella inside the cell with Earl's body. A solid door with a substantial lock on the outside had long ago replaced the original cheap maintenance room door. Laura could hear Sidella's muffled screams for Laura to open the door, but she didn't believe the sound was loud enough to be heard much beyond the hallway. Laura hurried into the main chapel to see if anyone else was around, but the place appeared deserted.

Free, at least temporarily. One benefit of her upbringing on the farm was the ability to think and plan. In schools today, they teach young people what to think, not how to think. On the farm, there are usually so many chores needing attention that unless a person can think and reason, the tasks go undone, or they get done haphazardly and have to be redone. It doesn't take long to learn that thinking and planning can save many problems later on. One quickly learns how to think, or one might die.

Okay, so Laura had just killed a man. Sure, he was one of her kidnappers, but she didn't feel the least little bit conflicted about ending his life. Her only regret was that it hadn't been Zack instead of Earl, although she had to admit that seeing the shock on Earl's face had its own reward.

She was temporarily free, naked, covered in blood, and in an unfamiliar house/church with no car. Now what?

CHAPTER TWENTY-NINE

Laura's Escape

First, she needed to wipe off the blood and get some clothes. Running around naked would not work for long, no matter how well one tried to hide in the shadows. Besides, it was now cold outside. Going back to the shower, Laura found a towel to wipe off most of the blood. She didn't dare take the time to shower.

She found Sidella's coat and purse on a table just inside the main chapel. In the purse were Sidella's phone and car keys. The coat barely covered her ass, and she needed something for her legs and feet. A search of the downstairs resulted in a pair of men's sneakers, but no pants. Undaunted, Laura found another blanket, which she tied under her arms like a sarong. The blanket hung down to her knees, but with the coat covering her upper body, it looked like she was wearing a fancy skirt, at least from a distance in the dark. Laura didn't plan on parading around in public, but she needed an excellent covering if it was necessary to interface with someone before she could get the proper clothing.

Taking Sidella's phone and car keys, Laura crept upstairs, keeping to the edge of the stairs next to the wall. She thanked the movies she had watched where the hero always chose the edge of the stairs, never the middle where the stairs might creak. Laura kept her fingers crossed, hoping there was no one else in the building. She didn't know if anyone lived in the establishment or if they used it strictly as a place for Satan's church. She walked on tiptoes to the main floor, which looked like an ordinary house. There was a kitchen, a living room, a family room which might have once been a library, a toilet and two bedrooms plus a stairway going upstairs. No one seemed to sleep on the main floor as both bedroom doors stood open, and it appeared as though they used the rooms as offices. She didn't care about upstairs. All she wanted to do was get out of the building without seeing anyone.

She tried the front door slowly, hoping it wouldn't squeak. Luck seemed on her side as the door opened silently, letting in the cold October night air. Quietly closing the door, Laura took her first breath of freedom.

Looking around, she tried to figure out which car was Sidella's. Walking away was possible, but if a vehicle was available, it would be nice to put some distance between her and the Church of Satan. There was a button on the key fob that would probably honk the horn, but Laura was afraid to try it out in case the horn aroused the wrong people. There was an older model Honda Civic across the street that looked like something Sidella might drive. Pushing the door unlock button on the key fob produced a satisfying click, which Laura could hear from across the street. It looked like she had a ride. Now what? Where to go and who to call?

The Civic had 213,045 miles on the odometer, but it ran just fine and seemed reasonably clean inside. Laura had been in some cars girls from her dorm drove, and they were like pigpens inside. She figured she had three or four hours before they reported someone had stolen the Honda. She had that much time to figure out her future.

What about the dead man? Would they turn her into the authorities? Laura didn't believe that would happen. If they reported the murder, it would raise all kinds of questions the Church of Satan was not prepared to answer.

How about going to the police? At first, that seemed like a good idea until Laura remembered seeing some uniforms among the worshipers. Police or county sheriffs or maybe both? If she ran into one of the church's men, they would take her back to Neter and the stinking cell.

Using some money she had taken from Sidella's purse, Laura drove through an all-night Mcdonald's for some coffee, a hamburger, and fries. They had fed her decent food to keep her healthy, but prison food tasted like prison food, and it couldn't compare to a big Mac.

Maybe she could call her roommate or her parents? However, the more she thought about it, the worse the idea sounded. The Church of Satan could not afford to have her reach the authorities. As soon as they discovered her missing, they would mount a search. Her room at the dorm and her parent's farm would be the first places they would search.

Who could she call or see that wouldn't bring harm to anyone else? Damn! She was free, at least temporarily, but she had the devil on her ass. Literally. Laura needed clothes and a place to hang out while figuring out her next move. There wasn't enough cash in Sidella's purse for a motel room, and she didn't dare use one of her stolen credit cards.

Sitting in the McDonald's parking lot sipping on hot coffee and munching on a burger, she remembered an old high school teacher who owned The Malad Motel. Mrs. Williams was a widow who taught trigonometry to the senior class. Most of the students hated her because she was a harsh taskmaster who graded on the curve. In every class she taught, Mrs. Williams believed there was at least one A student and one F student. Everyone else fell someplace in between. Laura loved math and consequently earned the A, making her one of Mrs. William's favorite students.

Malad was only fifty miles away. Less than an hour's drive. She knew the Malad Motel was on a dead-end street with plenty of trees behind in which to hide Sidella's car. Would Mrs. Williams hide her until she could figure things out? Would she be any danger to the teacher? Yes, and no. The Church of Satan would have no way to associate Laura with Mrs. Williams, and Laura knew Mrs. Williams loved her students, even if she was a harsh grader. When Laura graduated, didn't Mrs. Williams tell her that if she ever needed anything, please ask?

That settled the issue. Scrunching up the hamburger wrapper and French fry box, Laura tossed them into the back seat. She only felt a little guilty for trashing the car. Malad City Motel, here she comes.

CHAPTER THIRTY

The Identification

Hokee got up early to visit his office, check on the mail, and say hi to Hilda, his secretary/girl Friday. Glory wanted to sleep in after her sweat lodge experience the day before and a big dinner. Dressed in black denim trousers and a black turtleneck sweater, Hokee plunked his black Stetson from the hat rack just inside his front door on his way out. He almost reached the Explorer before having second thoughts. An instinct that Hokee had learned to heed warned him to get a gun. Hokee believed instincts were the way our subconsciousness talked to our brains.

Hokee rarely carried a gun with him when doing his detective business. In all of his years of searching for missing students, there were only two occasions when he wished for a weapon. Once in the Oasis Bar on Clark Street, three men molesting young college girls pulled knives when Hokee questioned their activities. Acting quickly, Hokee grabbed the nearest man, twisting his knife arm behind his back, dislocating his shoulder. The man's scream made the other two men turn and run like cowards.

He cornered a hit-and-run suspect in a dead-end alley one other time, and the man pulled a gun. This man seemed highly agitated and irrational, waving the gun about like he was holding a water pistol. The weapon was a Smith and Wesson M&P 9 M2.0 with a 5-inch barrel. When the man waved the gun in Hokee's face, Hokee saw the safety in the off position, so acting on impulse, Hokee snatched the weapon from the man's hands before he could pull the trigger. In both cases, with a gun in his hand, Hokee would have been more relaxed.

Shortly after returning from his Caribbean adventure with Glory, Hokee had retrieved his old favorite, the Colt 45, from the cougar's den, where he had left it on a ledge above the underground river. The 45 is a big gun to hide under a coat, but Hokee is a big man, so he grabbed a pea coat to hide what he was carrying.

It thrilled Hilda to see the boss and insisted on making him a fresh pot of coffee.

There were several letters, either giving thanks or asking for favors. Hokee didn't expect to see anything relating to the missing girl case, and he wasn't disappointed. A ransom demand or even a threatening note would have been acceptable, but nothing was there to provide a clue. Instead, Hilda told him that Grant Olson had called with a thousand thanks. Grant had Hilda provide him with Hokee's business banking account information, into which he promptly transferred ten million dollars. After a previous large payout, when Hokee had rescued his daughter, the big deposit was not a total surprise, but Hokee neither needed nor wanted the money. He worked for Grant as a matter of friendship, but hell; he'd give Hilda a big raise and perhaps find some suitable charitable causes.

The morning went quickly, and Hokee was about to go home and see what Glory was up to when Hilda told him Curly was on the line. "It sounds important."

"Hello Curly. You trying to set up another date with Glory?"

"Hey Hokee. I wouldn't mind another outing, but I'm calling about your missing girl case. I think we got one of the kidnappers."

"Great, did he tell you where the girl is located?"

"No. He can't. He's dead. Somebody dumped his body out by the landfill."

"How do you know it's one of the kidnappers?"

"We're not positive, so I wonder if you could pick up Laura's roommate and bring her and Glory down to the morgue. I believe both women got a look at the men responsible, and I'd like to make sure. He fit the description, but I would like the girls to tell me for sure."

"Okay. Have you contacted the roommate?"

"Yeah, I just got off the phone with her. She's expecting me, but if you show up with Glory, she'll be okay with that."

"It will take me about a half-hour to go pick up Glory and then the roommate. Does that timing work for you?"

"Oh yeah. We're going to be here for a while trying to figure this thing out. Right now, we don't have a clue who killed him or what weapon they used. Hopefully, the coroner will have more information when you get here with the ladies."

"Thanks for calling Curly. We'll see you in about thirty."

"Later, Hokee."

The Pocatello coroner's building is a two-story white stone building on Memorial Drive. Hokee had collected both Glory and Diann and found the building where they saw Curly's Jeep Grand Cherokee in the parking lot. Curly was waiting for them in his Jeep.

"Wow. Such service. Didn't expect to see you outside to escort us in Curly." Hokee had a big grin on his face while addressing the deputy sheriff.

"Hi Glory. I see you're still slumming with the local bad guy. Hi Diann. It's nice to see you again, even in the company of this shamus. Hello Hokee. I wish I could say the same about seeing you. I can't wait to have you show us up again with your *detective* skills."

Curly was wearing his deputy's uniform, which appeared rumpled as though he had been sitting in a hot car all day despite the cold. Glory wore a stylish blue jumpsuit with a custom sheepskin coat from the leather factory in Sun Valley. She looked gorgeous, as usual. Diann wore simple jeans and an ISU sweatshirt with a long knee-length gray overcoat and stocking hat.

"Let's go look at the stiff Curly. Get these girls out of the chilly air." Hokee wrapped his arms around the shoulders of both ladies, walking them into the building.

Sheldon Bastion was the coroner, a fat man in a small man's body. He moved with grace and speed despite his bulk, making it appear easy. A large yellow rubber apron covered an ordinary pair of bib overalls and a long-sleeved green Pendelton woolen shirt. He had a wispy blond beard and lively blue eyes that seemed to twinkle. Sheldon invited them to follow him into the stiff's room with a voice that sounded like a foghorn. The Stiff's Room is what he called the room with all the lockers where they stored the dead bodies.

Walking down a row of stainless steel doors, he stopped in front of 3-C, pulling it open. As soon as he pulled the sheet back from the face of the corpse, both ladies said, "that's him." Then, Glory added, "that's the son-of-a-bitch I saw at the restaurant when I was with Curly."

"What can you tell us about the body, Sheldon?" Curly asked.

"We've only had him here for a little over an hour," Sheldon answered. "We won't cut into him until tomorrow, but this is what we know. He died sometime this morning around three A.M. from a neck wound. Somebody drove something very long and sharp into his carotid artery. He bled out almost immediately. They didn't kill him at the landfill. Thanks to Curly here, we know his name is Earl Anderson, but that is about the extent of our knowledge. We have no address, no next of kin."

Positioning himself for a closer look at the neck wound, Curly added, "we suspect his associates include Zack Carpenter and the other two kidnappers that Diann saw, but we have no address for any of them."

"Curly?" Hokee asked. "What do you make of the wound you seem to find so fascinating? I don't see any defensive wounds on his hands or arms."

"Well, it must have been somebody he knew to get that close to him. I would guess that whoever did it took him by surprise. Finding his body dumped way out of town in the landfill tells me nobody wanted to be identified with the body. We know they killed him elsewhere. Probably someplace we will never find."

"I wonder where Laura is?" Glory asked. "If this is one of her kidnappers, does it suggest maybe there isn't all sunshine, peace, and happiness in paradise?"

"Finding Laura is our business," Hokee answered. "I don't know what the death of this man means. I don't see that it gets us any nearer to finding Laura."

"Can we go someplace other than this house of death to discuss the case?" Glory asked. "I would like to propose a theory."

"Hey, am I invited?" Curly asked with a hopeful smile on his face.

"I don't see why not?" Hokee responded. "This sounds like Glory's party, so I guess it's up to her. The same thing goes for you, Diann. Do you want to take part in Glory's game playing? I believe this is how she won all of those awards back in the Big Apple."

"I'd like you all to come," Glory was quick to add. "When we do this kind of brainstorming, the more brains, the better. Too bad that leaves you out honey," Glory couldn't help but give her man a little jibe along with a wink and smile.

Until now, Diann had been quiet other than when she recognized Earl. "I would love to take part, Glory, if that's alright with you," she added in a shy voice.

"Hey, the Grounds for Coffee shop is just down the street. How about we all meet over there and have some Joe?" Curly suggested.

"Sounds good to me, studly," Glory teased Curly. "And Diann, it would be great if you could join us. But, of course, since you are riding with Hokee and me, he'll bring you along anyway unless you scream."

"Okay, everybody. Let's saddle up and head on over to the Coffee Grounds." Hokee led the way outside. Morgues always made him uncomfortable. It might have had something to do with his mother's death when he was a baby. When they found him, his mother's body was stiff and cold. Ever since growing up, even though he had no memory of the event being only a baby, he hated being around icy bodies.

CHAPTER THIRTY-ONE

Planning

They housed the Grounds for Coffee shop in an old Pullman dining car on W. Carson Street just around the Mad Mike's Trading Post corner. Originally railroad gray, the owners had painted the coach a garish orange and installed a white coffee cup rooftop sculpture. It wasn't the sort of establishment that appealed to Hokee, but apparently, it satisfies a cop's thirst for coffee. Plus, Hokee noticed sitting on a counter a large glass cake server filled with sugar-coated donuts—definitely a cop's kind of place. The coffee smelled fantastic, plus whatever they were cooking in their tiny kitchen added its aroma to the room.

As if his intuition needed further confirmation, inside were three patrol officers sitting together at a counter that runs down half of one side of the old dining car. There was a grouping of three small tables, just big enough to hold the coffee cups and a plate of donuts. The tables were all empty, so they chose one farthest from the police officers and settled in just as a small, pleasant-faced woman wearing an old-fashioned apron covered with stenciled pictures of coffee cups approached, asking if they wanted coffee.

Hokee thought about being cute and ordering scotch and water, but it didn't seem like the time for humor. Instead, they all ordered coffee, even the ISU student. It was all Hokee could do not to ask Curly if he wanted a donut, but he resisted the impulse. Sometimes he got it right.

Once they all had coffee, Glory began offering her theory.

"What if Earl was guarding Laura, and she found or made a weapon out of something? You see in the movies how prisoners are always making a shiv out of dinner forks or something. Suppose Laura fashioned a shiv, and Earl got too close. Maybe he was trying to rape her or something. The coroner said something pointy and sharp caused the fatal wound. Perhaps something that looked like an ice pick."

The other three people seemed interested and thoughtful while Glory proposed her theory.

"That would fit what we know about finding the body," Hokee said. "If what Glory suggested happened, whoever else it involves wouldn't want to go to the authorities to investigate his death. To avoid suspicion, they would dump the body as far away from them as they could."

"That's a lot a supposition," Curly said. "Then what happened to Laura?"

"My God. A literate deputy," Hokee responded with a grin. "Big four-syllable words. Hanging around with college students like Diann is paying dividends. You need to hire this girl to spend some time down at the sheriff's station, Curly."

"What if she escaped and is in hiding," Diann offered, ignoring Hokee's comment and reluctant to be kept out of the conversation.

"Yeah, that's good, Diann," Glory said. "She would be afraid of the kidnappers. If they found her again, the Lord only knows what would happen to her."

"Okay," Curly interjected. "Why doesn't she go to the police?"

No one said anything for a couple of minutes as they all thought about the possibilities. Somebody kidnapped Laura; that was definite. One kidnapper was almost certainly Earl, who shows up dead, stabbed in the neck by something pointy and sharp. Someone dumped his body far away from where he was killed. Laura was still missing, and so far, she had not contacted the police. Was she still a prisoner, or had she escaped? And if so, where was she?

"If we continue with Glory's hypothesis," Hokee said, then added with a grin. "See Curly; even gumshoes can occasionally cough up a four-syllable word. Anyway, to continue before I so rudely interrupted myself, what if a police officer is involved with the kidnapping and Laura knew of their involvement? We believe four men kidnapped Laura. They must be part of some organization, as this has been going on for at least three years, maybe longer. It's conceivable that one of Laura's guards or someone else in the organization is in law enforcement."

Again there was silence as all four drank some coffee, thinking about all the ramifications.

"Well," Curly said, breaking the silence, "that's still a lot of supposition. Who kidnapped Laura and why?"

"According to what you told Glory, this has been going on for at least three years, maybe longer," Hokee said. "It probably involves several people. Possibly some organization. Or at least a group of people with similar interests in young women. Does that ring any bells?"

"There are certain people who are interested in virgins. At least virgin blood," Diann said. "I read about that in a psych book. According to my professor, this is still going on and includes some pretty famous people, even movie stars." Diann added this last comment about movie stars with disappointment in her voice.

"Do we know if any of the girls were virgins? And who in the hell would know something like that?" Glory asked.

"I don't think any girl over eleven is a virgin anymore," Curly paused, "Except our lovely *co-investigator* here."

"Excuse the sorry innuendos, Diann, but would you have any knowledge or reason to believe that Laura was a virgin?" Glory seemed reluctant to ask, but determined to pursue her theory.

"Well," Diann hesitated. "We have only been roommates for a few weeks, and we both have a pretty heavy schedule. I don't believe either of us has had a date since school began. I know I haven't. Boys and dating were not usually part of the conversations I had with Laura, and I am uncertain, but I would say she is still a virgin if I had to guess. How anybody else would know this is beyond my knowledge. She never talked about a special boyfriend back home in Malad."

After a couple of minutes of awkward silence, Curly added, "one girl was from Europe and came here with a boyfriend. It is highly doubtful that she was a virgin."

"Okay," Hokee said. "We don't know about the virgin angle or if it is even a factor. The kidnappers may not have known about the European girl's boyfriend, or maybe they didn't care. If they were only interested in a certain look or particular kind of girl, they wouldn't know about her entire life. So they scout the college campus, looking for a certain type of girl. Once they find her, they make the kidnapping arrangements."

"Maybe that's why they keep kidnapping girls. Trying to find a virgin," Diann added.

Curly watched the other police officers eating their donuts and finally couldn't resist. He got up from their table and went over to the counter. "You guys want any donuts," he asked hopefully, speaking back towards their table. The three police officers looked at him, hoping maybe he was talking to them. Curly didn't want to be the only one at the table eating a donut. He didn't get any takers but brought back a half dozen anyway, just in case.

Glory persisted with her theory. "The coroner told us Earl died around three A.M. That would give the escaped prisoner idea some credence. At three in the morning, there might not be many people around wherever they held her. I can see Earl sneaking into her room, looking for a little side action. When he went to grab her, she stuck him with something. How about that?"

"I have to tell you, Glory," Hokee said, "your theory makes some sense. That would also explain why no one has seen her. If the police were in on the kidnapping, she wouldn't go to them. She would also know her kidnappers would be desperate to find her before anyone else in authority. They couldn't afford to have her talking, and they would want her back. So she wouldn't go back to Diann and the dorm, and she couldn't go home for the same reason."

"We are spinning some wild theories based on one dead kidnapper," Curly said.

"Maybe it isn't so wild," Diann said. "I saw the four men who I believe grabbed Laura. I don't know why they kidnapped her or if she is still alive. I continue to hope and pray, but we don't know. Whoever took her had a reason. Maybe for the same reason they took the other girls."

"I know that human trafficking is a big deal throughout the world," Glory said. "Is it possible they kidnap the girls for somebody's harem or something?"

"Sure. Anything's possible, Glory," Curly answered. "But this isn't California or the east coast where you read about all the missing girls. Three girls missing here in three years don't sound like a kidnapping ring. But I'm the first to admit I am not an authority on human trafficking."

"Human trafficking would explain why no one ever saw the girls again," Diann added.

"I don't buy the human trafficking concept," Hokee said. "Three young girls all disappeared during the first of October, a month after school resumes. Everything I know about the human trafficking thing is that while well organized, it is random. More like an act of convenience, rather than stalking, which is what Diann described happened at ISU with Laura."

"Maybe the kidnappers were fulfilling some kind of order," Diann suggested. "Some Saudi prince wants a voluptuous young blond for his harem."

"Good idea, Diann, but I'm still not buying. I don't see three contracts, all for girls from the same school and all at the same time of year. If what you suggest is the case, they could pick up girls whenever they wanted. Hell, there must be two or three hundred girls at the University who fit Laura's description. No. Now don't give me that look, Diann. I'm not disparaging your roommate. Maybe she is one in a million, but I still don't believe it."

Having busted a bubble, Hokee took one of Curly's donuts to salve over his conscience.

Getting into the police mode, Curly said, "Let's summarize. We have a dead kidnapper with no leads. Laura is still missing and may or may not have killed Earl. We don't know where the other kidnappers are or if they are still holding Laura. Playing along with Glory's theory, since it's the only theory we have; if it was Laura and she escaped, where should we be looking?"

It was quiet for a minute while Hokee and Curly munched on donuts. The girls both watched with hungry eyes they tried to hide until Diann, not all that worried about her figure, grabbed one and started her own munching. After a couple of seconds, Glory decided to hell with it and grabbed the last one herself.

"I've been chasing missing college kids for several years," Hokee said. "And when they want to get lost, they find some old friend or acquaintance and hide out with them. It is always somebody that almost no one else knows. It could be a distant relative, a cousin or aunt, or nearly anybody that Laura would be comfortable staying with and who would help her in any way possible. No one in her present life would know about this friend."

"Damn Hokee," Curly said, "but you make sense. No wonder the parents always call you instead of the sheriff's department. And how do you go about finding out who this missing student's friends are?"

Hokee put on his killer grin. "I would like to tell you Curly, but then I would have to kill you. Excuse the old cliché. Can't have you divulging detective secrets."

CHAPTER THIRTY-TWO

The Conference

The mood around the conference table felt grim. Calling the old spindly kitchen table a conference table seemed like a joke, as any table that had chairs around it to sit became a conference table. They covered this table with an ancient soiled red and white checker oilcloth, the kind they hadn't made in forty years. Neter, sitting at what would be titularly the table's head, was dressed all in black, his standard uniform it seemed, and the color matched his mood.

"Does anybody know what in the hell happened here?" Neter asked the table at large, but he looked at Sidella.

It was the afternoon on the same day Zack and Arlo dumped Earl's body in the landfill. Getting all the principal actors back together took some time: Zack, Arlo, and Harold with Raven, Alwina, Sidella, Zelda, Dakarba, and Karnilla. Nobody looked at Neter. They all had their heads down, staring at the checkered tablecloth, maybe hoping to see some inspiration in the patterns made by the stained blotches on the oilcloth.

Getting no answer to his initial question, Neter asked another. "Did anybody see you at the landfill, Zack?"

Still looking at the tabletop, Zack answered in a fawning voice, "There didn't appear to be anybody else around. No one saw us either coming or going."

"Sidella, how did you get locked in the room with Earl?" The tone in Neter's voice did not leave any room for equivocations.

"I looked in on the sacrifice earlier and she appeared to be asleep. I had to use the toilet. That must have been when Earl unlocked the door and went into her room. When I came back, I just sat down in the chair when the sacrifice opened the door and came out of the room. It surprised me, and I asked her how she got out when I saw blood running off her hand onto the floor. When I asked her if she got hurt, she said no, but Earl needed help; he was inside on the cot. When I opened the door to check, the sacrifice shoved me inside, locking the door."

"What happened to your security, Raven? I thought you had that handled." Neter still had a murderous look in his eyes.

"We got sloppy. It's all my fault. The girl was compliant and seemed to have accepted the circumstances. She had not attempted to escape and gave us no trouble. We, that is I, assumed she was not a serious candidate to escape. Again, it's my fault." At last, Raven looked up at Neter with hope in her eyes. Hoping he wouldn't punish her.

"Well, we're all a little at fault," Neter said in an unctuous tone. It was clear from the look on his face and the timber of his voice that he blamed the entire mess on those assembled at the *conference* table. There was no acceptance of blame in his tone of voice.

"But, what's done, is done. We need to find the sacrifice. It's doubtful that she will return to the dorm or her parents. But we have to make sure. Find out who her friends are and start searching. I'll alert our friends in the police department to be on the lookout. Sidella's car is missing, so the police can search for that as well. She undoubtedly saw their uniforms during our worship service and will avoid going to the law. Zack, organize the searches, starting now." Without looking at the troops surrounding the table, Neter left the room, a black cloud of anger still hovering around his head.

*****

The following day, with the same players sitting around the same table staring at the same stained oilcloth, Neter entered the room dressed all in white. Starting with white leather shoes, white cotton pants, and a blinding white silk shirt with long puffy sleeves, he looked like a TV evangelist except for the black look in his eyes and the Van Dyke beard.

"Does anybody have anything of value to announce? Zack, any leads in finding the sacrifice?" Having witnessed Neter's violent temperament in the past, Zack was hesitant to report they had achieved no positive results searching for their missing sacrifice. Last month, Neter had two police officers hold a woman caught stealing one of the wall sconces for her home. Taking a page from The Scarlet Letter, Neter used a red-hot poker from the fire to carve the letter T on the woman's forehead as she screamed in pain.

Squirming in fear, Zack reluctantly announced, "I'm sorry Master, but the sacrifice has not returned to the dorm or her home in Malad. So we don't have any other places to search."

"I will have our police friends conduct a search. Meanwhile, we have to have a sacrifice for Lucifer, our God. The celebration feast is nearly here. Zack, since you cannot find the woman who escaped, we need another virgin immediately. Can you get a replacement today?"

"We can grab another student," Zack responded, still cowering in fear. Before Neter could comment on his announcement, he continued, fearful of the response, "There is no way to prove that she is a virgin before we snatch her."

With a wicked smirk on his face, their leader responded, "That won't matter Zack, we'll purify the sacrifice once we get her. Won't we, Raven?"

"Yes, Master." Raven was quick to answer, hoping there was no punishment in store for allowing their previous sacrifice to escape.

"How much of the blood from the sacrifice do we have left Raven?"

"Six cups," she responded, grateful that she knew the answer.

"We may have to forgo our nightly tribute to Lucifer unless Zack is successful in bringing us another sacrifice today. What do you think, Zack? Can you do it today?"

Relaxing a little as the threat of punishment for failing to find the missing girl diminished, Zack was happy to respond. "Yes, Master. I would like to have a replacement for Earl. With four men, the abduction goes a lot smoother."

"Who do we have for a replacement, Alwina?" Of course, as the keeper of the membership book, she would have the answer.

Without a word, Alwina opened the sizeable red leather-covered book lying in front of her on the table. The book was oversized, 14 inches wide by 16 inches tall. Flipping through the book, she scanned each page for only a second before turning to a fresh one. They devoted one page to each member of the Church of Satan. After just a couple of seconds, stopping at a page, she responded, "Kyro Brooks looks like a suitable candidate. He's been with us for almost five years and has been very supportive with his contributions."

"Yes, I remember him," Neter responded. "Isn't he the man with the long red beard?"

"Yes. That's him," Alwina answered. She kept her answer short, having learned long ago you don't get in trouble by not talking.

"What do you think, Zack? Will Kyro work for you?" It was clear from Neter's expression that only one answer would be the correct one.

Zack had difficulty remembering the man they were discussing. His primary interest in the Church of Satan's members centered on the women he could fuck during their celebrations. Finally, recognizing the look on his master's face, Zack gave the only acceptable response. "Yes, Master. Of course. Kyro will work just fine. Can you please give me his contact information, Alwina?'

"Certainly, I'll write it out for you." As she was writing the information, Neter left the room without speaking.

CHAPTER THIRTY-THREE

The Killers

After returning to Luxor from Japan, Ahmad called three of his hired killers for a meeting. Ahmad realized it had been a mistake using his relatives watching Rashida in New York to kill Gene Olson, believing him to be the threat. Ahmad took no more chances. This time he wanted real killers.

They met in Ahmad's office, a spacious room with a wall-to-wall window featuring a Nile River view. Some call this section of the Nile Egypt's California coast.

Abdul Wahid is slender, and at five foot five, he weighs a mere 155 pounds, but he is one of the best knife men in Egypt, and that is saying a lot as Egypt produces some of the best knife fighters in the world. Along with some Mexican cartels notorious for their excessive knife work, Abdul would be one of the world's greatest knife assassins. A mop of black hair hanging down over his face gave him a whimsical look, causing people to misjudge his lethality until it was too late.

Farij Zahir was not only one of the most dangerous men on earth; the man even looked dangerous. Farij grew up in an orphanage in Cairo run by the Sisters of Magdalene. He was the bastard son of a prostitute in Manshiet, one of the world's ten largest slums. His mother dumped him on the street outside the orphanage where a sister found him the following morning. With a sizeable raspberry-colored birthmark on his right cheek, he was the butt of jokes and teasing, despite the sister's best efforts to shield him from ridicule. He grew up hating everyone, and at the tender age of eleven, killed one of the nuns with a table fork, jabbing it in her eye, all the way through to her brain.

As an adult, the birthmark rode on his face like a beacon of doom. Penetrating black eyes that seemed to have no pupils sat in recessed sockets, giving him a blind man's appearance. A perpetual sneer on his face made people shun him, never acknowledging him on the street in passing. Walking in Cairo's markets, Farij took what he wanted. The police wisely left him alone.

One night, Zahir met Abdul drinking in The Al Jazeera, a slum bar in one of Cairo's worst sections. Abdul was hunting for killers and boasted he was not afraid of anyone, including Allah. Seeing Farij, Abdul offered to buy him a drink and thus began a partnership of murder for hire.

Gaffor Ali, at thirty-six, was the oldest and perhaps the most dangerous of the three killers. A certified psychopath, he had no regard for human life or any other form of life. Born to wealth with doting parents, Gaffor could have been anybody he wanted to be and have anything he desired. Instead, he started killing small animals as a child, and when his parents tried to intervene, he killed them both while still a teenager. He put sleeping pills in their evening cocktails, then strangled them both in their sleep. Afterward, Ali set fire to the house, destroying any evidence of his crimes.

One day he stole a car on a whim. No reason, just to take a ride. Unfortunately, the owner was sleeping in the back seat. Excited at the prospects of driving a new car, Gaffor failed to see the man in the back. When the driver's door slammed shut, the owner woke up, and seeing a man sitting in the driver's seat, pulled a knife from his pocket, intending to slice the thief's neck. Gaffor sensed movement at the last second, jerking his head sideways. The knife missed his neck but cut his cheek from his eye to his chin, leaving a nasty-looking scar. Gaffor killed the driver but left the scar on his face. He correctly assumed it added to his deadly appearance.

Gaffor's parents had been friends of Ahmad Hassan. Ahmad is no stranger to killing, although so far not by his own hands. Ahmad recognized the killer in young Gaffor and suspected the truth about his parent's deaths. Later, when he wanted to eliminate some of his competition in the construction business, he hired Gaffor. Being in the killing business, you learn who your competitors are and their specialties. Most killers have a method they prefer, like Abdul Wahid and his knives. Farij Zahir would choose to suffocate his victims either by his own hands or using gas, whatever made the most sense. Gaffor was just a killer.

Any method that killed them was acceptable to him. Inevitably, the three killers became acquainted through the auspices of Ahmad Hassan.

"Gentlemen," Ahmad began, "I have here information on a man named Hokee Wolf. We have learned that he is a private detective who lives in Pocatello, Idaho. That's in the United States. I want him dead and a picture of his corpse. I don't care how you do it. I just want it done, and the sooner, the better. There is only one stipulation. Under no circumstances do I want his death associated with Hassan Construction or me personally. Can you get the job done?"

"Come on, Mr. Hassan, do you know to whom you are addressing?" This question was from Abdul, the man with a fear of no one.

For the first time, Ahmad contemplated the men in his study. He suddenly realized these three men might be the most lethal people in all the world. When this thought finally came to rest in his mind, he grew cold and felt a chill run down his spine.

"I'm sorry, gentlemen," he gasped, suddenly finding it hard to breathe. "Of course, you can get the job done."

"What's the reward?" Farij, the orphan and the man most accustomed to poverty, asked this question.

Without hesitation, Ahmad answered, "one hundred and fifty thousand pounds, (EGP) that's about ten thousand U.S. dollars for going to America. That's one hundred and fifty thousand pounds each. The man who kills Hokee Wolf and brings me proof will get fifteen million pounds, approximately one million U.S. dollars."

This was Ahmad's second mistake; only this mistake was gigantic. The first mistake was questioning the ability of his hired killers. A mistake, but not one to affect the outcome. This last mistake pitted each man against the others in competition for the big payoff. One million U.S. dollars would allow the victor to live comfortably anyplace in Egypt. Now, instead of the three men combining talents, they would compete for the prize. Ahmad would still owe the million dollars, but the competition could get messy. Ahmad did not know how chaotic or how disastrous the mistake would be in the end.

It was Gaffor who asked the most important questions. "How do we get to America? I have no papers. And how do we find this Hokee Wolf?"

"I will provide you with a private plane. All the papers you will need are here in these envelopes," he informed the men patting a stack of envelopes on his desk.

"I have here passports, visas, and traveling money in U.S. dollars. You will pay with cash for anything you require: no credit cards and no paper trail. You are visiting the U.S. for pleasure. My cousin Setka Hassan will meet you in Boise, Idaho. He will be your American contact and provide you with a car and a motel in Pocatello."

The men each picked up an envelope bearing their name and began examining the contents. "How do we find this Hokee Wolf?" Gaffor asked again, this time with a scowl.

"I have the address for his office. We included it in your envelopes. Unfortunately, we could not find a home address, but the office location should be all you need."

Ahmad was nervous with the three killers standing in his office questioning his arrangements. That Gaffor had to ask twice where to find Hokee caused him concern. Although his relatives had spent considerable time in Pocatello, they could find no one who knew where Hokee lived. Getting to Hokee at his home, where he was alone or at least out of the public eye, would have been preferable. It would have been less exposure for his killers with a reduced chance that anyone could ever associate the death of Hokee to Hassan Construction. Still, these men were professionals, and there was little to tie them to Ahmad.

"Your cousin speak good English?" Abdul had been quiet for some time, and Ahmad was starting to relax, but the question raised another concern Ahmad had glossed over in his presentation.

"His English is excellent. You will have no worries in that department." This was a lie as Setka spoke barely enough English to order a meal or book a motel room, but Abdul counted on that being plenty to point his killers in the right direction. How tough could it be? All they had to do was kill the bastard and come back home in a private plane.

The killers finally seemed satisfied, and after they left, Ahmad relaxed for the first time since they had entered his study. He had used the killers several times in the past, but they were not his friends, and he was almost positive that if anyone offered them money to kill him, they would be happy to do the job. They were professional killers. But that was a concern for another time. For now, all that mattered was that Hokee Wolf, the miserable half-breed bastard, only had a few more days in which to live.

CHAPTER THIRTY-FOUR

Diann

Hokee and Glory returned Diann to her dorm, then headed into the office to catch up on some paperwork. Hilda was on her annual *no damn caffeine* binge but offered to make a pot of lovely herbal mint tea, which they both accepted. Hilda still carried a yearning for a relationship with her boss but seemed resigned to relinquish her spot to Glory. All three sat in Hokee's office sipping tea, talking about the missing girl case. Glory's theory about a potential escape by Laura continued to be the most acceptable possibility.

"Hokee, how far away is Malad?" Glory had a sly smile on her face as she asked the question.

"It's about sixty miles. It takes roughly an hour to drive there. Why do you ask?"

"Well, Laura is from Malad. If she went into hiding, why not go home where she knows people? Laura probably knows a lot of potential hiding places in her hometown. She may have some neighbors or distant relatives where she is hiding out. It just makes sense to look for her there. I thought I'd go visit the town and ask around."

"That's a great idea. I know I shouldn't ask a trained investigative reporter how she would go about checking out the town, but how would you go about checking out the town?" Hokee couldn't help but return Glory's sly smile.

"You don't ask a professional to reveal her professional secrets, geez Hokee," Glory said, playing along.

"I was hoping for a few tips, you know, little trade secrets between a couple of professionals," Hokee smiled his killer smile as though that would turn the trick.

Standing up, Glory asked Hokee to take her to her car. Hokee's killer smile didn't faze the investigator for a second. Instead, she was eager to get started. "I may stay overnight if it looks promising. Don't wait up."

*****

Hokee took Glory back to his house so she could grab a bag and her own vehicle. After she drove off, Hokee went for a walk in the lava field with Shila. Often during these walks, Shila caught a jackrabbit for her dinner. It had been several days since their last walk, and Hokee found the exercise helped him meditate.

The concentration required to avoid stepping in a hole or thin lava bubble kept him alert, focusing his mind. There had been no attempt to repeat the walk that nearly ended his life, although he returned to the river from the back of his cave-like house to retrieve his Colt 45. It disappointed him to find that the cougar and her cub had left the cave. During his epic river walk, Hokee discovered a mother cougar and her cub. Across the underground river from each other, the mother cougar and Hokee had a staring match until Hokee decided it was safe to leave and try to find his way back home.

As he walked with Shila, Hokee used every technique he knew to find some new angle to pursue. Cougars are solitary animals, which is how Hokee considered himself. Glory was a recent ally who may or may not be here tomorrow. He knew she was only visiting temporarily to see how things between them developed.

Like the cougar, Hokee usually hunted alone, stalking his prey with single-minded determination. While accomplished in every facet of a private detective's skill set, it was Hokee's sweat lodge activities that separated him from everyone else. His last sweat with Glory was less than satisfying because he had to monitor her body's condition continually to keep her from getting lost. Now that she left for a few hours, or perhaps a day or more, this would be an ideal time for a private session. He wasn't getting anywhere in his ruminations while walking with Shila. Maybe a good sweat would provide him with some answers.

*****

Diann lived in the University Manor Apartments, a student housing complex on the south side of the university campus, about two blocks from the Student Union Building. The Manor is a three-story building covered with redwood siding featuring one and two-bedroom apartments. The school supplies a refrigerator and stoves. Students handle everything else. Diann's other roommates were visiting the library, so she walked over to the Student Union building for some company. Lounging on the steps was Zack, watching the students troll by. As soon as she saw him, Diann did an abrupt 180, heading back towards her dorm, her heart beating like the drums at a Rolling Stones concert. Diann didn't dare turn to see if he was following her with his eyes. It wasn't clear whether Zack noticed her as a lot of students were milling about.

Diann was pretty sure she wasn't a target for kidnapping, but she didn't know if the kidnappers had identified her as Laura's roommate. It was pleasant to be outdoors, and several students showed up to enjoy this brief spot of warm weather. Although pleasant at the moment, if you were paying attention, you could feel the weather shifting as the clouds drifted in overhead. Cold air was on its way.

Back at the dorm, Diann finally turned to look behind her. There was no sign of Zack, but she could still feel her legs shaking. Hurrying back to her room, she quickly called Curly as she had programmed his number into her phone.

"Deputy Belingsford, this is Diann. I just saw Zack here on the campus."

Curly could hear the fear in her voice. "Where did you see him, Diann, and are you safe?"

"He's sitting on the steps of the Student Union building. I'm here in my apartment. Can you come right away?"

"I'll leave right now. Don't leave your room and keep the door locked. Don't let anyone in but me before I get there. Okay?"

"Okay, but please hurry. I'm really terrified."

"I can be there in ten minutes. Will you be okay until I get there?" Even as he asked, Curly knew it was stupid. What in the hell could he do about it if she said no?

"I think so. Please hurry."

"I'm already on my way, Diann. Just hold on and keep the door locked. I'll see you soon."

As Curly got into his Jeep, he thumbed in Hokee's number from memory. He called the big man often enough. This time he got an answering message. No one was home. He didn't know it, but Hokee was already in his sweat lodge.

*****

By the time Curly got to the university campus, a freezing wind blew leaves and trash, reducing visibility to less than a hundred yards. Diann was back in her dorm with the door locked, shaking like the trees outside in the wind. When Curly knocked on the door, she made doubly sure it was the deputy before letting him in her room. She described Zack hoping to avoid a return trip to the student union. Diann feared Zack would see her and recognize Laura's roommate, but Curly assured her that wasn't an actual threat. Zack had no way of knowing who Laura's roommates were or if she even had a roommate.

With Curly present, Diann could stop shivering and began feeling safe. Since time was precious, Curly wanted to see Zack immediately. Recognizing the weather outside, Laura dressed in long blue jeans and a yellow pullover sweater. On the way out of her apartment, she grabbed a knit Denver Chargers stocking cap and a long-waisted watchman's coat before escorting Curly back to the student union. Diann pointed out where Zack had been reclining on the steps, but the weather had changed, and he was no longer there. On the off chance that Zack had wandered inside, they took a tour of the building, checking out the cafeteria, the lounges, and the bowling alley and study nooks. No Zack.

Curly escorted Diann back to her room on the slight chance that Zack was outside in their vicinity hunting. There was no question he had been looking for Laura's replacement. Neither knew that it had already happened. It would be several hours before they learned her name.

CHAPTER THIRTY-FIVE

Nancy Williams

Nancy Williams is a fourth-generation Williams from Clifton, Idaho, a small town; some call a village nestled in the north end of Cache Valley. The valley earned its name because the famous Jim Bridger cached his furs there in the winter months. As the great-granddaughter of a founding pioneer of the town, Nancy inherited much of her forebears' iron will and determination.

The original pioneers of the town harvested trees from the nearby mountains to build their homes. One founder brought a sawmill over the plains in a covered wagon, which the settlers used to mill the lumber. Cattlemen used the entire valley as a free range and resisted the early Mormon settlers. One night, three cowmen burned the sawmill to the ground, resulting in great hardship for the immigrants. A Mormon prophet swore vengeance upon those responsible for the fire. A few weeks later, one arsonist lost his eyes when his gun backfired. Shortly after that, another arsonist became paralyzed when his horse stepped into a gopher hole while chasing a stray calf, throwing the rider on the ground, breaking his back. Finally, a cattle stampede caused by a runaway campfire killed the third man.

Nancy's grandfather merged many of the old forty-acre farms into one gigantic fifteen-hundred-acre farm capable in today's economy of supporting a family in decent prosperity. Nancy became the first person in her family to attend a university. She was a stunning brunette with desert brown eyes and dimpled cheeks, and she was the small town's lead singer in the church choir. Nancy's fraternal Aunt Iris inherited the job of town historian. It's an unpaid job performed simply out of love for her little town and the people who live there. Nancy spent many happy hours listening to her aunt tell stories about the town's colorful past. So, after careful consideration, she accepted a scholarship from ISU to study ancient history. A subject that fascinated the young lady after reading the history of her own little town.

Nancy lived off-campus in an apartment she shared with two other freshmen girls. She often studied in the central library, and today, looking out of the large windows facing the parking lot, she noticed that the weather had changed. The morning that started with a bright blue sky and the *warmish* temperature had changed in a heartbeat to a dark cloudy sky with a severe wind blowing leaves and papers across the ground. The darkening skies looked fearsome, and Nancy decided she would rather snuggle up with her studies at home by the gas fireplace that came with their rental. Picking up her books, she stuffed them into her backpack and left the building, struggling against the chilly October wind.

Holding up her hand to shield her eyes from the grit blowing in the air, she didn't see the four unsavory characters walking towards her from the parking lot. Dressed in ISU sweatshirts with hoods, they could have passed for football players or perhaps members of the wrestling team from a distance. Still, up close, you could see they were beyond college age, and the mean look in their eyes and the snarling grins on their faces would have given them away as anything but students. The first surprise came when a hand clamped over her nose and mouth, followed briefly by powerful arms grabbing her body, holding down her arms and legs. Then, before passing out, the last thing she saw was the triumphant faces of two of her abductors.

*****

In Boise, a private Boeing 707 landed and taxied to the General Aviation terminal and a waiting Lincoln limousine. Three dark-skinned men looking like the movie portrayal of mafia thugs left the plane and walked over to the limousine. They were all dressed in dark suit pants with creases and white shirts tucked under their belts. It was the intense burning dark eyes that caused strangers to back away. Another unsavory-looking individual greeted them, then ushered them into their ride. They had bribed the Custom Officials as no one showed up to check for passports. The travelers and their greeter never exchanged names.

"How was your flight?" Ahmad's cousin Issa was one of Gene's New York attackers. Issa considered himself to be a bad man; someone others should fear. However, having been admonished by Ahmad for his failure in New York, he was determined to make up for it by being accommodating to these hired killers.

A stupid question asked only to instigate a conversation. It didn't rate an answer, so no one responded. How bad can a flight be on a private super jet airline complete with alcohol and pretty girls to fuck?

"How long to Pocatello?" At least one traveler could speak English.

"Not long. Maybe three and a half to four hours. I have three motel rooms reserved for you. I only rented one car, which is parked by the motel. If you require more vehicles, I can help you each get one if that is desired."

This announcement also did not elicit a response.

"Why do we not fly to Pocatello?" Gaffor asked. "This drive seems unnecessary."

"The Pocatello airport does not have the facilities to take care of Ahmad's airplane properly. The drive will also give you a chance to get a feel for the area."

They drove on in silence for the rest of the trip. Looking out of the windows at the passing countryside, the four killers looked out on a gray country. They were comparing the scenery to that of the fertile valleys along the Nile near Luxor. The bleak deserts, desolate Craters of the Moon National Monument, and stark lava plains did little to bring warmth to their black hearts. Instead, in each man's mind was how ugly this country was and how soon he could collect the million-dollar fee for killing Hokee and leave the God-forsaken place. But, of course, this meant keeping his associates from doing the collecting. The darkening skies reflected the somber expression on the four killers' faces, and chilly winds did little to brighten the trip.

Issa had booked rooms at the Hampton by Hilton just off I-15 close to E. Clark Street, a major downtown street close to Hokee's office. He helped get the four killers registered and showed them their rooms. Before leaving, he explained they could not determine where Hokee lived but that he would show them his office tomorrow. So it was a relief when the three men bid him good evening with a promise of getting together in the morning for breakfast. They fully expected to kill the Wolf tomorrow early and get back out of this infidel's hell hole.

****

Glory found few options for hotel/motel accommodations in Malad. She drove by the Hotel Malad and saw an unattractive two-story flat-roofed yellow brick building downtown that looked a hundred years old with little modern upgrading. Not to her liking.

And just like that, she drove within fifty feet of Laura, missing a chance to solve the missing girl case on her first day in town. After driving around, Glory decided the Village Inn on the edge of town offered her the most promising room.

The first project was to search for a public library, but Malad was too small to provide that public benefit. The next stop was at the Malad High School in search of one of Laura's teachers. By the time Glory found the school, the lessons had ended for the day, and everyone but the janitors had vacated the building. With no other brilliant ideas, she went back to visit with Laura's parents. Perhaps they could provide a list of potential hiding places Laura might be using. Glory's parents got a list of Laura's high school teachers who might befriend the girl. She was halfway through the list before the cold evening forced her to seek refuge in a restaurant, looking for a hot cup of coffee. Me and Lou's Diner, just off I-15, looked like the most promising prospect. She found the establishment clean and the cooking, home-style, just the ticket on a crisp October night. Maybe tomorrow. Isn't that the mantra of all searchers?

CHAPTER THIRTY-SIX

One Down

Neter stood beneath the Sigil of Baphomet, and behind his podium tied to the cross hung the naked girl. On the far wall, the fireplace crackled with the pine logs burning brightly, while all the sconces along the walls featured the glowing eyes of demons shining behind their red glass masks from the candles glowing within. The faithful stood before their prophet, waiting for him to speak. This was the first time the entire congregation had seen the new sacrifice.

"Our Beloved Master," Neter spoke, pointing to the sky, "has provided us with another sacrifice," he continued sweeping his arms back, motioning towards the naked girl on the cross, "to replace the one so foolishly lost to one man's greed. Let's not let that happen again." A chorus of "hear hear" and "amen," by members of the congregation, followed the prophet's words.

"Karnilla is now the official minder, and she has provided us with a cup of the new sacrifice's blood. Enough for everyone to take a brief sip. On our next meeting, we can expect a more dignified reward."

Nancy hung with her head down on the cross, denying the audience a look at her face and eyes. Sorrow and tears and finally defiance had replaced the fear. Small town girls have a more incredible feeling of independence than their counterparts from large cities. Out in the country where everybody knows everybody else, a girl feels safe leaving home and exploring by herself. In a town where everybody helps when someone is in trouble or sick, everyone naturally feels safer to experience fresh adventures. Nancy knew she was in trouble with seriously sick people. There was nothing she could do at present to alter the circumstances. From the chatter heard in her closet and the big room, she knew they had someone locked up before her, and this person had escaped. In Nancy's mind, if another girl had done it, she could do it as well. All she had to do was wait for her chance.

Shortly after Nancy went missing, nearly every student at ISU knew that someone had kidnapped another girl. Therefore, when Nancy failed to return to her apartment, her roommates immediately called the campus police who notified the county sheriff. Curly called Hokee's office, but the phone went unanswered.

*****

At that moment, someone had wrapped Hilda in duct tape while three dark-skinned thugs ransacked her desk and Hokee's office looking for Hokee's home address. Hilda had honestly proclaimed she did not know where Hokee lived, a protestation the three men did not believe. Hokee provided Hilda with directions to his house before leaving for Nampa, which she wrote under the label; _Directions to Shila_. Since Hilda never traveled to that part of the lava flat, she honestly did not know where Hokee lived.

As their search progressed and finding not one piece of paper with the detective's home address, they started believing in her words. They knew it was commonplace for management to keep their home address private. The questions then became when she expected Hokee to return. Again, she had to tell them she did not know. He did not have any specific schedule and might stay away from the office for several days, checking in from time to time for messages.

Hokee finished his sweat and played roughhouse with Shila for a few minutes before calling the office to check for messages. When Hilda failed to answer, he knew something was wrong. Hilda always answered the phone. Loading Shila in the Explorer, Hokee drove to the office.

E Clark Street in Pocatello is one of the main exits off I-15 that runs straight through to the old town where Judy Garland claimed to be born in a costume trunk in the musical _A Star Is Born_. Hokee drove south down N 4th Ave., turning left on E Clark going past the Idaho First National Bank Building, where he has an office on the second floor above the bank. He was about to turn into the parking lot across the street when Shila growled. Being warned by the wolf,

Hokee looked more carefully and saw a man sitting in a new car in front of the bank. Usually, this would not have raised any flags, but since Hilda wasn't answering her phone, it seemed unusual as the bank was closed. The man had a dark complexion and seemed focused on the door leading to the stairway and Hokee's office.

Over the years, Hokee had made several enemies, but they knew enough to keep away from the shaman. Many who tried to kill him disappeared. Shila continued a low growl, and when Hokee saw the man watching the street, he kept driving, nearly running over another dark-skinned man running across the street. So, at least two men are hunting him. Could there be more? And why now? Who were they, and who sent them?

His first concern was Hilda. What had they done to her?

Hokee drove around the block, parking on E Lander St. behind the bank. There were spaces between the building forming a small alley leading to the building fronting E Clark. An old fire escape led to the second floor on the bank building's backside, which Hokee climbed. The fire escape ended at a window in the hallway leading to Hokee's office. He checked the window first to see if he could spot anyone in the hall. Seeing it empty, he opened the window and climbed in.

Hilda's office door was open, and Hokee could see no one was visible in her room. Creeping down the hallway, staying close to the wall in case the floor squeaked, Hokee made it to Hilda's office, seeing no one. He was just about to enter his office when a man came at him from inside with a knife poised to stab at his heart. Hokee had spent too much time working on his martial arts programs to be so quickly taken.

Turning sideways, deflecting the thrust while chopping down with a hand made hard by pounding on sandbags, Hokee knocked the knife out of the assailant's hand, breaking his wrist, causing the man to howl in pain. The assailant expected the knife thrust to succeed, so Hokee used his momentum to grab the man, pulling him close then twisting his arm viciously behind his back while pushing him to the floor. Hokee followed him down as the man fell, driving both knees into the man's back then grabbing his head, giving it a swift, severe twist, breaking his neck.

The entire sequence of events lasted only three seconds, after which Hokee rushed into his office where he saw Hilda swathed in duct tape. Grabbing the assailant's knife from the floor, Hokee hurried to cut his secretary free. After freeing her mouth and arms, he gave her the knife to finish cutting herself loose while dragging the would-be knife killer into his office and then shutting the door.

Hokee didn't want anyone walking into his office with a dead man on the floor, especially someone from the bank downstairs. So, glancing to see if Hilda was getting free of her sticky wraps, Hokee went through the killer's pockets. Inside of the man's wallet was his driver's license. The killer's name was Abdul Wahid; his nationality was Egyptian, and coincidentally, Hokee had just returned from visiting an Egyptian. It was too much of a coincidence, and Hokee vowed to take at least one of the man's mates downstairs alive for questioning. His question was how?

Going over to Hilda, Hokee asked how she was feeling; if the man had hurt her?

"No. I'm okay. Just a little shaken up. Getting this damn tape off was the worst part," she said, pointing to a pile of scraps lying on the floor. "Is he dead?" She asked, pointing to the man lying on the floor.

"Yes. I believe Olson's Egyptian nemesis, Ahmad Hassan, is a little angry with me. I may have to do something about him. But now, I need to take care of those two men downstairs. I presume you met them."

"Oh! Lordy, Hokee. Yes. Three scary-looking men came in here together demanding to know where you live. One guy, the man you killed, never stood still. He weaved in and out, waving his knife in the air like he wanted to stab me or cut me somehow. Another man had a long scar from his eye down to his chin. All three had an angry, frightening look in their eyes. They scared the life out of me. They wouldn't believe I didn't know where you lived. The three of them searched my office and yours, looking everywhere for someplace you may have written your address. Thankfully, when you called with directions to your house, I wrote it on a piece of paper, labeling it directions to Shila."

"I'm sorry you had to go through that experience, Hilda. I don't want you leaving until we deal with those guys downstairs. Those men downstairs may not take kindly to you waltzing out when you're supposed to be tied up. Why don't you make yourself a cup of tea while I develop a plan to deal with the problem?"

Hilda, careful to sneak a peek out of the door before leaving, went into her office, where a cupboard and counter against one wall held the tea supplies. Hokee went back to finish searching the body while figuring out what to do when the phone on his office desk rang. He heard Hilda enter the room, so let her answer it.

"It's Curly for you," she said, handing him the phone.

"Oh God, not again," he spoke into the phone. To Hilda, he said, "they kidnapped another girl. Nancy Williams, a girl from Clifton, Idaho. That's over the mountains to the east from Malad."

"Curly, can you come to my office right now? There's something here you need to see. Be careful outside on the street. There are two murderous thugs outside looking for me." He listened for a minute, then continued, "no, just come on upstairs and ignore them unless they give you a problem. We'll talk about taking some action once you arrive. Later," he said, returning the handset to the receiver.

CHAPTER THIRTY-SEVEN

Hokee and Curly

Hokee was sitting with Hilda drinking a cup of peppermint tea when Curly knocked on his office door. Getting up and stepping over the body on the floor, Hokee let the deputy into his office. To Curly's credit, he took one look at the body, then asked how they were both feeling?

"He had this in his hand when I came to see why Hilda wasn't answering the phone," Hokee said, handing Curly the killer's knife. It was six inches of long shining metal, slim, and sharp on both sides. "I don't recognize the make," Hokee continued. "He may have had it custom made in Egypt."

"Yeah, it looks like a killer's knife, alright," Curly suggested. "What happened? He tried to knife you?"

"Yeah, I suspected someone might be here, as Hilda wasn't answering the phone. So I crept up the fire escape and checked her vacant office. I was about to check my office when he came at me real quick. I dodged the thrust, breaking his wrist; then I broke his neck." Hokee related the incident as though describing a scene from a movie.

Curly had known Hokee for many years and knew of his legendary fighting skills, although he never saw him in action. He said nothing about the man on the floor, knowing there was more to it than what Hokee related, but it didn't matter. "Hilda, I see all this duct tape piled up. Is that what they used to secure you?"

"Yes. Thank God Hokee came and set me loose. He used the killer's knife to cut the tape off. Those three men scared me half to death, Curly. You've got to help Hokee get those two downstairs."

"Do you know who they are, Hokee?" Curly asked as he inspected the body on the floor.

"The knifeman lying on the floor is, or was, Abdul Wahid, an Egyptian. The two downstairs have the same look about them. I suspect my recent trip overseas may have brought this trouble home. My guess is they are Ahmad Hassan's paid assassins. Wahid there," he added, pointing to the man on the floor, "had almost ten thousand dollars in his pockets."

"How did he get that knife through airport security?" Curly wondered.

"The man who hired him is a billionaire with his own airplane fleet," Hokee answered. "I imagine he flew them here on his private plane. I suspect the plane is still in Boise. We may want to check that out later."

"Well, we need to get this body out of your office, Hokee. But first, I guess we need to deal with those two outside. Got any ideas?"

"I'm not sure how much heat they might pack, Curly. This one only had a knife, but I doubt the others came without bringing more powerful hardware. Hilda said they came here looking for me, so I'm sure they have seen my picture. They know my looks. I think you should go down first. They are not looking for you, and you should be okay if you ignore them. They do not know I am here, so my coming downstairs would be a surprise. When I drove by, one man was parked by the door leading up the stairs, and the other one was across the street."

"I didn't see the one across the street. The man by the door was still there when I came up the stairs. He was a mean-looking bugger with a big strawberry birthmark on his cheek."

"That's one of the men," Hilda spoke up. "Of the three, I think he had the most frightening eyes."

"You could arrest them. I'm sure they are carrying something illegal. The problem is, if you grab the man in the car at the door, the other one may scoot or come at you shooting. Then, I want to question at least one of them, and you probably don't want to be around for that part, Curly."

"If we corner them and have to shoot it out, what difference does it make?"

"I believe I know who sent them, but I need to be sure before I go to Egypt and kill somebody. I cannot continue to live freely knowing there is a wealthy asshole willing to pay for my death."

"Let me slip back down Curly and go around the block. I think I can sneak up on the guy across the street. Give me ten minutes, then you come downstairs and throw a gun on the guy in the car. After I see you, I'll put the other one on the ground. Hopefully alive."

Hokee told Hilda to hang tough for a few minutes. Fortunately, the dead body on the floor didn't bother her, at least not so much she was eager to leave and face the men downstairs.

After speaking to his secretary, he went back down the hall to the fire escape. Seven minutes later, he was across the street from the bank. Many years ago, the city planted Box Elder trees in the grassy median between the road and sidewalk. Directly across the street from the bank was a vacant lot where several merchants parked their cars. Hokee weaved through the cars until he could see the man hiding behind a tree, watching his partner across the street by the door going upstairs.

The big Colt 45 was in Hokee's hand as he watched for Curly. The man by the tree was looking across the street, giving Hokee a chance to sneak up behind him. Hokee had followed his subconscious mind's suggestions and wore his moccasins, allowing him to move in close enough to club the killer on the head. Both men were watching as Curly clamored down the stairs, making enough noise to be heard across the street. The killer by the door was not looking for Curly, so he was unprepared when Curly stepped onto the sidewalk, thrusting his service revolver into the car saying, "put your hands in the sky or die."

He practically yelled the words, so Hokee and the killer by the tree heard him yell from across the street.

The killer by the tree raised his gun, an act Hokee interpreted as an intent to shoot Curly. Without hesitation, Hokee struck him on the back of his head with the butt of his heavy Colt, knocking him unconscious.

Curly expertly removed the guns and knives from the killer on the sidewalk. The man was a walking arsenal. He carried a silenced Israeli Mossad.22 LRS pistol, an assassin's gun, plus a snub-nosed 9mm Israeli Desert Eagle. Hanging down the back of his neck on a nylon string was a Rainy Vallotton custom 4-inch knife so sharp you could cut your eyes just by glancing along its edges. In his coat pocket, Curly found a Browning Wicked Wing Framelock Stiletto, a 3.5-inch switchblade. Why so much hardware? Curly could only shake his head.

Hokee watched Curly across the street subdue and search the killer on the sidewalk, securing his weapons. Once he had the man's arms handcuffed behind his back, Hokee signaled Curly to walk the man across the street where he had his own man lying on the ground.

"Good job, Curly. It looks like you collected one hell of an arsenal. I wouldn't mind having that man's knives. The guns look pretty decent as well. Anyway, I want to question these killers. Do you want to take them to your jail or a vacant spot out on the lava flats?"

"Is it going to be messy? I can't have you torturing these jerks in the jailhouse. Too many witnesses."

"I don't know Curly. It depends on them. If they tell me what I want to know without having to beat them to death, then the jail would be okay. Otherwise, I want to put them in a hole in the ground someplace."

Farij Zahir, the most dangerous one of the three killers with the strawberry birthmark on his cheek, stood listening to Curly and Hokee talk about torture and holes in the ground. "What you want to know? I talk."

Curly was busy searching both men, collecting wallets, and a picture of Hokee. "These boys were carrying a lot of money, and your picture, Hokee. I don't think they were here to sell you life insurance."

Taking Zahir's wallet from Curly, Hokee looked for the man's name then said, "I only have one question, Mr. Zahir, who sent you?"

"What will you do to me if I tell you?" There was no fear in the man's eyes. He had stared death in the eyes many times and knew it would be his turn at some point. Whether it was today or in the future, only Allah knows. He asked to see if they would prolong his life by telling the truth or die regardless of what he said.

Hokee looked at Curly, who nodded, then answered. "If you tell me the truth, this man who is a sheriff will take you to jail. From there, it depends on the charges and the judge. If you lie, I will kill you as I killed your friend upstairs in my office. Then I will throw your bodies down in a pen full of pigs."

"How can you do this?" The man asked. "In America, we have rights. How can you kill me in front of an officer of the law?"

"Americans have rights. Your driver's license tells me you are Egyptian. You have no passport or immigration stamp for visiting here. You have no rights. You are here illegally and have already committed many crimes. Who will ever know if I break your neck and dispose of the body?"

This statement was enough to get the man talking. "Ahmad Hassan hired the three of us to kill you, Mr. Wolf. We were each given ten thousand dollars for coming here on Mr. Hassan's private plane, and the one who killed you would get one million U.S. dollars."

"Such a courteous, polite killer, Curly. I'll hold them here while you get your vehicle."

"That's all you need, Hokee?" Curly was acting a little disappointed there wouldn't be more excitement. "What about the man upstairs?"

"Well, hell, Curly. You're the damned law. What do you suggest? I can get rid of the body once it gets dark. Or we can load him in your vehicle and haul his ass to the coroner. I don't want to get involved in a lot of legal horseshit Curly or a long, drawn-out investigation."

"The only people who know for sure how he died are you and Hilda," Curly spoke, thinking out loud. "We know they are here illegally. They assaulted Hilda and tried to kill you. I saw the evidence of Hilda's ordeal in your office. I think the easiest way forward is to let the coroner hold his inquest on the dead man. We have all their illegal weapons, and I heard Zahir's testimony regarding how they were all hired to kill you. Of course, you and Hilda would need to testify, but it shouldn't take more than a few minutes."

"Alright. Shit. At least I ain't dead yet. Get your vehicle, Curly. I'll watch these gents and get the one upstairs after we get these two loaded. It looks like sleeping beauty here might be stirring. Got any more handcuffs in your truck?"

"No, but I have plenty of flex cuffs. Here," he said, digging several from his pocket and handing them to Hokee. "I'll go get my vehicle."

Hokee quickly bound his reviving killer's wrists behind his back while the killer moaned, trying to sit up. With his arms tied, he had a hard time, mostly as he was still groggy. Finally, Hokee helped him sit up with his back against the tree.

"So Gaffor, how's your day going so far?" Hokee asked while Curly went for his vehicle. The killer's black eyes were filled with hate, and the white scar running the length of his cheek pulsed with his heartbeat. There was no answer to Hokee's question.

After Curly pulled his Jeep Cherokee up to the curb, Hokee helped him load the two prisoners, then went upstairs to get the dead man. Hilda had watched the show on the street below from the window in Hokee's office, so she was ready when he came through the door.

"Are you okay to drive home, Hilda? I can take you if you like. We have the men downstairs in handcuffs, so you're safe to leave now."

"No. I'm doing okay, boss. That tea really helped. I got terrified, but I'm doing okay now. I'll be just fine driving myself. Thank God you got them all, and they didn't kill you."

"Yeah, I'm kind of happy about that myself. But, listen, if you want to take a few days off, that's okay by me."

"No, we have another missing girl, if you remember right, and I can help. I'll see you tomorrow."

"Okay then, if you're sure. Thanks Hilda. I'm sorry you had to go through this; I guess it worked out alright. Have a good night."

"Good night, Hokee."

After Hilda left, Hokee searched around his office, making sure everything was as it should be. He straightened out a few papers and the desk drawers the killers left in a mess. He had to smile when he saw the note Hilda had written to herself. *Directions to Shila.* Hilda had cleaned up all the items thrown on the floor along with the duct tape, so it didn't take long. After a good look around, Hokee picked up the dead body and threw it over his shoulder in a fireman's carry, hauling it downstairs to Curly's waiting Jeep.

After throwing the body in the back, Hokee said to Curly, "Let's meet at ReNee's Diner and talk about this latest missing girl."

"Sure thing. Oh, and Hokee,"

"Yeah."

"I'm glad they didn't kill ya."

CHAPTER THIRTY-EIGHT

Hokee Sees Evil

In some ways, a sweat lodge experience is not that much different from a sauna; they both have heat and steam. The difference is primarily the ceremony, the ritual. Those who use a sauna make no preparations other than getting the room hot and jumping in to sweat out the alcohol, loosen the muscles and relax. On the other hand, a sweat lodge requires preparation—first, the fire.

Fire alone is a meditation exercise. Once man discovered fire, he sat staring into the light, mesmerized by the dancing flames. We know this because that's what we do, and we are not that different from those spear chuckers from long ago. Stare into the embers long enough, and one sees the beginning of the universe. Infinity lies in the glowing embers, the birth, and the passing of time. People throughout the millennia have sat transfixed, lost in time and space before a fire.

Next come the lava rocks set in the flames, which become the furnace in the pit. As the stones are heating, the shaman sits by the fire, meditating on the problem or question for which he seeks answers. By the time he feels comfortable with the quest in his mind, the rocks are ready. Before the shaman moves them inside the lodge, he purifies his body with a cold shower followed by a quick aura sweep, then a sage smoke smudge to cleanse the body's energy field. Some call this energy field the body's aura. He then moves the rocks from the fire into the lodge, setting them in the open pit.

And finally, the tools. An experienced shaman has them handy. Sage, sandalwood, cedar, and marijuana, plus other exotic herbs used to stimulate consciousness. Something akin to LSD. Today, the shaman in certain places uses a little katalata found in the roots of particular plants. Something akin to the THC in marijuana. The shaman's *holy* water contains a liquid version of these same exotic herbs.

These items wait just inside the lodge opening, which the shaman closes with an animal hide after crawling inside. Preferably the skin of an animal killed and dressed by the shaman in another ritual.

The shaman enters the lodge, closes the opening, trapping the heat, which soon becomes intense. He calls forth the help of his spiritual guides offering a greeting and thanks to the Gods handling the four corners of the universe. He sits for a moment in quiet contemplation before throwing a few plant leaves and wood chips onto the glowing rocks. He inhales the smoke and scents, allowing them to work their magic, setting up the body for its grand adventure through time and space. When the time is right, the shaman pours a cup of the holy water onto the white-hot rocks. This is the instant steam shock drives his consciousness into far distant states. Other dimensions exist beyond the ability of our tongues to express. Only by experience can one get this information. Never by word of mouth.

Hokee followed this path today, looking for answers to the missing girl. Who took her? Why? Where did they keep her, or is she still there? In the holiest of all holy places are kept the thoughts, words, and deeds of everyone on the planet from the time man first walked the earth. There are many names for this place and the information stored there. The term most often used is the Akashic Chronicles.

Skeptics claim that such a place cannot exist. However, in today's world, the most inept physicist knows it is impossible to destroy energy. We can only change it in form. Therefore, our thoughts are energy that exists forever.

Some really can channel information from other dimensions, although most who claim this ability are frauds. Those with genuine knowledge get their information from this data bank. In Hokee's sweat lodge reality, he uses this information, but his spirit goes way beyond this vault of dimensional storage to dimensions and universes beyond the one we call home. He used to fear getting lost, but over time learned that there is nothing but God, our Creator, everywhere he went, and coming back to this reality meant relaxing into the void. While it sounds easy, it is a gained skill.

There is never a beautifully painted sign saying here is what you are looking for in this realm. English is a product of this world. In the sweat lodge, the information is in vibrations and can only be accessed by one willing and able to vibrate in harmony with that being sought. If the shaman's quest is to find evil, he must experience the evil in his soul's vibrational patterns, hopefully without letting these vibrations become a permanent part of his being. Stories abound about the shaman who returned from this journey and becomes evil.

Hokee sought the evil. He imagined it first, then felt it take over his being. The horror, the spectacle, the ugly, selfish, ego-driven mania interested in subjugating all those in its presence. The thoughtless, wanton destruction of other souls and lives for self-gratification.

The trick taught by his mentor and employed by Hokee to remain unscathed in this wickedness was to carry in his consciousness the concept of unconditional love. Loving the individuals engaged in evil-doing does not mean condoning their acts. Instead, it is a recognition that this life is an illusion. As Shakespeare noted, "All the world's a stage, and all the men and women merely players." When watching a drama, you do not condemn the actor, only the acts they perform. The same principle applies to hunting evil. It's how you find the villain without having to become villainous.

Today Hokee saw the face of a man with empty dark eyes. He had big red lips twisted in a perpetual sneer below a hook nose. Long stringy black hair hung over his face like a veil, hiding the ravaged look of one who feeds on souls. The face reminded Hokee of a painting entitled Beelzebub by a Spanish artist. He couldn't remember the artist's name, but he remembered the horns on the subject's head. The man Hokee saw in his vision did not have horns, but he still looked evil.

That was all Hokee saw, and with reluctance, he came back into his body thirsty and wet with sweat. He couldn't wait to shower and rinse off the feeling he experienced when seeing the hideous head. It felt like slime had adhered to his body, and it took several soapings before Hokee felt clean. Now all he had to do was find someone who looked like Satan.

CHAPTER THIRTY-NINE

Glory's Search

Glory's first day in Malad searching for Laura was a bust. Seeking in desperation for a place to stay the night, she looked at the Red Rooster Bed and Breakfast Inn on lower Bannock St. The Red Rooster is an unlikely-looking B & B. It's a single-story yellow brick building that looks like a comfortable but older, three bed, two bath home. With some misgivings, she drove into the yard and walked to the front door. She figured looking didn't mean she had to stay there. After all, famous, or at least semi-famous, N Y investigative television reporters didn't sleep in trash heaps.

A petite silver-haired lady of about sixty wearing a good-looking cream-colored pantsuit answered the door. "Come in, please. Were you looking to spend the night?"

"Hello. Yes, I wanted to look at your accommodations, if I may. Your house doesn't resemble any of the B & Bs I've stayed in before."

"Yes, I know. Let me explain. My name is LuAnn McIntire. I've lived here most of my life. This house is where my husband and I raised our three boys, now scattered in the wind. My husband, Cecil, died a few years ago, and I don't have any marketable skills, so my sons helped me turn our home into a B & B. I have a small apartment in the back, and we remodeled the master bedroom and bath into an elegant suite. Please come in and see for yourself."

"I would love to see the room. This is a beautiful living room. These watercolor pictures of the Redwoods appear to be originals. Oh, my name is Gloria, although everyone calls me Glory."

"Yes, one of my sons is an artist. Justin. He lives in San Francisco. Those are his paintings."

"I'm no expert, but they are beautiful pictures. I've never seen the actual trees. These pictures make me want to go visit them."

"Follow me, Glory, and I'll show you to your room. I know you're going to love it."

Glory followed LuAnn down a wide carpeted hall lined with pictures and a long wall hanging depicting a cougar crouched in a tree looking over a scenic valley. The image was calming, considering the principal subject. The valley seemed so peaceful, and the cougar looked contented.

"Your wall hanging is beautiful, but such a strange scene."

"They stationed my husband Cecil in India, where he bought that hanging. It must have been over forty years ago now. I can't seem to part with it. Here's the guest suite," she said, opening a door.

Glory walked into one of the prettiest and well-designed suites she had ever seen; a giant king bed with a white velvet bedspread dominated the room. They had removed several walls from what were once bedrooms, which now served as a sitting room with comfortable recliners and a large flat-screened television. A vast picture window overlooked a small flower garden with several yellow and white mums in full blossom. An oversized bathroom had a sunken Jacuzzi and a large serpentine shower with twin showerheads. The suite looked barely lived in; everything seemed fresh. Altogether, it was one of the most comfortable bedrooms Glory had visited outside of the Waldorf in New York City.

"I love it," Glory said. "Let me go get my overnight bag."

"You go on, get your things and come on back in when you're ready. I serve breakfast at eight in the morning. You have a coffee maker here in your room, and I also put fresh coffee in the thermos on the dining table. So you may help yourself to that if you don't want to make any coffee yourself."

Glory congratulated herself for thinking ahead and bringing an overnight case. Then, in her car, she called Hokee to let him know her plans and see how the hunt was progressing on his end. Hokee told her about Nancy but didn't mention the killers. There was no need to alarm her, and besides, the danger was past for the time being. No telling what Ahmad would do when his killers failed to check-in or return to Egypt. But that too could wait. The search was on for the second missing girl.

Glory couldn't do anything about Nancy, and she was tired. A splendid dinner and a long night's rest were in order. Dinner was at The Pines, a family-style restaurant close to the exit from I-15. Tonight's special was homemade spaghetti and meatballs, and although she was reluctant to order a dish perfected in NY restaurants, she tried it. It didn't have the spices and seasoning found in the NY version, but it was tasty and filling. What more could a girl stranded in Malad, Idaho, possibly ask for? Well, maybe a nice dry martini, but forget that. Not here. Still, Glory went to bed with high expectations about tomorrow. Somehow she just knew that a big break in the story was just about to happen. A honed investigator's instincts, or perhaps merely dreaming?

When Glory got around to finishing getting dressed the following day, she almost missed breakfast, a real country breakfast found in farm country. She was served a large ham steak, hash browns, fried eggs, fresh-baked bread, plus their famous scones and homemade chokecherry jelly. Glory almost went giddy over the jelly, something she had never tasted before. Liking company when she ate, Glory asked LuAnn to join her for breakfast. LuAnn tried to demur, but Glory insisted, so LuAnn reluctantly sat down across the table. Having already eaten, she poured herself a cup of coffee.

On an impulse, Glory asked, "LuAnn, do you know a family named the Taylor's with a girl called Laura."

"Why land's sake. But, of course, I do. We go to the same church, although Laura is away to college now. She's going to Idaho State University." LuAnn spoke with pride in her voice as she talked about Laura. Apparently, it was a big deal for a girl from Malad to attend a university.

"Well, did you know Laura was kidnapped and has been missing for a few days?"

"Oh, my goodness no. When did this happen?"

"They took her from the school campus several days ago. We don't know all the men involved for sure. We found one of her kidnappers dead a couple of days ago. Laura is still missing. And now they kidnapped another girl. We suspect it is the same group who took Laura. Perhaps Laura escaped, which might be the reason we found one of the kidnappers. That's why I'm in Malad, trying to get a line on where Laura might have gone."

"You sound as though you think Laura escaped from her kidnappers?"

"Oh, I'm sorry. The evidence suggests that Laura might be responsible for killing the kidnapper we found dumped in a garbage heap outside of town. If that is the case, she escaped from wherever she was being held. We know Laura is pretty self-reliant and quite intelligent. If she escaped, she poses a serious risk to the other kidnappers. They would want her dead, and Laura must realize that. We believe she is hiding somewhere in a place the kidnappers are unlikely to look. I wonder if you might have any idea where she might be hiding?"

LuAnn took a sip of her coffee and thought for a minute or two before answering. "Why are you looking for Laura, Glory?"

"I'm glad you asked. I work with Hokee Wolf, who specializes in finding missing children. We want to see if Laura can help us find the other kidnappers. If she remembers the place they held her, or perhaps has some other information that might help us find them, we might save the other girl."

"I've heard about Mr. Wolf. He's pretty famous for an Idaho boy." LuAnn once again smiled that shy smile, showing her pride in being an Idaho gal.

"Yes, I understand he has solved some interesting cases. It's a pleasure working with him. So, are you able to help?"

"Laura was an excellent student in school. She was always a whiz at her arithmetic. Her old math teacher, Mrs. Williams, owns the Malad City Motel just up the street a few blocks. You might stop in and talk with her. I believe she and Laura got along well together, both of them liking arithmetic and everything."

Luann sat wringing her hand, hoping she was doing the right thing, giving this almost stranger the information on Mrs. Williams. Seeing the discomfort, Glory was quick to respond.

"Don't worry, LuAnn. I'm really one of the good guys, honest. I won't mention you to Mrs. Williams if you don't wish me to."

"No. That's okay. Lois and I go back many years. It probably won't help much, but you can tell her you stayed here. That old fleabag she calls a hotel should have been torn down years ago. I'm not sure how she pays for the upkeep. I never hear of anyone staying there."

As great as the breakfast was, Glory was eager to visit with Mrs. Williams. It felt like the tip she had been seeking. Making an apology for leaving so much food uneaten, she went to her room, picking up the overnight bag already packed. Saying goodbye, she left the Red Rooster heading for the Malad Hotel.

CHAPTER FORTY

Ahmad, Neter, and Laura

Luxor sits at the top of a big horseshoe bend in the Nile River, 80 miles west of the Red Sea. Ahmad maintains a strict regime about his early morning rituals, despite his various eating and drinking sins. He was always up in time to see the sunrise above the Nile, sending orange and yellow rays of sunlight streaming into his office. A morning airplane bringing fish from the Red Sea to Luxor's fancy restaurants skimmed over the river near Ahmad's house, its twin-engine drone like a morning wake-up call.

His killers left three days ago, and there had been no word. It wasn't panic time, but it seemed strange that there had been no contact since they landed in Boise. Perhaps he should call one of them for a status report. The question was, which one to call? He realized his mistake in announcing the big bonus to the one who bagged Hokee Wolf. It wasn't brilliant pitting them against each other like that. Too late now. Perhaps he could rectify the mistake by giving them *each* a million dollars for Hokee's head. Yeah. That's what he would do. Maybe he should call.

Farij had been with him the longest. Although the lethal killer caused Ahmad some tense moments whenever they were alone together, it would show him some respect by calling him first.

The call went unanswered.

Curly heard the phone ring, but by the time he had sorted through all the pocket litter and weapons on the table, it had stopped ringing. Unfamiliar with the Egyptian symbols on the phones, he couldn't tell which phone had been ringing and could not tell who had been calling. Although curious, the killers were no longer his primary concern. He had another missing girl to find, and the killers would keep no matter who was calling.

Upset but not yet alarmed, Ahmad tried calling Abdul's number with the same result.

Curly had just settled back into his desk chair when he heard another of the killer's phones ringing. He made it to the table this time just when the phone died, so he still did not know which phone had been ringing. Suspecting that it was Ahmad calling, the man one killer claimed had sent them to kill Hokee, Curly waited by the table to see if the third phone started ringing.

By now, Ahmad felt uneasy about his killers well-being. What was going on? He knew they had landed and taken a car to Pocatello. But then the updates had ended. True, he did not ask them to make frequent calls home, but it should not have been necessary to request a courtesy call. Sort of a thoughtful acknowledgment. Not that the killers concerned themselves with that habit. Still? Saying to hell with it and throwing caution out the door, Ahmad called Ali while looking at the enormous balloon of a yellow sun rising over the Nile. A sight that usually brightened his day, but now worry kept the joy at bay across the river. The blazing sun seemed an omen of evil instead of a sign of warmth.

Curly was ready when the third phone began ringing. After fiddling for a second, he picked it up and figured out which control he needed to select to answer.

"Hello. Can I help you?" It sounded pathetic even to his ears.

"Who is this, please?" Ahmad was sweating, even though it was a pleasant 70 degrees in his office.

"This is Deputy Sheriff, Curly Belingsford. Who is this, and who were you calling?" Curly didn't know which phone went with which killer.

"Let me talk with the man who owns that phone," Ahmad demanded.

"You need to tell me who you want to talk with," Curly countered. He wanted verification of the killers' claim that a man named Ahmad Hassan hired these three killers.

"I want to talk with the man who owns that phone. Put him on now." Ahmad seemed to think that he could bully anyone into doing his bidding, even a county sheriff in Pocatello.

"Tell me your name and the business you have with the owner of this phone, and I'll decide whether to let you talk with him."

The line went dead. Curly held the phone for a couple of minutes before deciding he needed someone familiar with the Egyptian language to help him with the phone. He wanted to see if they could find out who the caller had been. Curly was afraid to push buttons in case he accidentally erased something important.

Ahmad was sick with dread. An American sheriff. Not good. Somehow it appears his men had failed. It was almost incomprehensible that someone had captured three of the most vicious killers alive. He did not know that one of his killers was dead at Hokee's hand. He would gladly give up his sixth wife to find out what was happening.

Did they kill Hokee Wolf?

*****

The congregation was all standing when Neter came down the stairs in his black wardrobe. He never smiled, but tonight his countenance was more severe than usual, which said a lot as he always wore a fierce scowl on his face. The faithful all had looks of ecstasy on their faces as tonight was their night to get close and fondle the new sacrifice. When Neter took his place behind the altar, their faces changed to one of concern. If Neter wasn't happy, nobody was happy.

"We have been unsuccessful in locating the escaped girl." She was no longer considered a sacrifice. "Despite our friends on the police force and our own efforts, we have found no trace of her. As long as she is running free, she is a huge risk to everyone here. She could destroy what we have spent a lifetime building. I want everyone to take tomorrow off and search for her. Scour that hick town she came from, Malad, I believe. She must have gone to ground there someplace. She wasn't here in Pocatello long enough to develop any convenient allies or hiding spots. I am almost positive she is with someone she knows in Malad. Find her and drag her here. We must punish her."

They proceeded with the opening ceremony, paying tribute to Satan as he had taught them. Then they performed the chants and songs with all the emotion they could sustain. As promised previously, they all had a couple of sips of fresh blood for tonight's sacrament, after which it entitled each of them to spend a couple of minutes examining the new sacrifice.

Nancy was no longer embarrassed by her nudity. However, she was unprepared for the groping and sheer delight the men and women seemed to have in probing and stroking her body. All the while whispering some part of a satanic slogan such as 'pr an-weh say-tanas' meaning 'hail Satan' or 'Avete onmes Satanam' meaning 'all hail Satan.' In Nancy's mind, she wondered, *what the hell? Do they think Satan only speaks Latin?'*

The women were even worse than the men as they kept probing her vagina, trying to see if she was still a virgin. She felt weak from all the blood they had been taking. She had lost count of the number of pints Karnilla had drawn. They were good at giving her plenty of fluids, mostly apple juice and water, but sometimes some orange juice. Like Laura before her, Nancy quickly figured out they were saving her for some big celebration on Halloween, the day they called All Hallows Eve. It took little imagination to figure out they meant to offer her as a literal sacrifice to their God, Satan.

*****

Glory drove back to the Malad Hotel, a place she drove by yesterday. She parked and went into the lobby, which was a pleasant surprise. The building's exterior seemed shabby and rundown, but the inside was homey and clean with a small-town atmosphere. Today's edition of Malad's local paper sat on a coffee table in front of a soft brown leather couch. A deer head with a four-point set of antlers hung over a fireplace with a crackling wood fire. There was no one behind the oiled oak check-in counter, but there was a push bell to summon help. Glory pushed the bell, and about three minutes went by before a matronly older woman with long white hair cut in a fashionable page boy and a beautiful complexion often seen in older women came hurrying into the room, wiping her hands on an old-fashioned rose-patterned apron with oversized pockets used for holding everything, primarily fresh garden produce for supper.

"I'm so sorry," she began flashing a friendly smile. "I was upstairs cleaning a room when you rang. We rarely get visitors this early in the morning." She said, explaining her absence at the counter. "Were you looking for a room?"

The older woman's beauty intrigued Glory, and she studied the lady a few seconds before answering. The woman wore her old-fashioned apron over a pretty blue gingham dress. The apron reminded Glory of the farmer's wife in that famous painting *American Gothic* by Grant Wood, although this lady was much prettier.

"No, but thank you. I've just come from visiting with LuAnn McIntire over at the Red Rooster, and she suggested you might help me. My name is Gloria Bingham, although everyone knows me as Glory."

"Oh yes. Ann and I are good friends, although competitors, as you might have guessed. How can I be of service?"

Glory marveled that two older women, obviously widows, could appear so serene and complacent in a world gone mad. "I am an investigative reporter from New York City, currently assisting Hokee Wolf in trying to locate a college girl missing from her room in Pocatello. We believe that the missing girl is one you know well, having taught her in high school. Her name is Laura Taylor."

"Yes. I know Laura. A lovely young lady. Very smart. She has a brain on her head that one does."

"Mrs. Williams, it is Mrs. Williams, isn't it? Can you help me get in touch with Laura? It's imperative. They kidnapped another young girl recently. We believe Laura escaped from the same kidnappers, so they replaced Laura with a new girl. If Laura can help us find the kidnappers, we may save this new girl."

"If I could put you in touch with Laura, what would you have her do?"

For the first time, Glory felt like singing. The way Mrs. Williams answered the question told Glory she had struck gold. She could feel that Mrs. Williams knew all about Laura and where she might be hiding. Most likely, right here in the Malad Hotel.

"My associates would like to find out if Laura could describe the place they held her. We want any information she can provide regarding her kidnappers' nature and why they kidnapped her. Laura was not the first girl who has disappeared from the University. This seems to be a regular occurrence every October. We must find these criminals and put a stop to their kidnapping."

"These people sound dangerous. Will Laura be in any danger?"

"We suspect the men who kidnapped Laura are quite dangerous. I believe I saw them in a restaurant a few days ago, and if those were the kidnappers, they looked especially mean."

"Well, I would like to help you, young lady, Gloria, was it? But before I could promise anything, I would have to speak with Laura. It really must be up to her to decide to see you."

"It's just Glory, madam. And if you could get in touch with Laura right away, time is critical. We don't know what they are doing with these young ladies, but we are pretty sure it isn't pleasant for the girls. So we want to end this as quickly as possible."

"Would you mind waiting for a minute, dearie? Let me go see what I can do."

Glory didn't much like being called dearie, but the excitement about possibly seeing Laura overshadowed any negative feelings. For what seemed like hours, but was only five minutes, the lovely old lady returned with a beautiful, fresh-looking girl Glory immediately knew was Laura. Glory stood up as the pair entered the room.

"Glory, this is Laura Taylor. Laura, this is the lady I told you about; her name is Glory."

With a smile on her face that would definitely launch a thousand ships, Glory held out a hand, "Hello Laura. I am so thrilled to meet you."

CHAPTER FORTY-ONE

The hunt is on

Hokee was back in his office, sitting with Curly and Hilda, waiting for Laura. They were all delighted that Glory had been victorious in locating the missing girl. Laura's initial reluctance at a meeting with the sheriff disappeared when Glory explained no one was interested in blaming her for Earl's death. As far as the law was concerned, Earl met his death while performing an illegal act at the hands of a person or persons unknown. The law was not interested in punishing anyone for killing a kidnapper. They only wanted Laura's help in locating the other kidnappers and whoever ordered the kidnapping.

Laura hung back when Glory brought her upstairs to Hokee's office. Her ordeal with the kidnappers still traumatized her, and she could not trust others as she had before. Nevertheless, Glory held her hand, assuring the young lady that these were the good guys.

"Laura, you don't know how hard these men have been looking for you. We know you were not the first person kidnapped by these monsters, and now another girl has been taken."

"Hello, Laura. I'm Hokee Wolf." While speaking, Hokee stood and gave the girl his brightest smile as he took her in a gentle hug. "And this bald-headed gentlemen from the sheriff's office is Robert Belingsford, but we call him Curly because of his beautiful curly locks. You may not believe this Laura, but seeing you here alive is maybe the best present in the world. We both want to thank you for having the courage to speak with us."

A timid Laura, looking like an angel in one of Glory's white pantsuits, gave a shy smile as she said, "I'm happy to help. I hope you can catch the others."

"Let's all sit down and get comfortable," Hokee suggested. While he was speaking, Hilda came in carrying a tray laden with coffee, tea, water, and doughnuts in Curly's honor.

Glory sat with Laura on Hokee's office couch while the men pulled up the two visitors' chairs to face the ladies. Hokee wore blue jeans and a long-sleeved blue sweater to appear less threatening, and Curly was out of uniform in jeans and a white shirt with an open neck. Neither man was visibly armed.

Hilda sat in Hokee's desk chair, which she pulled close to the girls after placing the tray of goodies on the coffee table in front of the couch.

Glory was the one to open the meeting. "I have already heard most of the story from Laura, so I'm familiar with her testimony. Let me summarize for everyone what I have learned and then ask Laura the questions if you don't mind."

During the next hour, they listened as Laura relived her kidnapping and subsequent defilement while confined in the basement. Even Glory shuddered as Laura talked about the bloodletting and shaving episodes. Listening to the harrowing tale of imprisonment and sexual abuse, Hokee's jaw stiffened along with his resolve not only to find but administer some Hokee punishment on those responsible. Curly sat shaking his head in disgust at his fellow man's treatment of this beautiful girl.

"Can you find the house where they held you?" Hokee asked.

"I believe so. It may take a little while. When I left, I was pretty upset and in a hurry driving a stolen car." It spoke volumes that she didn't mention Earl's death in recounting her difficulty in locating the building.

"What do we know about the church of Satan, Curly," Hokee inquired. "Have you had any dealings with them in the past?"

"No, this is the first I've heard of them. I didn't even know there was such a church. Although, of course, I ain't no church-going man; even so, you would have thought. And to hear Laura tell about police officers at the mass. Drinking her blood. Oh, my God. How thoroughly disgusting."

In the far northwest section of Pocatello, where W Siphon Rd. intersects N Axel Ln., there are several old farmhouses and a few old railroad bosses' mansions. It is in one of the old RR mansions that the Church of Satan has its services. There is no sign outside of the house, and unless someone brought you there, it would be difficult to find. They had converted several old mansions to apartment houses, so having several cars parked outside the building was not unusual. When Laura left there in the dark, driving her stolen car, she just drove randomly until running into a major street that finally led her to a road she recognized as one connecting to the freeway. Driving around town in Curly's Jeep with Glory, Laura, and Hokee, it had been impossible to determine which building housed the Church of Satan. Everything looks different in the sunlight, and poking along rubbernecking to see everything at once also changes the perspective.

They gave up after two hours, having narrowed the possibilities down to the northwest section of Pocatello. About a dozen houses of interest were unfortunately too separated to keep under surveillance by Hokee or Curly. Knowing there were members of the law enforcement community who were members of the church meant that they couldn't count on fellow officers' help to keep watch. They had excellent descriptions of the kidnappers, Neter, and several members, especially the women, but no addresses. Hokee was reasonably sure that Nancy was in one house they identified, but which one? Time was getting short, and Nancy must be in a genuine panic.

In the meantime, they had to secure Laura. There was undoubtedly a major search by the Church to recover their missing sacrifice and close her mouth for good. It was Glory who suggested hiding her in Hokee's place. She would have Shila for protection while Glory helped Hokee. It was inconceivable that anyone could find Hokee's place without help, and no one could get past the hundred and twenty pounds of pure wolf. They decided it for sure when Shila ran right up to Laura when she got out of the car, rubbing his enormous body against her legs. For Laura, it was love at first sight. There is nothing more majestic and beautiful than a full-grown wolf with a smile on his face. Shila reminded Laura of the wolf in her dreams and she felt completely safe for the first time in weeks.

After Glory installed Laura in Hokee's place, she called the Taylors to let them know they had found Laura, and she was healthy and safe. They understood why she needed to stay in hiding until they had dealt with the kidnappers, and since they had met and liked Glory, they trusted her judgment. Laura talked with her parents and assured them she was okay and would be home and then back in school real soon.

Hokee and Curly talked until late at night, trying to develop a plan to find the kidnappers. If they could have relied on some local police or sheriff's officers for help, it would have made their job much more straightforward. Keep all the suspect houses under surveillance until spotting Neter or one of the kidnappers. There was no way just the two of them could accomplish the same thing.

It was Hokee who asked. "Curly, if they have a big Halloween party, an All Hallows Eve thing, where would they have such an event? Surely not in the basement of an old mansion."

"That might be something to consider. Laura said something about a hole. Some reference to somebody being dumped or thrown into some deep hole. That has me thinking. I've lived here my entire life, and I know little about a hole, but one time we had this deputy from McCammon. He mentioned, oh years ago, something about the McCammon Hole. From what I remember, that place has a sordid history. It might be worth checking out. I believe it's pretty remote."

"Do you have any idea where it is? My God, Curly, I was around these parts nearly as long as you, and I've never heard of the hole. Although, I rarely visit McCammon."

"I don't have a clue, but hell Hokee, it can't be that tough to find. Let me see if I can contact that old deputy. Maybe he can show us or get someone else to do the job."

"Let's hit it tomorrow, Curly. I'm bushed, and you must be tired as well. See about the hole first thing, okay?"

"You got it, Hokee. Goodnight."

They bedded Laura down on the couch next to Shila, and as Hokee laid his head down next to Glory, he smelled the luxurious lavender scent from the hair shampoo and rinse she used. Being a bachelor for so many years, this was still a fresh experience and one he found most pleasing. Then, just before drifting into sleep, an old refrain from a Longfellow poem ran through his head.

'And the cares that infest the day, shall fold their tents, like the Arabs, and as silently steal away.'

CHAPTER FORTY-TWO

Ahmad and Neter

Ahmad felt like he needed protection. His hired killers were all either dead or in the custody of the local county sheriff in Idaho. This meant that bastard Hokee Wolf knew he had tried to have him killed along with the earlier hit on Olson's son.

How his cousins fucked up by putting a hit on Olson's son instead of Hokee Wolf was beyond belief. Of course, *he* would never have put a hit on the boy; what's his name, Gene? My God. Gene would never hurt his beloved Rashida, although as far as he was aware, Gene only knew her as Opal.

And now?

He had little information about the Indian. Okay, Hokee found him in Japan and knew of his deceitful practices, making the Indian a formidable enemy, one he had tried to have killed. At some point, the Wolfman would come for his revenge, if only to be sure no more killers were on his trail. The safe move for Ahmad was to disappear, and this was something he could not do. He had an empire to run. The alternative was to surround himself with guards and hope for the best. And that would most likely not stop the man he now feared more than death.

When the man named Hokee came calling, and it was only a matter of when, not if, someone or something must stop him before he reached Luxor.

*****

Neter was not a man who lives in fear. He makes others fear him. In the world of sages and saints, they would consider Neter an energy vampire. One who sucks the energy from others. The Church of Satan provided an excellent venue to instill fear in everyone who came in contact with the church. Neter feeds on the fear of others. He cultivated his entire persona to provide the fear that feeds his twisted soul. America has always been a Christian country, and nobody scares a good Christian like Satan. Although most of his followers never considered themselves Christian, living in a Christian community instilled some community beliefs, the big one being a fear of Satan.

He no longer knows what he believes, or if he even has a belief. The Church and his role as the High Priest are his life. Neter's soul belongs to the church and Satan. Without the church, he is nothing. And now, it is all in jeopardy because of that little bitch. That God damned Earl and his lust.

Laura was no longer a missing sacrifice, a virgin for Satan, a delightful pleasure-filled evening of sexual gratification for everyone to enjoy. She was now just that farm girl bitch.

And now, for the first time in his life, Neter felt the cold coils of fear wrap themselves around his twisted black heart. Unless they found the bitch before she could get to the authorities, his entire life's work could vanish along with his life. Over the years, they had sacrificed many virgins to their God, Satan. However, agents of civility in the community would not view their sacrifices in the same manner. Therefore, they must find the missing bitch.

If she had not killed that bastard Earl, he would kill him with his own hands. And that bitch, Raven, for allowing it all to happen. Maybe he should take her to his private quarters for some alone time with the High Priest. She was always a good fuck. Then sacrifice the bitch to Satan. Wouldn't that shake up the congregants? Yeah, this year, Satan might get two for one. Sadly, only one a real virgin. Possibly, but definitely a virgin by decree.

*****

An early riser, Hokee performed the sun salute ten times before going for a ten-mile run with Shila, then made his first pot of coffee. The smell of freshly made coffee brought Glory out of the bedroom while Shila nuzzled Laura awake. Wearing Hokee's royal blue bathrobe that swallowed her up, Glory had an elfin look peeking out of the folds. Laura usually wore a silk babydoll nightshirt to sleep in, but given the circumstances, she had on a pair of pink shorts and a rainbow-colored tee shirt also borrowed from Glory. With everyone awake and ready to begin the day, Hokee asked Laura if any deputy sheriffs took part in The Church of Satan.

She thought for a minute before responding. "I'm not sure if they were from the sheriff's office or the city police. They had guns and wore uniforms. The situation wasn't ideal for observation. Mostly I didn't look at the people who groped me. With my head hanging down, I saw their shoes and pants and, like I said, their guns."

Glory asked, "Would you be able to recognize any of the officers if you saw them again?"

"There was this one man, a real beast. He had the foulest mouth and wouldn't stop squeezing my breasts. I looked at his face. Him I would recognize."

"Laura, I would like for you to ride with either Glory or me and sit outside of the sheriff's office and watch the officers entering and leaving. We will make you up so no one can recognize you. Would you be willing to do that?"

Her response was hesitant, "Maybe. I would have to feel really safe."

Hokee gave her a chance to think about it for a minute before proceeding. "Laura, we both know you have undergone a genuinely traumatic and frightening experience. There may not be any other person who could have your experience and still feel like a whole human being. We certainly do not want to put you under any stress. If you only want to hang out here with Shila, that will be fine with us. We're concerned for Nancy and want to do everything we can to get her away from those monsters who molested you. Think about it, Laura. I'm going to make you my famous *eggs ala goldenrod*. I don't think I've even made it for Glory."

"No, you have not," sniped Glory. "Do I have time to take a shower?"

"Sure, you can both shower and get dressed. Breakfast will be in about thirty minutes. I have to boil the eggs first so take your time. But not too much."

Hokee pulled some deer sausage from his freezer to thaw out while the eggs were in boiling water on the stove. Then, after shredding potatoes for hash browns and waiting for the eggs to cook, he called Curly.

"My God, Hokee, why so early? I'm still on my first cup."

"I'm wondering about Ahmad's plane up there in Boise. Can you call your buddies and find out if the plane is still there? I may want to return it to the owner."

"Is that all you want to do with the plane, Hokee?"

"Well, I might keep it after taking it back to Egypt. It depends on the state the present owner is in after my visit."

CHAPTER FORTY-THREE

Glory and Laura

The dawn came with an overcast of dark clouds turning daylight into a shadowy affair, making it into a dreary, cold, overcoat kind of day. Driving her rental, Glory hauled Laura out-of-town to the sheriff's office. The old highway runs in front of the office, and next to it are the railroad tracks opposite the sheriff's building.

The highway department or some philanthropic citizen planted a row of Jack Pine trees along the road that grew into eighty-foot specimens with massive trunks. Glory parked her Lincoln Navigator under the trees with the vehicle hidden from the sheriff's office by their huge trunks. From the front of their building, the deputies could glimpse the Navigator if they were looking in that direction, but even if they saw the vehicle, it would have been next to impossible to see who was inside.

Laura was wearing a black woolen watch cap covering her hair and some wrap-around shades that almost hid her face. She was unrecognizable except for someone next to the car who knew her. Glory sat next to her with a 9mm Glock resting on her lap to comfort Laura.

Hokee had fixed a thermos of hot coffee and hot chocolate and some homemade chicken salad sandwiches if they got hungry. In the big Lincoln, the ladies rested easily, relaxed, and comfortable. Laura felt safe, and whenever someone new entered or left the building, they had an old pair of Hokee's Nikon Prostaff 10 x 30 compact field glasses to study their images. Then, towards the middle of the afternoon, when both ladies were about to give up, they struck gold.

"Oh my God, I think that's one of them," Laura exclaimed. "Let me see the glasses, quick."

Glory handed her the glasses, and Laura studied the man's face as he left the building. "Yes. YES! That's one of the bastards. He kept ramming his fingers up my vagina like he was searching for a diamond in a bowl of jellybeans. He is one sick son-of-a-bitch."

"Oh shit," Glory exploded. "What do we do now? Follow your man or go inside to see who he is? From Curly, we can find his name and address. If we follow him, he may lead us to the house where they held you prisoner."

"You won't leave me here in the car alone, will you?" Laura's body was trembling, and she acted frightened after seeing the man.

"Never Laura. We're in this together until we stop all of those Satan bastards for good. I'm just wondering what our best move is now, and we need to decide before he drives away."

Still trembling and white with fright, Laura mumbled, "Would it be okay if we let him drive away and then go inside and see who he is?"

"We can do that, Laura, but we don't know that he is the only one of the Satanists in the sheriff's office. I would hate to take you inside and run into another one. Of course, I would shoot the bastard before he could cause us a problem, but that might not be the smartest play right now."

"I'm scared, Glory. Sorry, but I can't do this." Laura started shaking hard, so Glory wrapped her arms around the girl, comforting her in the best way she knew how.

"That's okay, Laura. I'll tell you what. We can wait and have Curly give us a picture of all the sheriff's deputies. We now know that at least one deputy belongs to the Church of Satan. We will find out who he is and have Hokee use his magic to find out where they are holding Nancy."

"Hokee does magic?" Laura asked in a trembling voice.

"Well, it's a kind of magic. Of course, not the type of magic show you see on the television, but believe me, when he asks a question, he *will* get answers."

Laura stopped shaking, so Glory poured her a cup of hot chocolate, then reached for her phone and called Curly.

"Curly here." Short and a little curt.

"Curly, Glory calling, you handsome dog. Okay, wait, I'm sorry for slurring our four-footed friends, but hopefully, Shila will never find out."

"What did I do to deserve such foul treatment from such a beautiful lady?"

"Aw, now you've gone and hurt my feelings by being so nice. How can I possibly be cruel to you now?"

"My God Glory, did you call me and interrupt my busy day to shoot the shit? I'm a busy man."

"I'm almost sorry, but to cut out the BS, we need to see pictures of all your deputies. Laura just saw one man who violated her in the house of Satan come out of the sheriff's office. I parked us across the highway next to the railroad tracks under the pine trees. Laura is afraid to follow, and we can't be sure there isn't another member inside of the building."

"Okay, I'm across town right now and can't get away for a few minutes. After that, I'll drop by the office and get the pictures, say, in about sixty minutes. Do you want to wait there, or meet me at Sherry's? I'm due for some food and hot coffee."

"We're good in the food and drink department, but waiting in Sherry's will be a lot nicer than sitting here in a cold car. See you there."

"Bye Glory," but she was already gone.

"Is that okay with you, Laura? I should have asked before agreeing. I'm just used to operating alone and deciding on the fly."

"I'm okay now, Glory. Thanks for the comfort. I didn't realize it would be so frightening. Sure, let's go meet Curly at Sherry's."

It took more than an hour and a half before Curly pulled into Sherry's parking lot and parked next to Glory's Lincoln. Going inside, he saw the two ladies sitting in a booth where they could both watch the entrance, just in case.

Sliding into the booth next to Laura, Curly had this self-satisfied grin on his face that always infuriated the New York journalist. It's the grin that says, '*look at me, ain't I special*,' while he slid a folder of pictures across the table.

Glory and Laura immediately tore into the pictures, looking for the deputy they saw exit the building. They found it. And two others.

Curly had a hard time assimilating the revelations about his co-workers. "How sure are you, Laura?"

The question was senseless, rude, and demeaning, but that didn't occur to Curly. He had just learned that three of his 'friends' were sick bastards who tormented innocent girls, then killed them.

Before Laura could speak, Glory erupted, "My God, Curly. Don't you think you might recognize some ladies that played with your precious pecker while they tied you to a cross, unable to resist or prevent their groping?"

"Sorry, sorry. I'm sorry, Laura. It just hit me kind of hard. I know these guys. I work with them. And I did not know. It makes me feel sick. I want to kill the bastards."

Not waiting for Curly to finish his pity party, Glory plowed on, "What's next, Curly?"

*****

Neter's persistence finally paid off as one of his people stumbled across the Malad Hotel and Mrs. Williams. Posing as a concerned friend looking for her missing roommate, Zelda learned Laura had been staying there but had already been rescued by another lovely lady.

Racing back to Pocatello, Zelda reported her findings. Believing their location would soon be discovered, Neter had them move Nancy and their entire church belongings to another building he had purchased and been remodeling into a more beautiful facility. The new facility was in an industrial park, making it almost anonymous. And now it was nearly finished. Neter planned on making the announcement a surprise on All Hallows Eve. Moving in a couple of days early would not seriously inconvenience the contractors, and best of all, the new building featured a special holding cell for their sacrifice. In addition, the new prison cell had a toilet, so the prisoner didn't have to squish her stools down the industrial drain anymore.

The members were all notified of the change immediately and told to stay away from the old building. Knowing that Laura would identify the law officers involved with the church, Neter ordered all the officers to take immediate leave and stay in the new building until they could make other arrangements.

Mrs. Williams thought about the recent visit with the new girl looking for Laura and wondered why they were still looking as that investigator lady took the girl. Then, deciding something didn't seem right, she called Glory on the number written on her notepad. Glory took the call, which alarmed her immediately. This meant that the Church of Satan bastards knew someone had found Laura, and they would scurry around for a new hiding place.

Two of the compromised deputy sheriffs were family men, and Curly had no trouble getting the Church of Satan's address from one of the wives. However, later that evening, when Curly finally located their old facility, he saw they had abandoned the building. There was no sign of their new location.

CHAPTER FORTY-FOUR

Hokee

Hokee met Ivan Ostegar in the lobby of the McCammon Hotel. To his surprise, the hotel's inside looked modern and brand new—Parque floors with woven Indian rugs and ornate wall hangings. Not at all what you would expect in a small town off the main highway. Fifty years ago, when Salt Lake City's main road to Boise, Idaho, went through McCammon, the hotel must have been a convenient stopover choice for the long drive. The gray limestone building's exterior showed its age, but inside was another story.

Ivan is Curly's old retired deputy friend from McCammon who told stories about *the hole.* Entering the spacious modern-looking lobby, Hokee spotted an older man dressed in levis and a long-sleeved red woolen Pendleton shirt and black cowboy boots with run-down heels. The man had shoulder-length white hair and a beard to match on a face sporting clear blue eyes. Crossing the lobby, Hokee held out his hand, "Mr. Ostegar, I'm Hokee Wolf, Curly's friend."

The old man creaked to a wobbly standing, holding out a hand in response, "Glad to meet you, Mr. Wolf."

With a grin, Hokee responded, "Call me Hokee, Mr. Ostegar; everybody does."

"Well then," the old man countered, "Ya best call me Ivan. Although most folks just call me the old fart."

"Okay then, Ivan it is. They say you can show me this mysterious hole in the ground."

"Ay, yep. That ole hole has quite the history. So what's your interest, anyway? And what kind of name is Hokee?"

"Well, Ivan, to answer your last question first, that name also has quite the history. Briefly, the name Hokee is a Navajo name for abandoned. Maybe I'll tell you the story sometime. My interest in the hole has to do with some missing girls and a case I'm working on."

"Well, sir, you've come to the right place. Rumors go, oh... ah, all the way back to the Indian days. They say that ole hole is home to quite a passel of missing folks."

"I know you're old Ivan, but even you ain't that old." Hokee couldn't help but tease the man a little. He seemed like such a friendly old cuss.

"No, but my granddad and papa had to deal with them heathens, no offense Hokee, and they had some stories to tell, I'll say."

"I'll bet they're interesting, and maybe when we solve this case, I can come back and buy you a beer and listen to your stories."

"I'd like that Hokee, except I'm a Jim Beam fan. Don't drink nothen but whisky."

"I will bring a bottle, Ivan. Now let's go look at your hole."

The two men went out of the hotel to Hokee's Explorer parked just outside the door. Hokee drove, with Ivan giving him directions.

Leaving the center of town, Ivan directed Hokee to a road, leaving the highway crossing the railroad tracks going east. The road started with an asphalt base that soon turned into gravel, and then after a couple more miles, it turned into dirt and lava rocks. They passed the last ranch house, then kept going up a gully into a lava flat. The ground was black rock and brown earth. The lava field had undulations much like the land around Hokee's house, except here, the lava field seemed much older and more worn down by the ages. Snow, ice, wind, and rain had smoothed over much of the rough edges, making the trail bumpy but passable. After driving a good ten miles, Ivan pointed out a rough parking spot that looked capable of holding several vehicles.

Hokee parked and, looking at the ground, could see that someone had parked there in the recent past. Ivan joined him and directed him to a path through the lava to a place that nearly brought Hokee to his knees. The vibrations of evil were so strong that Hokee had to stop for a few seconds to breathe and build up his defenses. He had purposefully worn his moccasins to feel the earth, but had neglected to shield himself with the proper ceremony. Through his feet, Hokee could feel the terror of the victims who had died in the hole. He observed fire pits surrounding the hole with a simple crude table placed near the hole's edge before reaching the hole itself. The scene's most telling aspect was that the fire pits were all set with kindling and logs ready to light up.

"These fire pits haven't always been here," Ivan said, waving his arms around. "Ain't been here for years, but it didn't use to look like this. Somebody made this smooth path all around the hole as they march around the damn thing."

"I believe Ivan; we have stumbled on to the site used by sick people to murder young ladies in some kind of evil ceremony."

"Why would folks do that?" It seemed the concept of what happened here was too much for Ivan to handle.

Walking over to the hole, Hokee dropped in a piece of lava, listening for it to hit bottom. Instead, they never heard the rock stop falling.

"It's some kind of cult, Ivan. I believe they come out here on Halloween and sacrifice a young girl. God knows what they do to her first; then they throw her in the pit."

"Well, from the stories I heard as a boy, there's quite a few people were tossed down that ole hole. I never thought it was still happening."

"It shouldn't be, and it will stop this year." The grim look of determination on Hokee's face would have chilled even the great Neter. Hokee was used to confronting evil, but nothing in the past could compare with the vibrations he felt here. The face of the evil he saw in his last sweat lodge was taking shape.

"Is it okay to leave now, Hokee? This place gives me the willies."

"Yeah, Ivan. Let's go. I've seen what I came to see. I believe we might find a good use for that hole on Halloween. Thanks for showing this site to me."

During the drive back to McCammon, Hokee was silent and sensing his new friend's mood; Ivan kept to himself.

When they were near the hotel, Hokee's phone rang. Glory told him about finding the house where they had held Laura prisoner, but they had already abandoned the place. So the Church of Satan discovered that someone other than a church member found Laura.

Hokee left Ivan by his pickup with a promise to call him again soon for that drink of whisky and the stories. Then, leaving the town of McCammon, Hokee pounded his fists on the steering wheel. *God damn. I hope we can find Nancy before Halloween. It's going to be an ugly night for the church.*

CHAPTER FORTY-FIVE

Conference

On the way back to Pocatello, Hokee called Curly, inviting him to dinner. He then called Glory to tell her of his plans and to alert Laura. After that, it was time to compare information and make plans.

Glory and Laura were already home when Hokee arrived, and he forgot that Curly had never been to his place, so he called back, giving him directions.

Laura seemed to have bonded with Shila, giving her peace of mind for the first time in many days. Something about the giant wolf and his protective nature made her feel safe. With Shila around, no damn Satanist was going to frighten her. Instead, the wolf would tear them to shreds.

Setting out a few elk steaks to thaw and putting some famous Idaho spuds in the oven to bake, Hokee excused himself to go wash off the feelings he had carried since visiting the hole. Something about the feel of evil seemed to stick in his pores. So after the shower, he did a sage cleanse to wash out his aura. Next, he went into the river behind his bedroom for the finishing touch and sat on the river bottom for five minutes. There is nothing like sitting on the bottom of an icy cold underground river in the dark to cleanse the soul.

Hokee dressed in a pair of comfortable soft leather pants and a doeskin shirt. While dressing, he could hear Curly holding court with the ladies. Hokee had a new pair of moccasins he put on to be comfortable. The old pair were the ones he had worn at the hole. They no longer felt right. Too many negative vibrations had worked their way into the soft leather. In thinking about these acts, Hokee had to smile at himself. He realized that most people would consider his actions careless and stupid. Yet, he knew inanimate objects collected vibrations. How many healers used crystals to draw out the poisons in people's bodies and auras? His smile was wry as he was only smiling at his peculiar behavior.

Joining the ladies and Curly in the living room, Hokee bandied about with the deputy, asking, "Where the hell is my drink, Curly? My God, I invite you to dinner and should at least expect a cocktail when I finished getting cleaned up."

"Oh, sorry, Bawana? I didn't realize you allowed the servants to prepare your drink. Something about slipping in a bit of poison, maybe?" Curly was having a hard time holding a straight face.

"Yeah, good thinking, and while we got the brain cells cooking, what would you all like to drink? Glory, you know what we have. Laura, would you like a cocktail or some wine? We could also make some tea. I don't have any carbonated drinks here. I know Curly drinks bourbon, but maybe tonight you would like something else?"

Drinks made and passed around, Hokee pulled salad makings from the refrigerator and started pulling apart some head lettuce while sipping on a scotch.

"While waiting for the spuds and the meat to thaw, let's compare notes."

"I'll go first," Glory volunteered. "We know three deputy sheriffs are in the Church of Satan. They fear us finding them. I don't see that the sheriff's department has any option but to arrest all three."

"I agree, Glory," Curly was quick to concur. "We staked their homes out. However, we don't believe they know we are on to them, so they should go home when this new emergency gets sorted out. At that point, we may find out why they moved the church and where it is now located."

"I visited the McCammon hole today," Hokee added. "I'm positive that is the site of their All Hallows Eve festival when they chuck the girl down the hole. I am going to be there and read to them from the book of Hokee."

"Not without me, buddy?" Curly chimed in.

"You are welcome, Curly, but not as a deputy. I may not strictly adhere to the law, which I know you are well aware of from our experiences together. I don't want to jeopardize your standing in the sheriff's office."

"Hell Hokee, I've already broken a dozen laws on this damn case. Ever since we maltreated those Egyptian killers and dealt with the Earl situation."

"I know that Curly, but when I dispense justice according to Hokee rules, you may not want to be present."

"Ya know, friend, after listening to Laura's story, I might just help administer some ole Hokee punishment."

"They must be running scared," Glory suggested. "Knowing that somebody found Laura, and she has probably talked."

"I think little frightens that leader, the Prophet or Divine Leader or whatever the hell they call him," Laura thought out loud. "He doesn't strike me as a man who scares easily."

"Changing subjects, Curly, but did you find anything about Ahmad's airplane in Boise?"

"Oh yeah. Thanks for reminding me. The plane is there, a Boeing 707, and the airport will not let it leave without talking with our department first."

"Oh, great. Thanks. I'm going to have to visit Egypt just as soon as we wrap up the Satan business. Ahmad must know his hired killers have failed by now, especially after Curly shot the shit with him on the phone. I want to put an end to this business before he mounts another charge."

"Hey, the damn phones kept ringing. Besides, I wanted to confirm your theory."

"I know I've made a few enemies, but when three Egyptians want to kill me, it ain't because I pissed off some pervert making a living off duping college kids. Come on, Curly. Did you honestly doubt me?"

"Well, no, but we in the sheriff's department try to validate everything."

"Just don't let bureaucracy dull your senses, my friend. You know the devil lives in the details."

"Ugh!. Got any more ugly cliches you can use, Hokee?" Glory kidded, half-serious.

"Okay, the steaks are ready for the grill. Glory, would you mind putting the rolls in the oven with the potatoes? The spuds should be about done. Just shove them over a little. I'll take the steaks outside. Are you coming Curly or staying in with the beauties?"

With dinner finished and the dishes put away, they sat around drinking coffee, discussing their next moves.

"Laura, I would like you to stay here with Shila if you don't mind. Only four people know how to find this place, and they are all in this room. The Church of Satan has no way of finding its way here. Even Hilda doesn't know where I live."

"I hate to miss any more school, but a few more days won't make that much difference. And I sure love hanging out with Shila. I have never felt so safe."

"With only two more days to Halloween, it would be nice to rescue Nancy before they take her to the hole. Otherwise, I'll need you there, Glory, to help with Nancy. She may be in a bad way."

"I would also like to help, Mr. Wolf," Laura suggested. "I'm sure I could help with Nancy after she gets rescued."

"It might be frightening, Laura. And please call me Hokee. Are you ready to face those maniacs?"

"We will take Shila, won't we," she almost pleaded.

"You bet. He won't leave your side until you go back to school. You may have to come back and visit him from time to time. He's going to miss you."

"Oh, I love that wolf. I never knew they could be so protective and friendly."

"There are those who believe that a wolf was the very first domesticated dog. However, all dog breeds can trace their origins back to the wolf."

"How did you come to get Shila, Hokee?"

"My teacher and friend gave him to me when I decided to become a private investigator. He always wanted me to become a shaman, like him. I guess he thought I needed the protection."

Standing up to show that the conference was over, Hokee said to Curly, "Step outside with me for a few Curly, I need to stretch my legs and give Shila a chance to run. I may need help to finish this cult, and I don't want any legal wash back."

CHAPTER FORTY-SIX

Neter

On the outside, the building looked like it might belong to a cement contractor or plumbing company. There were two large roll-up doors next to the pedestrian entrance. The roll-up doors were dummy, sealed shut, with the inside studded out by 2 x 4s and drywall covered by pebbles, giving it a garden-like appearance. On the inside, the building looked like a massive church, complete with stained glass windows. The windows were genuinely stained glass, backed by indirect lighting mimicking the sun. The stained glass scenes were like nothing ever seen on a Christian building. Instead of biblical scenes featuring prophets, Jesus, and the saints, they were pictures of demons, naked people copulating, and one particularly gruesome scene showing people drinking the blood of dying victims.

Here the chapel was on the main floor, with the basement reserved for *other* functions besides the prison.

A fireplace blazed against one wall, and wall sconces with their demonic eyes hung on the others. Neter had a new pulpit with the figure of Satan carved into the front. A cross stood over to one side, permanently mounted in the floor upon which hung Nancy, their latest sacrifice.

Neter entered, garnering the attention of all, "Welcome to the new home for The Church of Satan. I had planned on making this a surprise on the weekend, but circumstances have forced our hands. You are now all familiar with the reasons for this sudden move. The little bitch under Raven's care escaped and has now been found by parties or a party unknown. We assume she has spilled her guts. She escaped in Raven's car, so she probably knows where to find our old chapel, which called for our early move."

Pointing to Nancy, he continued, "We have a new sacrifice for our Lord and Master. She is beautiful beyond words and a glorious gift for our God. Tonight we shall all have a ceremonial sip of her blood to honor both her and our God, Lucifer. Look at her and admire her beauty. The weather report for All Hallows Eve is perfect. Our celebration and feast will be the best we have ever had."

Neter sought the law enforcement members of the congregation. "I am afraid there is bad news for our police and sheriff's members. Our escaped sacrifice may have noticed your uniform and could identify you. If they arrest you, they may force you to divulge the location of our new facility. As a precaution, please remain here in the church until after our celebration, after which we will assess the possible damage. There are bedrooms downstairs where you can stay until then." Then, to lighten the mood, he added, "Just don't molest our sacrifice until the festival when we can all take part."

Hanging on the cross with her arm wrapped around the crossbar and her legs spread apart, Nancy could see and hear everything. Although naked and vulnerable, she felt deep inside that her God would not let these sick bastards defile her. She kept thinking about the girl who escaped and hoped that this girl could help her avoid being sacrificed. Although this jerk at the pulpit talked a good story, Nancy could feel the fear seeping through his words. The girl who had escaped was a significant problem for the church. These people were guilty of so many crimes they must know couldn't continue forever. All she could do, hanging on the cross, was watch and wait for her opportunity.

Karnilla had extracted almost six pints of blood from the latest sacrifice, giving them a whole quart to enjoy tonight, adding the rest to the blood they had accumulated for the big celebration. Tonight, Neter had again provided a human skull from which everyone could take a sip of Nancy's blood. He never said where the head came from, and no one dared asked whose skull held the blood they were drinking? Somehow, drinking blood from a human skull was a big turn-on for the congregation, and they all wanted a piece of Nancy. Neter had to admonish the congregation to leave the sacrifice alone. They were free to look and admire, but tonight it was strictly hands-off. They had all physically examined the gift before; tonight, it was for looking only.

As the skull made its way around the room, Neter led the congregation in a series of chants and prayers. When the head came back to Neter, there was still a little blood left in the bottom. In defiance of his earlier order, Neter poured the blood over Nancy's breasts and invited the girls in the audience to lick it off her body. This act turned the congregation into a frenzy of sexual wantonness. The women and men all shed their clothes and seeking partners; the church became an orgy. Neter stood by his pulpit, not taking part until a naked Raven came up to him and boldly grabbed his penis. Although he had ravished her only a couple of days earlier, remembering how much he enjoyed her sexual appetite, he let her undress him and fuck him standing by the pulpit.

Ladies would stop by Nancy, lick the blood on her breasts, then flop on the floor with some man. Of course, the men all wanted a chance to lick Nancy as well, but Neter's strong warning led them to be satisfied coupling with some other woman.

The entire floor was covered with naked bodies, grunting and squealing like pigs enjoying a meal of dead rabbits. As a man satisfied himself with one woman, he looked for another. If none were presently available and women were as apt to be with another woman as with a man, the men would dance in front of Nancy shaking their stiff shafts at her with the warning, "Just wait until it's your turn, sweetmeat."

Poor, innocent Nancy could hardly believe her eyes. Beyond embarrassment and shame, she felt violated but no longer discouraged. Watching men and women crazy with lust behaving in mindless sexual gratification made her feel grateful for a different sort of teaching. All Hallows Eve was approaching, and she could not imagine any affair which could top what she was witnessing tonight. The girls who administered to her in her tiny prison said nothing specific, yet their veiled remarks made it sound like the grandest spectacle on earth. Without them saying anything, it became apparent that what she was witnessing tonight was a sample of what happened on All Hallows Eve. Except then, she would be the star attraction. She couldn't help but ponder. Would Neter be the first one to stick his penis into her? Would all the men take turns? And what about the women? Her rescue better happen soon. She wasn't sure how much longer her faith would last. It was one thing to be an optimist and brave, but as the time drew near, little fears started creeping in, tearing down her confidence. If she could only hold out a little longer.

CHAPTER FORTY-SEVEN

All Hallows Eve

Halloween approaches, and Hokee had no luck locating the Church of Satan's new building. He hoped the married deputies would reveal their new location, but they never returned home, warned by others to stay away. Hokee met with Curly in the early afternoon to complete the evening plans. Glory wanted to be at the celebration, and so did Laura, which was a worry to Hokee. He didn't know what went on at such an affair, and it worried him the church members might be on drugs. The men who abducted Laura were all husky guys, and a few dozen crazy men on drugs built like that could be a problem. Hokee and Curly both tried, but they could not talk the girls into staying home. Both of the women wanted to be there for Nancy.

Feeling the need for some otherworldly advice, Hokee spent a few minutes in the cold river. He would have preferred a sweat lodge session, but there wasn't time for that before they had to leave for the hole.

A silent underground river runs behind the back wall in Hokee's bedroom. This river was the seep source that first attracted Hokee to this barren lava plain years ago when he was on a vision quest. Getting undressed, Hokee sat by the river's edge and began his breathing exercises, saturating the body with oxygen while building up his core temperature. When ready, he slipped into the water, sinking to the bottom, sitting in the lotus position. The so-called Lost River is icy cold, but Hokee's body had adjusted to the cold within a few seconds. Now began the hard part.

We only learn this meditative exercise through much practice and dedication. Most people start out practicing in a warm swimming pool or hot tub. However, once perfected, there is no better way to communicate with your higher being. Hokee didn't use words like higher being, which is a new age term. In Hokee's world, he was communicating with the souls of ancient shamans.

The river is only about four feet deep, and over the centuries, it has worn the walls and floor smooth, giving the water a laminar flow resulting in its silent passage. Sitting on the river bottom immersed in Hokee's world, it cuts him off from every worldly distraction. Before long, the images of ancient shamans began appearing in his mind's eye. Posing the question in his mind, Hokee sat waiting for the answer. Before long, he imagined an herb sometimes used in the sweat lodge. This herb comes from the root of a local plant found in the surrounding mountains. It causes hallucinations and is used cautiously and only under the supervision of a trained shaman. Having his answer, Hokee left the river. His sojourn on the bottom lasted only fourteen minutes. He often sat for thirty minutes or more.

Hokee had everybody dress in black clothing. Black jeans, black pullover sweaters, and a black watch cap. Hokee had his Colt 45, and Curly wore a Browning 9mm on his hip. Curly provided them both with short barrel 12 gauge shotguns loaded with 00 buckshot. Glory had her own snub-nosed Smith and Wesson 38, and they found a similar gun for Laura. Hokee was reluctant to let her have a gun until he watched her take it apart and put it back together in less than a minute.

"I used to hunt and shoot with my dad and brothers," she informed the group with a small satisfied smile. "My dad instilled in me the practice of cleaning my gun after hunting." The gun made her feel part of the group and gave her confidence. Growing up in deer country with coyotes and jackrabbits, everyone learned how to shoot. "Besides," she said, "I'm a farm girl, and farm girls ain't afraid of nothing but God, and him only a little," she added with a grin.

Hokee loaded the Explorer with a tarp for ground cover and a few old blankets. Glory made a couple pots of coffee for their thermoses, and with everyone carrying coats, just in case, they loaded up Shila and headed for the hole.

Hokee worried that some early church members might be at the site arranging for the evening festivities. And he was right. Hokee used his binoculars to watch men and women prepare the evening fires from a high-ground vantage point a couple of miles away. After seeing them set the fires, the silent watchers saw them cover the table with a white sheet. Then they carpeted the entire area around the hole with ground covers and blankets, giving the site a somewhat festive appearance. Finally, when their preparations were complete, the men and women got into a sheriff's Jeep Grand Cherokee and drove off, leaving the site vacant.

Curly and Hokee discussed driving to the site and dropping the girls off, but afraid someone from the church might come back early, they opted to find someplace to stash the Explorer where it would not be seen by the church members when they returned. Driving back to the trail leading to the hole, Hokee followed it until he saw a tall outcropping of lava offering concealment behind which he parked, about a mile from the site. Then, carrying blankets, ground covers, coffee, and coats, Hokee led them on a circuitous route to the hole. He aimed to be close enough to watch, but he wanted to remain hidden until everyone who was coming had arrived.

This lava plain was much older than at Hokee's house, and the ground was almost smooth in spots, making for easier walking. There were still several rough spots easily avoided. Hokee took them to the hole so they could all see the bottomless pit and the preparations for this evening's mass. It almost made Laura cry when she saw the preparations for tonight's festival. Especially the linen-draped table where she was supposed to lose her virginity. If Shila had not been by her side, she might have bolted back to Hokee's Explorer.

Curly set about finding convenient hiding places for everyone while Hokee doctored the fire kindling with a few of his magic herbs. Testing the slight breeze, Hokee warned the others to watch for a shift in the wind, which could bring campfire smoke in their direction. He told them that the herbs would burn away within a few minutes, after which there would be no problem. Hopefully, the herbs would put the celebrants into a different ecstasy from the one they had expected.

Satisfied that the festival celebrants could not see where Curly or the girls and Shila were hiding from the area around the hole, Hokee joined them to wait for the party to begin. This waiting was the hard part. It was still an hour before dark, and no one expected the Satanists to arrive before then. As the day ended, the air turned chilly, and the group huddled behind the lava outcropping were grateful for blankets and coats. By the time it was completely dark, the coffee was gone, and the watchers were getting restless. A few minutes later, they could see the caravan's lights bouncing down the road coming towards them. It looked like at least twenty vehicles were coming down the road in a funeral procession. The long line of cars gave pause to Hokee, who wondered silently how many funerals they would hold after tonight's festival ended.

Glory and Laura could feel the adrenalin flood through their veins, sharpening their senses. They could hardly wait to rescue Nancy.

The first two vehicles were pickups with extended cabs carrying six burly men. The men immediately started fires, lighting up the circle around the table and the bottomless hole. As the men moved around lighting fires, Shila let loose a few soft growls silenced by a command from Hokee. The wolf knew some bad stuff was happening.

By the time the fires were burning, throwing flames three feet into the sky, the other cars had unloaded men and women who were laughing and teasing about the festivities about to begin. The last vehicle, a Lincoln Navigator, carried Neter and three girls who walked Nancy into the circle of fires. They had wrapped Nancy in a colorful blanket adorned with images of a man's penis and a woman's vagina. Nancy walked with her head held high. It was as though she knew in her heart that her God would somehow save her from this mounting spectacle. Watching the girls march Nancy over to the table, it was all Glory and Laura could do to keep from shooting them. It was Hokee's restraining looks that held them in check.

Neter went to the table covered with a white sheet, beckoning the girls to bring the sacrifice to the table. Then church members began dancing around the table, chanting *Sanctus Satanas, Ave Satanas, Ave Satanas*. Holy Satan. Hail Satan. While dancing, they began stripping off their clothes, throwing them on the blankets.

The girls and Neter put Nancy on the table, covering her temporarily with the blanket. There was a girl on each of Nancy's arms and one on each leg holding her down. While the crowd danced around the table chanting, Dakarba opened a bag containing the skull and a jar with two full quarts of the sacrifice's blood.

The men who started the fires dropped suddenly out of the circle of chanting people, sitting on the ground in some sort of stupor. Then the dancers started stumbling, falling to the ground in giggles and wonder. The people stared at their hands as though they were the most beautiful things on earth. Dakarba dropped the skull, which bounced on the table, then onto the ground, shattering into pieces. In grabbing for the relic, she knocked over the jug holding Nancy's blood, which spilled over the table, soaking the blanket, then Nancy, before running onto the ground.

Neter seemed oblivious to what was happening until he also slumped to the ground. He then began babbling in some strange tongue which no one could understand. So now it was Hokee time.

CHAPTER FORTY-EIGHT

Hokee and Neter

As soon as Neter fell to the ground, Hokee gave the signal for the others to move. Glory and Laura went immediately to take care of Nancy. The drugs Hokee had put into the fires also affected her, but lying down, most of the smoke went above her head, so she didn't get affected to the same extent as the others. Pulling the blood-soaked blanket off Nancy, Glory reached down on the ground and grabbed a woman's cotton sweater, which she used to wipe the blood off from Nancy. Then, with Laura's help, Glory found discarded clothes to cover Nancy until they could get her out of here to some safe place. Laura gave Nancy a big hug, telling her she was the one who had escaped earlier.

Nancy's first thought was to give a big thanks to Jesus, who she believed sent these good Samaritans to save her. But Glory and Laura urged her to move and let Hokee and Curly take care of the Satanists.

With Hokee's blessing, Glory and Laura walked Nancy to Neter's Lincoln Navigator, which they borrowed to drive Nancy back to Hokee's place. Neter wouldn't be driving it again, and Glory felt that taking his ride was only fair for Nancy and Laura, who had both suffered from his hospitality. They would need some time to decompress Nancy while they figured out their next moves. Hokee and Curly stayed behind to clean up. But first, Curly called in more sheriff's deputies and the local police to help with the arrests.

Then he and Hokee went around the table with plastic cuffs, tying up both the naked men and women. Everyone seemed happy and didn't mind being restrained, except for Neter. Neter was relaxed from the drugs Hokee had put in the fire, but he had not lost his mind or voice. Either he had a higher tolerance for the drug Hokee put into the fire, or his metabolism processed the drug out of his system at a faster rate. He began cursing Hokee and Curly with language neither could understand, but the intent was clear. If he could have killed them with words, they would die horrible deaths. Cursing Hokee with all the fury he could summon, Neter ranted and raved about how Satan was going to curse both Hokee and Curly with hell-fire and damnation. Curly tried handcuffing a squirming Neter to the table, but the aggressive leader kept throwing him off, so Curly tapped him on the head with the butt of his pistol, putting him to sleep. Neter woke up and was still ranting twenty minutes later when the police and sheriff's deputies began arriving.

Every church member was guilty of sexual molestation, helping to hide a kidnapped victim and accomplice to attempted murder. Some men and women faced more severe charges, and of course, Neter was guilty of damn near everything they could imagine.

Instead of sorting out the clothing issue, the police just had the people grab blankets and coats from the ground to cover themselves for the jail trip. Getting them dressed would mean removing the restraints, and as the men were coming around, it seemed wiser just to leave them tied up in Curly's plastic tie wraps. People were being hauled away in small groups by the police until it was just Hokee, Curly, and Neter. The police wanted to take Neter, but as Curly also represented the law, they left him at the hole while they took the rest downtown.

Working around the fires, Hokee and Curly had received a small residual dose of the drug Hokee used, giving them both sluggish mental powers. For Curly, who was not used to such drugs, the effects were pretty startling, making him almost giddy. Hokee also felt the effect, but in his case, he used similar drugs to stimulate that part of the brain he activated in the sweat lodge when he saw the face of evil. Looking at Neter through these eyes, Hokee could see the evil behind the mask, recognizing the face from his visions in the sweat lodge.

Neter saw the change come over Hokee's face as he stood looking at the disgraced leader. The Satanist knew then that this was the famous shaman detective he had heard about for years, the man who trained as a shaman before becoming a local legend. As Hokee watched, Neter stood wrenching the table leg away from the table, freeing his hands with a surprising burst of strength. Then, knowing he could not reason or sway these two men away from their mission to destroy him, he did the only thing possible. Taking a running jump, he hit the hole dead center, never making a sound all the way down.

"It's probably just as well," Curly almost giggled as he spoke. "It saves me a hell of a lot of paperwork and the taxpayers a ton of money."

"Yeah. I know that, Curly. But it still pisses me off. I wanted to talk to that bastard before skinning him alive, which is the *only* reason I had the cops leave him here for us."

"Oh, Hokee, you are such a knight in shining armor. You want to solve all the world's problems and punish the evildoers. Maybe you should read more of the Christian Bible. Leave justice to me, sez the Lord. Or something or the other like that."

"I believe Curly, the quote you seek is in Deuteronomy, 'To me belongeth vengeance.'"

"I didn't think Navajo shaman read the Christian Bible, let alone knew enough of it to quote chapter and verse."

"Don't remember the verse, Curly, but I think it was chapter 32," Hokee added with a grin. "Someone searching for wisdom will seek it wherever it can be found."

"Well, hell, partner," Curly grumbled, "what are we going to do with all of this shit lying around?"

"Well, hell, Curly, that's why God made bottomless holes. Let's dump these clothes, ground cloths, and the table into the hole. Clean this place up. The fires will burn down, and there won't be anything left here but ashes. Let's keep the sheet with Nancy's blood for evidence of the church members' physical abuse. We probably won't need it, but it won't hurt."

They left all the member's cars, parked, and drove Hokee's Explorer back to Hokee's place. By the time they got back home, the drug's effects had worn off, and they found Nancy and Laura sitting at the table drinking hot cocoa while Glory was sipping on a gin and tonic.

Back at Hokee's, Nancy took a long hot shower cleaning off as much blood and psychic muck from her body as possible. When Hokee returned with Curly and took one look at Nancy, he immediately went to a sideboard and grabbed a sage smudge. Then, having Nancy stand up, he doused her entire physical and energy bodies with sage smoke, after which he brushed her aura with an eagle's feather. Everyone in the room could see the girl's transformation as her color returned and she began glowing.

They had Nancy call her parents when she informed them that angels had saved her, just like angels spared Daniel from danger in the lion's den. The three ladies then all had a good cry along with the parents, while Hokee and Curly stood by, trying not to look foolish. Nothing in the police or detective's work is more satisfying than successfully reuniting kidnapped victims with their loved ones. With promises to return both girls tomorrow, Hokee set about making one of his famous rabbit stews. Notable, at least with Glory, who couldn't stop telling the two girls how much they would love dinner. Both girls had more than likely grown up eating rabbits most of their lives, but were too polite to mention it to Glory.

Both girls were eager to see their roommates, and Nancy wanted to get into her own clothes, so Hokee drove them all back to town to drop off the girls and Curly. Both girls had their own cars and promised their parents to go home tomorrow, so Hokee and Glory dropped them off at their rooms, bidding the girls a good evening. Curly had previously reminded the girls that they may have to testify in court, but it wouldn't be for some time and maybe never.

Hokee took Glory to a club downtown whose owner he had helped by catching a thieving bartender. Rarely drinking in a bar or nightclub, Hokee felt the time was right for a celebration. But, unfortunately, they had no sooner sat down and been served than Glory asked him about this business concerning his going to Egypt?

It had been pleasant until then, at which time the chill would have frozen vodka. With no way to avoid the issue, Hokee explained why he had to go. Unless he wanted to live for the rest of his life waiting for Ahmad to send in another team, he had to visit the man explaining life's facts, according to the Wolf.

Glory could see reasons for the trip, although she wasn't sure the risks warranted the danger. Luxor was Ahmad's home turf. He probably knew hundreds and was known about town by several hundred people. It was a reported fact that life throughout most of Egypt was cheap. You could buy a person's death for only the price of a cheap meal. Hokee and a beautiful blond lady would stand out in Luxor like a penguin on an iceberg. Ahmad would have word of their being in town long before the pair could even find his palace. To Glory, it was a fool's errand. But then, Hokee was her fool.

The following day, they made plans for the trip to Egypt. Hokee didn't plan on spending more than a day at most in Luxor, so they each packed a small overnight case. They left before noon, driving to Boise to find Ahmad's plane.

They had parked the plane close to the airport terminals because the airport authorities could find no one to pay the fuel and docking fees. Ahmad's cousin Setka Hassan was still in Pocatello, trying to find some way to free the two killers from Curly's jail, and the pilots could not be located. Setka had talked with Ahmad, but the latter's anger made him almost incomprehensible, and Setka's English kept him from understanding exactly the procedures taking place. He also didn't want to seem connected with the killers, afraid the police would accuse him of some crime.

Hokee kept the money liberated from the killer's wallets, which he used to pay Ahmad's plane's fuel and storage charges. Then, rather than deal with the Egyptian pilots, Hokee called Grant to see if he could help find some qualified pilots. Within thirty minutes, two men wearing pilot uniforms for an airline no longer in business entered the General Aviation terminal.

Meeting the pilots, Glory joked that hopefully, the old air carrier's demise did not reflect on their piloting skills. "Nah," the most senior pilot, a skinny man named Philip with white hair worn in a buzz cut quipped, "we were still flying simulators when they folded. But they gave us these snazzy uniforms." "Yeah," his muscular friend chimed in, showing a sense of humor, "they were going to let us practice with real planes before that happened." Muscle man with a full head of shoulder-length black hair tied in a ponytail wore the name Albert.

"It's getting late," Hokee mentioned. "How about you men getting our plane checked out tonight and loaded with refreshments for a long ride? Let's plan on leaving here at O seven hundred."

"Hey?" Philip asked, "I understand they registered our plane to a firm in Egypt. Will there be a problem getting permission to fly it back out of the country?"

"I don't think so," Hokee replied. "I talked with Grant, and he seems to have a little say in how they do things around here. The FAA was making some stink, but they assured me that has all been resolved. I'll check again before we leave, but it isn't here that bothers me. It's landing in Egypt."

"Anything we need to worry about?" Albert asked.

"Not for you guys. Glory and I may have a different situation, but we'll talk about that tomorrow."

"Well, lover boy, it looks like you're taking me on another excursion into hell," Glory said to Hokee on the way to their hotel. "Hopefully, your magic will work on these Egyptians."

"Oh honey, don't you worry, I'll come up with something."

Neither one knew how hairy it would get.

CHAPTER FORTY-NINE

Egypt

Getting the FAA to release Ahmad's airplane to Hokee was a minor problem compared to keeping Ahmad from receiving the information. International protocols dictated that someone notify the owner if his aircraft gets released to someone other than his representatives, in this case, his pilots. So it didn't come as a total surprise to Hokee when Egyptian authorities arrested him and Glory as soon as they set foot on the ground in Luxor.

The authorities soon released the two airline pilots who were innocent of any wrongdoing. They ushered Hokee and Glory into a holding cell inside the airport where air marshals held them for interrogation. The wait wasn't long before a man and woman wearing airport authority uniforms entered, dismissing the marshals.

The lady was 45, with wisps of gray hair showing under her police cap. She was small, five-foot-five, weighing about 125 pounds, with a pinched face and bushy eyebrows. Although small in stature, her attitude would have filled a football stadium. Airplane piracy is a serious crime.

Her senior partner was not much larger, maybe five-foot-seven with a stiff 150-pound body. He had a buzz-cut under his cap, on top of a face pockmarked with smallpox or acne. Maybe pushing sixty, the man paced around the room, moving with the grace of an Olympian athlete as he yelled at the two miscreants threatening life in an Egyptian prison.

When he had a chance to speak, Hokee asked, "Do either of you know a Mr. Ahmad Hassan?"

The older man named Mohammed Ipi answered with a sneer, "of course we know, Mr. Ahmad. He is one of our leading citizens."

"Well then," Hokee said with a big grin, "you know that the airplane you accused us of stealing belongs to him."

"Of course, we know the plane belongs to Mr. Hassan," added the woman, getting into the action. The woman named Aria wore a self-satisfied look, as though she always lunched with this icon of Egyptian royalty. "The air controllers alerted us as soon as the plane entered Egyptian air control."

"Well, what you may not know is that his pilots abandoned the aircraft in the state of Idaho in the USA, where those responsible for the plane being in America got arrested. Having dealt with Ahmad only a few weeks ago in Japan, I thought it would be neighborly of us to return the aircraft to him here in Luxor. Since my beautiful partner has never had the opportunity of visiting your lovely country before, we thought it would be a good time to return Mr. Hassan's plane to him and do a little sightseeing."

You could see the painful realization on the faces of the two officials. Here they were arresting two people for stealing an airplane when all they were doing was returning the plane to its rightful owner.

"How come you never informed Mr. Hassan of your intentions?" Mohammed asked.

"We meant for it to be a surprise," Hokee replied. "Ahmad was so gracious with his hospitality to me when we last visited; I wanted to do something for him."

Hokee hoped these officious people would not call Ahmad to question his statements. On the contrary, he counted on his familiarity with the vital contractor to persuade them to let them go free. But it doesn't hurt to be sure, "I hope you don't feel the need to call him and spoil our surprise."

Now that it appeared the Egyptian officials were holding friends of Egypt's most famous contractor hostage in a holding cell, the two officials couldn't have been more courteous.

"Oh, we don't have to bother the man," Aria said, looking at her partner for confirmation. "Let us help you get through customs and find some transportation."

Glory, who surprisingly had not said a word, couldn't help but give Hokee a big grin while squeezing his hand, "Not too bad, Tonto," she whispered so the agents couldn't hear. Then, the officials escorted the two former prisoners who held hands out of the airport into a waiting limousine.

Fortunately, their driver could speak English, so Hokee asked him if he knew where Ahmad Hassan lived?

"Most assuredly yes, Mr. Sir," the driver responded.

"Could you drive by his residence so we might look at it?" Hokee asked.

"We don't want to stop and bother the busy man," added Glory. "We just want to view his beautiful home."

"Yes, missy. Very wonderful home."

The international airport, handling primarily charter flights, was six kilometers from downtown Luxor and another two miles to Ahmad's palace by the Nile. Situated on the river bank about 80 feet above the river, the palace looked like the same men who designed the Taj Mahal in India designed it. Fashioned out of white marble with a blue tile roof, the building was impressive by any standards. They had their driver stop ostensibly to take pictures, but primarily to give Hokee a chance to study the layout. Ahmad's property appeared to run all the way down the river bank to the water.

Satisfied they had seen all they could view from the road, Hokee had their driver take them to the Al Moudira Hotel, one of Egypt's most refined. Then, using more of the money taken from Ahmad's hired killers, Hokee splurged on a luxury suite, a room you have to see to believe. Guests could be so pampered. It impressed even the New Yorker.

"Maybe we should move your business here to Luxor, Hokee," Glory teased as she changed, dumping her clothes for one of the hotel's soft cotton robes.

"My poor detective business couldn't afford this place, Glory. I'd have to put you out on the street. I hear they favor blonds in this country."

Hokee had to duck the hairbrush Glory flung in his direction. "Just remember, wise guy, I brought my gun along, and I hear it is legal to shoot pimps *in this country*."

"Okay, Okay. Truce. I hope you can help me figure out how to get close to Ahmad now that we've seen his fortress. Any ideas?"

"Maybe, but you have to buy this girl a drink to loosen her up if you expect a reasonable answer."

"Well, they have one hell of a mini-bar here; what's your pleasure?"

What Hokee and Glory didn't know was that the hotel had a secret arrangement with Mr. Hassan. Whenever a distinguished guest showed up, the hotel notified Ahmad. They did so because much of the hotel business was catering to guests of the great contractor.

The hotel staff told the manager about this strange dark Indian and his beautiful blond companion. After reading the names from the hotel guest list, the manager called the Rain Man, Hassan himself, to inform him that Mr. Hokee Wolf and Gloria Bingham stayed at his hotel.

Thanking the manager and promising him a case of his favorite champagne, Ahmad ended the call. Now all he had to do was get someone to kill that bastard, Hokee Wolf. He missed ole Wahid, the knifeman, but perhaps he could find someone even better qualified.

CHAPTER FIFTY

Killing Hokee

While relaxing in their room, Hokee called Curly to ask him to drive out and check on Shila. They expected to be back before the wolf ran out of rabbits to chase, but Hokee never liked to take a chance with his brother. As she listened to Hokee on the telephone with Curly talking about Shila and the power of her scenting abilities, Glory remembered learning Shila was the Navajo word for brother. And she remembered wondering how Hokee got his last name, Wolf. Did he get it from Shila and is there something relating man and wolf in some blood sense?

Even now, she had to wonder as Hokee sat there talking about scents. Hokee sat in a chair with his long black hair hanging down to his shoulders and a blue headband holding it from his face. His brooding, dark eyes reminded her of Shila. But, na, that is silly. There was no way the wolf and Wolf shared the same blood, even if they had the same name. Although watching him in her mind's eyes tromp around the bread truck robbery site in his moccasins, he seemed half animal.

What could she be thinking? Although, damn, at times, Hokee seemed more wolf than man. She remembered hearing a story a long time ago about some wolf raising a child as her own pup. Did a she-wolf raise her lover?

Later, he and Glory walked around the swimming pool to the dining room for an authentic Egyptian dinner. Dinner was almost over, and the couple sat eating baklava for dessert and drinking Turkish coffee when the alarm bell sounded.

Their servers vanished. Two had been young men dressed in colorful clothes similar to the Three Musketeers with their baggy silk pants and high topped polished black boots. One minute they hovered around the periphery of the room, waiting to be summoned or watching to see if someone needed something, then they disappeared. Suddenly. Too suddenly for Hokee to ignore.

Attuned to his surroundings, Hokee noticed the two boys leave the room as though summoned. Suspecting something was about to happen, he stood up, telling Glory to get up with him and leave. *Now*! But, instead of going out the front as expected, he took Glory's hand, leading her into the alcove where the servers vanished.

This nook was an archway with heavy red velvet drapes hanging from the top of the arch and fastened at the sides with a sash. The drapes were perfect for hiding behind while watching to see what transpired. They barely got themselves concealed when three men rushed into the room seconds later, waving pistols, shouting, "Where's the Indian and his white bitch?"

Glory could feel Hokee trembling as he fought the urge to step out and blow away all three gunmen. He had his Colt 45 in his hand, held down by his pant leg, and knew he could kill all three men with ease. But then what? This was Egypt. They were staying here at this hotel. The hotel knew their names. There was no place to hide from the police who were sure to be called, and if Ahmad had police connections, and you could bet he did, then the law would only cause them more problems. So they remained hidden, peeking out to see what the assassins were doing.

Three short, powerfully built men in baggy white clothes ran around the room, waving their guns and shouting. While the three men were chasing around, Hokee wondered, '*What is it with Ahmad and the number three? Always three killers. Is that some Egyptian thing or just Ahmad using numerology and being careful?*'

The other guests, who must have observed Hokee and Glory's dash to the arch, remained mute, afraid to say anything. Then, thinking their query must have run out the back, all three men went chasing through the kitchen. Using the reprieve, Hokee grabbed Glory and hustled out the front. They had nothing worth going back to the room for, so they jumped into a cab with instructions to hurry, hoping the cabbie understood English.

It didn't take many brains to figure out how the killers knew where to find them. Hokee figured that stiffing the hotel out of a meal barely made up for the hotel's treachery. The question now became, where to go, and what to do with their cab driver? Wherever he dropped them off, he would undoubtedly report to somebody who would tell Ahmad and his killers. Asking in English, Hokee asked their driver to take them to someplace he could rent a car. Fortunately, like most cabbies, he had picked up enough foreign language to understand the request. Nodding his head in assent, the driver sped down the highway.

So okay, Hokee reasoned, Ahmad knew they were in town and could guess why they were here. Hokee had not expected this to be easy, and this setback didn't come as a complete surprise. They were on Ahmad's home court. He probably owned most of the town, including the police. To kill or permanently disable the bastard so he would no longer be a threat was going to be difficult.

For now, they needed to find someplace where they could rest and make plans. Hokee didn't enjoy having Glory with him at times like these. He operated alone better when he didn't have to divide his concentration. He worried she would get killed. Alone, he could disappear. But Hokee knew he had to deal with reality. She was here, and she was his responsibility. Sure, she was capable, intelligent, and a warrior, but Hokee found it better to be alone when you were in the killing field.

Two hours later, they found a quiet little hotel in Nagaa Al Uwaydat, twenty-five miles upriver from Luxor. The fugitives didn't believe Ahmad's influence reached this far, not that someone who spotted them wouldn't turn them in if they knew Ahmad wanted them. They registered under false names, claiming that their luggage and their passports got lost by the airline. They always carried their passports on their physical body when in a foreign country. But fortunately, their hotel, the Anakato II, wasn't in the top tier and allowed them to register with no identification. This hotel was not a place that would be familiar to Ahmad. Still, they both went to bed with their pistols close by on the nightstand.

One thing that always fascinated Hokee was the scents you got from different people and different countries. Any dog could tell you, if they spoke English, that every human carries a unique scent. Likewise, every culture has its distinctive smell. Our diets seep into the pores of our skin. Hokee could remember studying with some Chinese students when he was in college, and they told him that every American carried a foul odor that almost made them sick. They attributed the smell to the American's diet of meat while China's primary dish was rice. Even in America, New York smells different from Atlanta and San

Francisco. Regional diets vary along with local industries, giving each area its unique scent.

Lying in the hotel bed with Glory, Hokee was restless. He knew Ahmad would not stop hunting him unless he stopped Ahmad. Remembering his discussion with the Chinese students from long ago, Hokee recalled the scents in the hotel dining room when the three killers rushed in the room shouting. The smell of fear, sweat, and foul body odor overcame the pleasant aroma of Egyptian spices, cumin, coriander, and bay leaf. At the time, Hokee was too concerned about being spotted to think about the scents, but now he wondered if he could somehow use that information.

The sense of smell lays dormant in modern humans. It no longer serves as a warning or helps us find food. Sure, women wear expensive perfumes to attract the male species, and if you pass someone on the street with an awful body odor, you notice the scent. But mostly, today, we humans ignore this vital sense that helped keep our ancient cave-dwelling ancestors alive.

Was there some way to use this information against Ahmad and his killers? They would rely on their eyes and ears to search for Hokee. One of the earliest lessons Way ay' looh had taught his young apprentice was to use his nostrils. The final test was for Hokee to find some field mice's home using only his sense of smell. For the test, Hokee wore a blindfold and had to stand upright. His mentor took him to a large field and instructed Hokee to find a mouse's nest. It took many tries and almost two years, but ultimately Hokee passed the test. It had been a long time since that training, but maybe he could focus his mind and recapture some of that training.

In thinking about it, Hokee realized that as he and Glory had walked the streets, he was aware of the different body scents they passed, but it was subtle, riding just below his other conscious senses. Now he thought this might be a way to defeat Ahmad. He would use his extra senses.

CHAPTER FIFTY-ONE

Stalking

Upon arising the following day and breakfasting in their room, Hokee and Glory discussed their problems. Ahmad would have his minions; however many, be on the lookout for a giant mixed-race native American with a pretty blond lady companion. To navigate around the area, and Luxor in particular, they needed to change their looks. Using cabs or limousines was likewise out of the question. Hell, for all they knew, Ahmad owned the damn companies, anyway.

Penetrating the Hassan palace would not be easy, and they could think of no subterfuge to get Ahmad to leave his home. They had to get past whatever guards Ahmad might keep around his palace, find the bastard, and render him impotent, even if it meant killing the corrupt contractor.

The pair left the hotel by a rear door to avoid being seen by anyone working the desk or reception area. Then they drove around Nagaa Al Uwaydat looking for a costume shop, a theatrical supply business, or a place selling women's wigs. Unable to speak modern standard Arabic, which is the most prevalent language in Egypt, they had to constrain themselves to look in windows hoping to see something of interest.

Colonization of Egypt resulted in the elite and affluent speaking English, so Hokee kept his eyes roaming around looking for a wealthy merchant out on the street. Driving by a jewelry store, Glory spotted a man she thought might be the owner. Indeed, from his clothes and the way he carried himself, he was an elite. Jabbing Hokee in the side to get his attention, Glory pointed out the man she had spotted. Hokee pulled to the side of the road and got out of the car, hurrying to catch up with the man. There was a risk the man had ties to Hassan industries, but being in a different town made this seem unlikely; at least it was worth the risk.

"Good afternoon sir, do you speak English?" Hokee asked, catching up with the man.

"Well, yes, I do. How can I assist you?" Very formal and stiff. One of the privileged.

"Some dear friends invited my wife and me to a birthday party, and we need to find a costume shop or perhaps a theatrical supply company. I noticed that you have several lovely theaters in your town." It never hurts to try a little flattery when asking for help.

"You are in luck. Not 30 kilometers from here is the Luxor Bazaar in central Luxor. There you can find everything you may desire." The elite-looking man delivered the information like a master informing the servants where to find the trash basket for emptying.

Hokee thanked the proper man, and getting back into their rental, Hokee told Glory what he had learned as they discussed their plans while driving back to Luxor.

"We need to cover your head and find something for you to wear. I can't go into the bazaar without a costume. So let's fix you up to do some shopping for us."

Forty-five minutes later, Hokee parked their rental one block from the Luxor Bazaar. Hokee tore up his shirt to make a headscarf for Glory's blond hair, and Glory used her eyeliner to paint wrinkles on her face, aging her appearance. Then, with last-minute shopping instructions, Glory left to buy clothes, costumes, and toiletries.

Hokee had to stay low in the car to avoid being seen by someone looking for an American Indian, and after an hour, he worried for her safety. It seemed like Glory took too long, and Hokee was about to get out and search when he saw her weaving down the road carrying several packages. He opened the door and helped her get into the car with all the bundles she was carrying.

For Hokee, Glory purchased a long white cotton robe and matching skull cap. Next, she found a theatrical supply vendor and bought Hokee a full-length beard. For herself, she found a long black wig that looked like Elvira's hair in the old television show *The Munsters*. Completing the costume was a pair of wireframe glasses with clear lenses. She had also purchased a change of clothes and toiletries for each of them.

Hokee got out of the car to check himself out in reflections from the car windows after pulling on the robe and wig and clipping the beard over his ears. He also needed to stretch out his legs after being cramped up in the car for an hour. Once Glory had the black wig covering her blond hair, Glory also got out of the car and put on the glasses. After checking each other out, they walked down the street, getting comfortable in their costumes and stretching Hokee's legs.

They walked past a McDonald's, and feeling hungry, they entered and ordered breakfast. It was their thinking that ordering food in a regular restaurant would tip off the employees that they were American. But, despite their costumes, they didn't want to take a chance on being spotted by some of Ahmad's communication networks.

The menu looked similar to what you might see in Pocatello, and the food looked identical. Ordering was simple as most menu items were pronounced the same, making it possible to order without seeming strange. The flavor was also similar, but slanted towards the Egyptian diet. It might have been the grease or perhaps the catsup, but it was tasty and filled the holes in their stomachs.

Between Ahmad's palace and the Nile river, a walkway led to a small park a block away. Parking downriver from Ahmad's place, Hokee and Glory walked along the river's edge, passing Ahmad's without gawking at the magnificent structure. Then, using only his peripheral vision, Hokee determined that Ahmad's office was here on the river's side of the palace so the master could see the water and boats passing while giving instructions to his far-flung empire. Ahmad probably spent most of his time in the office, but how would they get inside?

As they walked, Hokee concentrated on the scents in the air. Here, the river dominated the nasal sense; its musky odor colored everything within several hundred yards. The river barges and boats lent their aromas to the mix with diesel, gasoline, and exhaust fumes. By concentrating, Hokee could also smell the birds, those on the river and in the bushes, plus the grass along the walkway.

The pair seemingly wandered aimlessly, with no apparent motive for their actions. Hokee wanted to catalog every scent he could identify before going into Ahmad's palace. All the scents prevalent here would also be inside his home, although not in the same strength. Once inside, he could focus his attention on those odors peculiar to the dwelling and not those coming in from outside.

Satisfied that they had learned all they could from the walk, Hokee led Glory back to their vehicle to begin the wait. Parking in a visitor's lot two blocks from the palace, they had a perfect view of Ahmad's driveway, front door, and servant's entrance. They wanted to get a feel for how many guards Ahmad had stationed inside and outside. They could see two men sitting in the portico's shade, men who periodically wandered around the estate. The men had semi-automatic pistols strapped to their sides, and each carried an AK-47.

The pair of watchers sat for several hours until Hokee decided they needed to eat. They flipped a coin to see who went for food and drinks and who continued with the watch. Hokee lost, meaning he had to walk about a mile back into town to find a food vendor while Glory kept watching.

It was nearly dark when a large SUV drove into the driveway. Eight men got out of the vehicle, stretching and joking about their cushy jobs. The men appeared to be well trained. They carried themselves with pride and purpose. They were all armed precisely like the two guards doing outside duty. The two outside men got into the SUV as two newcomers took their place. The other six went inside and disappeared. A few minutes later, the six men they replaced came stomping out of the palace, getting into the SUV, which they then drove away.

Knowing the makeup of Ahmad's guards, Hokee and Glory needed a plan for getting inside. It was getting dark, and the pair needed to find a place to eat dinner and stay for the night while making plans for tomorrow. Staying in Luxor was probably not possible. Ahmad was sure to have the local hotels all call him about any recent check-ins.

They drove back to Nagaa Al Uwaydat, but a different hotel. Hokee didn't want the desk clerk to see last night's guests dressed like an "imam" and his partner. With little difficulty, they found suitable lodging with an excellent restaurant next door. Satiated, the pair went to bed, hoping to live through tomorrow.

Chapter Fifty-Two

Getting Inside

Ahmad knew Hokee was in Luxor, or at least somewhere nearby. His spies in Luxor were silent, yet he assumed his enemy was close. In retrospect, sending his killers to America had been a mistake. Used to having everything his own way, Ahmad could not let go of the fact that Hokee had made him dole out one hundred million dollars to that upstart Olson. This payoff wasn't the first time his ego had gotten him in trouble, but this time it might cost him more than he wanted to pay. He had guards outside patrolling around the palace and six more inside. Not even a damned American half-breed could get to him here. Yet, he sat in his office sweating, fearing every time he heard an unfamiliar sound that the Indian bastard had somehow crept inside.

Hokee had Glory take him to the Luxor Bazaar, where she had purchased their clothes yesterday. They wandered the streets until Hokee found the merchant's stall he was seeking. What looked like an old-time apothecary in America was tucked in between a stall selling Hookah pipes on one side and another selling hand-knit Berber rugs on the other.

The stall was tiny, six feet wide, and eight feet deep, yet they jammed its shelves full from the floor up to seven feet high. The shelves held bottles, bags, small jars of ointments, and wrapped bundles of herbs. Hokee couldn't read the labels, but he knew what he was seeking.

The proprietor sat in a corner on a high stool, watching the strange big dark man with a fake beard examine the offerings on each shelf. The man would smell the herb or ointment, then put it back on the shelf. Occasionally he would take a tiny piece on his tongue to taste. Finally, after what seemed like an hour but was only about ten minutes, the big man selected a jar from one of the top shelves and two bundles of herbs he found tucked back into a dark corner. These herbs were exceptional, meant only for a medicine man or medical professional, and the proprietor kept them isolated in a deep, dark corner for a reason.

The proprietor hoped the big man knew what he was doing. The top shelf from which he selected his jar held exceptionally potent herbs and concoctions. And only the wisest of all sages used the small bundles the man plucked from the dark corner. But then the man overpaid, the stupid foreigner. If he killed himself, it wouldn't be the shop owner's fault.

On the other side of the rug shop was a stall selling bamboo products. There were window shades, rugs, tables, chairs, cabinets, and plain bamboo poles of every thickness and length. Hokee bought a hollow bamboo stick about four feet long and three-quarters of an inch thick. Moving on down the row of stalls, they found a lady who had set up in an alley a small table covered with homemade jewelry. Hokee selected a pair of pierced earrings with feathers dangling from a silver chain.

On the way back to the car was a stall selling finished model airplanes and boats, plus the kits to make your own. Here Hokee purchased a tube of airplane glue.

Glory had been silent the entire time Hokee had been searching stalls for the supplies he purchased. But finally, with the earrings and glue, her patience wore thin.

"Hokee, what in the hell are you doing? Woman's earrings and airplane glue, for God's sake."

Putting his big arm around her shoulders and hugging her, he said, "Ah, honey, I'd tell you, but then I'd have to let you help me, and you know I'm a do-it-yourself kind of guy."

Glory jabbed him in the side with her elbow, "Ah hell, honey; I just wanted to help a little," she kidded with a smile. "What are you going to do with those supplies, anyway?"

"Let's get back to the car, and you can help me," he replied. Hokee stopped several times to pick up sticks on the way back, throwing most away but keeping those he found useful.

He pulled the earrings from their package and handed them to Glory. "Use that emery board you bought for your nails and sharpen the points on these earrings, please," he asked, giving her the feathered beauties. "Oh, and use this knife to cut off the feathers," he added, handing her a pocket knife. "Be careful not to damage the feathers. We'll use them later."

While Glory was busy sharpening points on the earrings, Hokee carefully set the apothecary jar on the floor of their rental between his feet. Then, using a stick he picked up, Hokee began mixing his packaged herbs with the jar of potions. Telling Glory to remain extremely quiet, Hokee closed his eyes and went into what Glory would call a trance.

After a few minutes, Hokee opened his eyes and told Glory that this was a meditation method he sometimes used when a sweat lodge was unavailable. Over the next several minutes, he repeated this procedure many times. Hokee would mix herbs into the potion jar, then go into his meditation. He would mix, then meditate. Mix, then meditate. Finally, he pronounced the mixing completed. Careful to screw the lid on the jar, touching none of the contents, Hokee told Glory that whatever she did, she could not handle the jar or the stick he had used to stir the contents.

With that chore completed, Hokee took the earrings from Glory. Then, lying the earrings on some cardboard from their earlier purchases, he used the Swiss knife to cut off the stems from the glass bowl to which they were originally attached.

Taking more of the sticks he had picked up, Hokee selected two, which he fashioned into matchsticks about an inch long. Then, giving Glory the airplane glue, he had her squeeze a drop onto the end of each stick while he stuck the blunt end of the earring stud onto the match stick, holding it for a few seconds allowing the glue to dry. In a couple of minutes, they had two miniature spears.

Using the Swiss Army knife's scissors, Hokee cut fletchers from the earring feathers for his miniature darts. Then, with Glory holding the small wooden shaft, Hokee carefully attached the fletching at an angle like the feathers on an arrow. They now had two tiny darts. Next came the hard part.

Driving back to the river, they went towards Ahmad's palace. By now, it was midafternoon, and a bright hot sun fired up the river in a silver glow. The river traffic was heavy with barges, pleasure boats, fishing boats, and tourists on water skies. A 75-foot yacht was tied to a boat deck on the river below the palace. The craft had not been there yesterday, and Hokee worried maybe Ahmad was on the boat, but then as they drove past, they could see no guards. If that were his yacht, it was unlikely that Ahmad would be on board without guards. Looking back at the palace, they could see one of the roving guards walk past the windows to Ahmad's office. Hokee's plan was still in place.

They parked on the street down a few hundred yards from the palace while they finished getting ready. Deciding not to take any chances, Hokee drove away and went back to the bazaar, instructing Glory to please buy a pair of rubber gloves. He was reluctant to experiment with his concoction without some protection.

Going back to the street where he had parked earlier, Hokee put on the gloves Glory found, then reached for his homemade poison. Setting the jar on the console between the seats, Hokee removed the lid, then took the darts from Glory she had been holding in her palm. He dipped the point of both darts into the mixture, thoroughly coating the shafts and ends, then laid the darts on a piece of paper to dry.

Hokee carefully put away the jar of poison while waiting for his darts to dry.

Making a tube out of the cardboard, Hokee used the airplane glue to hold it in shape like a small toilet paper roll. He then stuck the two darts into the tube so that their points were inside the tube, which he placed into cutouts he previously made in the Koran. He figured disfiguring their holy bible was in keeping with his disdain for Ahmad's religious practices. However, knowing how some people might take great offense to the defacing of a sacred book, Hokee had been careful to cut the tube slot for the darts in the margin, safely away from any holy words.

His long white robe made hiding his Colt 45 impossible, so he had Glory put it in her purse.

In keeping with their religious theme, Glory was also wearing a white robe and carrying their copy of the Koran in one hand and her bag in the other. Then, getting out of the car, they walked to Ahmad's palace, side by side, Hokee carrying his bamboo shaft like a walking stick.

Hokee and Glory took the long way around the palace, watching for the guards. Finally, they entered the yard from the backside where the servants entered, keeping an eye out for the guards and being careful to avoid any windows from which someone might notice them.

They stopped in an alcove by an arched doorway leading to the kitchen, waiting for a guard to appear. Now Hokee had Glory open the Koran in which he had cut the slot to hold the tube of poisoned darts.

Being very careful, Hokee slipped a dart into one end of the bamboo rod. Within seconds, a guard came around the building, walking towards the pair standing in the doorway.

The guard looked like a seasoned veteran, not one of the young, arrogant kids they might easily fool. Seeing what appeared to be a religious cleric and his companion, the guard relaxed and approached the pair with a smile. Hokee swung the bamboo rod around when the guard was within ten feet and, putting it to his lips, blew the dart into the guard's neck. The guard jumped back, grabbing for the dart, but before he could remove it, he dropped to the ground without moving.

Quickly, lying down his bamboo rod, Hokee dragged the unconscious guard into the doorway where he was not visible unless someone was very close to the door. He removed the dart, replacing it in the cardboard tube. So later, it would be challenging to determine what caused the man to be unconscious.

They then waited for the other guard to come around the building. The second guard came around the palace from the opposite corner, heading towards Hokee and Glory, standing in the doorway. Like the first guard seeing a holy man, he relaxed and smiled while Hokee put him to sleep. Then they repeated the moves made earlier with the first guard. They hid him in the same alcove and removed the dart from his neck.

Speaking in a whisper, Glory asked, "Did you kill them?"

Whispering back, Hokee replied, "I don't know. I hope not, but this isn't an exact science. I only wanted to make them unconscious for a few hours, but there was no way to test the efficacy. So now, you know what to do when we get inside, right?"

"Yes, darling. Don't worry," she whispered with a smile in her eyes.

Picking up the two AK-47s from the downed guards and giving one to Glory, Hokee marched around the palace towards the river and Ahmad's office with Glory in tow. With any luck, the big man would be there, just inside the office window at his desk, watching the world float by on his river. With even more luck, Ahmad would not have bulletproof windows in his office.

Halting his march just around the corner away from the windows, Hokee poked his head around to view the situation. There was no one on this side of the palace, and the way looked clear. The first big window was five feet from the corner. With a quick look at the office from yesterday's river walk, Hokee figured Ahmad's desk to be more in the middle of the room behind the second large window. Signaling Glory to be ready, Hokee quickly stepped around the corner and, in two steps, swung an AK-47 into the window with all of his might. The resounding crash was music to their ears.

Seeing no glass to impede his entrance into the room, Hokee immediately stepped into Ahmad's office with a stern, loud command to the fat man behind the desk, "Put your hands into the air immediately." He then stepped aside for Glory to enter the room.

The loud crash as the window broke brought the inside guards running towards Ahmad's office. As the first guard came rushing into the office, Hokee sprayed the air above his head with bullets from the automatic rifle, driving the guards back outside. Then, asking Glory to be on the alert for a guard trying to sneak into Ahmad's office from outside through the broken window, Hokee instructed Ahmad to tell his guards to stay away. Tell them if they entered the room, I will kill you immediately.

"Glory, close the door and guard it while I talk with Mr. Hassan."

Hassan sat with his hands high above his head, shaking like a bobblehead doll on a washboard road. Dressed in a long blue satin robe, Ahmad looked like he was one of those Jack-in-the-Box jumping jacks from kids' toys that popped up from a wind-up box.

"Ahmad, if you signaled the police with some silent alarm, I will kill you when the first car arrives. Did you send for the police?"

Shaking in fear with an ashen face, Ahmad said, "No, no. I swear. No police. Are you going to kill me?"

Hokee kicked one of the side chairs around, so there was no desk between him and Ahmad; then, sitting down, he instructed Ahmad, "Call your guards to enter the room one at a time, holding their guns above their heads. First, they are to lay their guns on the floor by Glory; then, they are to lie down on their stomachs with their arms held above their heads. After the first one complies, we will call for the next one. Do it now."

In a loud quivering voice, Ahmad did as instructed. As the guards entered one by one, all six dropped their rifles on the floor by Glory, then found a place to lie down with their arms straight above their heads.

"Glory, move the guns over into the corner, then stand guard. If one of them twitches, kill Ahmad."

Confused, Glory asked, "But you're watching Ahmad. So why don't I shoot the guards?"

"Because Mr. Ahmad is a tad too clever, and I need to find out what he is up to before we can continue."

"Ahmad, stand up and hold your hands above your head, and don't move unless I ask you to move. Do it now."

"Why don't you kill me and get it over with infidel? You're nothing but a piece of American garbage." Ahmad followed Hokee's instructions, but he was still running his mouth.

"Quiet, let me think. There's something a little off here, Glory. Give me a minute to figure out what we are missing. Then, while you are keeping everyone covered with your gun, I need to close my eyes for a little while."

Hokee shoved his chair a couple of feet away, then sat in quiet contemplation for a couple of minutes.

"Okay, Glory. We have a problem, but I think I can fix it. We may have to kill this toad and his little private army. Give me another minute."

CHAPTER FIFTY-THREE

The Surprise

Hokee sat unmoving with his eyes closed in Ahmad's office for several minutes. Glory was getting concerned, as he hadn't moved in all that time. Ahmad had a beautiful antique grandfather clock standing against one wall that monotonously banged out each minute with a bit of a twang, like hitting a symphony symbol with a hammer. Glory was getting antsy, and the clock rubbed against her nerves. She was about to say something when Hokee opened his eyes and spoke to Ahmad.

"Call in the woman Ahmad, or I'll start putting bullets in your body one leg at a time."

"I don't know what you're ta... **BANG.**"

Hokee's Colt 45 made one hell of a racket, followed instantly by a scream from Ahmad.

"Oh, you fucker. You absolute bastard. You shot me in the leg. Call a doctor."

"Glory, do not let anyone into this room and keep the shooters on the floor."

Hokee walked over to the squirming Ahmad, who had both hands wrapped around his leg with blood oozing out between his fingers. "Call in the woman Ahmad, or I'll put the next one in your other leg."

"No, don't you halfbreed bastard, don't shoot. I can't call her in. That is one of our safety protocols. We pay her not to come into this room when there are hostile people inside. So no matter what I say, she will not enter this room."

238

"Well, Ahmad, you better hope she disobeys your commands because unless she is inside of this room in thirty seconds, you will lose your other leg at the hip. If she still doesn't come in after that, I'll start with your arms."

"Okay! Okay! I need to use the intercom. She may not hear me if I yell." He seemed sincere, so Hokee went over to the men lying on the floor and, picking on one, turned him over on his back. "Keep your hands above your head."

"Now!"

Hokee barked. With the man suitably chastised, Hokee kneeled and pulled off the man's belt, which he took over to Ahmad.

"Tie this around your leg to staunch the flow of blood. Then call in your woman."

If Glory had questions about Hokee's behavior, she kept them to herself. Hokee figured she must wonder about this woman. How did Hokee know about her? It would have served him well if he had taken the time to help her see the scene a little better.

With his leg in a makeshift tourniquet, Ahmad got on his speakerphone. "Faaria, come in here, please. The man knows you are out there and has promised to do nasty things unless you come here now. Please." To Hokee, "Give her a minute; she may be on the other side of the palace."

A few seconds there was a knock on the door.

"Come in, please, Faaria. Don't shoot. Just give your gun to the lady here in my office."

The door swung open, revealing a tall, beautiful Egyptian woman with long black hair. She looked like a young Sophia Loren, with all the statuesque curves and a glorious smile. She wore a floor-long Hawaiian-style mumu with bright colors featuring the bird of paradise plant. She stood with her legs slightly parted, holding out a little snub-nosed Smith and Wesson 9mm for Glory to take. But before Glory could get the gun, the folds between the girl's legs parted, and a gun appeared, which immediately fired a bullet into Hokee Wolf.

Hokee caught the sight of the gun out of the corner of his eyes just as the weapon came into view from between Faaria's legs. Turning, he caught the bullet in his right shoulder instead of his heart. When the gun went off, Glory reacted by shooting Faaria, and as she fell, exposing the second girl lying on the floor with a smoking gun in her hand, Glory shot her as well.

Ahmad moved when Hokee got shot, but as Hokee turned, he slammed his pistol into Ahmad's face, starting a gusher as his nose splintered. Ahmad howled with pain, swearing at Hokee as Glory rushed over to check on her wounded companion. Instead, Hokee told her to go back and guard the men lying on the floor and make sure she got both of the girl's guns.

Pulling his chair back with a foot, Hokee fell into it with a thud, facing Ahmad.

"You know, Hassan, if you would have just stayed on your side of the pond and not sent a bunch of killers after me, none of this would have been necessary. However, I obviously cannot allow you to repeat yourself, so you force me to put you out of business."

Although in obvious pain, Ahmad could not help but scoff. "You? How are *you* going to put me out of business? You're nothing but a fucking half-breed infidel from Idaho. You can't do shit here in Egypt without my knowledge and approval."

"Well," Hokee said in response, "we're doing pretty good in the shitting department so far. We breached your castle, removed your guards, and shot your insurance."

"Glory, I am going to need some help to staunch the blood flow to my shoulder, so we need to make sure we immobilize these men. There's a bar over against the back wall with some towels. Rip some towels and tie the men's legs together, then their arms, keeping them straight out on the floor."

Hokee watched as Glory tied up all six men. The bullet was still inside of his shoulder, but they didn't believe it hit any bones, although Hokee didn't move his arm enough to scrutinize it. Instead, he had Glory give him a towel to soak up the blood while putting pressure on the wound to staunch the blood flow. Then when she finished tying up the guards, he had her come over and help with his jacket.

Hokee grabbed Ahmad's ledger from his desk and, thumbing through it for a minute, found the number he wanted. Then, pulling over the telephone, he placed a call to London.

"Greetings. Archibald McKenzie here."

"Mr. McKenzie. My name is Zahur Fahmy. I'm calling from Egypt with some unpleasant news, I'm afraid. You have a contract with Hassan Construction for your new airport. Unfortunately, Mr. Hassan has had a terrible accident and can no longer manage his company. Under the circumstances, we are in no position to continue with your project and will have to default on our contract."

Ahmad listened to the call, but before he could complain, Hokee had already issued the sentence.

After listening to the phone for a second, Hokee continued, "Yes, I know it's a terrible inconvenience. I'm going to be calling our on-site managers to give them the news, but I wanted you to be the first one to know."

And after another pause, "Yes, yes, I'll let him know. I must go now and make some other calls. We are sorry for the inconvenience. Several quality, world-class contractors could come in and finish the job for you.

"No, no. Mr. Ahmad is expected to make a full recovery, but not for a long time, and unfortunately, our contracting days are over. Well, so long."

Using Ahmad's directory, Hokee called Ahmad's man in London, the one heading up the airport construction project, giving him the same sad news before telling him to pull the men out of London. They had ended the airport contract.

With Ahmad listening, Hokee repeated the calls to India, canceling the dam and Japan, canceling the nuclear reactor.

There were another dozen small jobs on the ledger, but none of them caught Hokee's eye as worth the trouble to bother canceling. What he needed was to put a severe hole in Ahmad's finances. Hokee found it hard to concentrate with a throbbing shoulder, but he wanted to finish the days this sucker Ahmad ruled the universe once and for all. He just needed a little more time.

Ahmad's banking arrangements were also in the ledger. After searching for a few minutes, Hokee found what he was looking for.

Since the London stock exchange was open, Hokee called Warren, his investment broker in Pocatello. "Warren, I have here the banking information for Hassan Construction. I'm going to give you all the information I have. I want you to buy every single Hassan Construction stock share you can find using Ahmad's money. The company has excellent financials. Borrow all the company's money the banks and brokers will allow you to spend to buy as many shares as possible. Thanks, Warren. Send the final tally to this email address." He then read off Ahmad's email address.

"Oh, you bastard," Ahmad wailed. "You fucking bastard. You've ruined me. My stock will plummet, and I'll be broke and in debt, and I won't be able to bid on another contract."

Ahmad seemed ready to cry, and not just from a broken nose and a bullet in his leg.

"Sorry about the girls, Ahmad. You shouldn't have tried to pull a ringer on me. Put your wives to work. You probably need to sell this dump, but it's got a busted window, and anyway, there's blood all over the place."

"Are we finished here, Hokee?" Glory asked, almost as much in shock as Ahmad and eager to leave.

"We can't leave those rifles sitting over there. Once these guys on the floor get loose, they are going to be mad as Hades. Empty the magazines and make sure there are no shells in the chamber. Then smash the guns against the door frame, breaking them up."

After she finished, Hokee stood up. Then, reaching over, he pulled the phone cord from the wall so Ahmad could not place a call. Weaving a little, he let Glory help him walk over to the window they had entered what seemed like hours ago, but was less than sixty minutes. They made it back to their rental car before Hokee collapsed in the passenger's seat.

"Get us out of here, Glory. We need to find a place to hole up."

CHAPTER FIFTY-FOUR

Peace

Glory drove out of Luxor towards Nagaa Al Uwaydat, where they had been staying, looking for something that looked like a doctor's office or a drugstore. They didn't think Hassan or the people in the palace knew what kind of car they were driving, so Glory wasn't worried about being pulled over, but she worried about Hokee; he looked pale and weak.

"What are we going to do, Hokee? We need a doctor."

"Our best hope is to drive to Aswan; it's about 80 miles south. We're going in the right direction, but I'm not sure about the road. We need a map. Let me look in the glove box. Sometimes these rentals have a cheap map."

Sure enough, there was a rental car map with just enough information for Glory to navigate her way to Aswan. The road hugged the river Nile for most of the way, so she should be good to drive without too many problems.

"Okay, Mr. Wolf, we have about an hour's drive, and I want some answers. How in the hell did you know there were some women shooters?"

"I didn't. At least not at first. Yesterday when we saw the changing of the guard, we saw eight guys, right? Then, a few minutes later, this statuesque woman with long black hair came out of the palace and spent a few seconds talking with the guards who were going off duty. I thought it strange but didn't give it much thought at the time."

After a few seconds, Glory responded, "I didn't see the girl until today, just before I shot her."

"Yeah, it happened sort of casually yesterday. It wasn't a big deal, and I only noticed it because of the woman's unique build. She was quite tall."

"Okay, but today, you seemed so sure there was a woman shooter. How did you know?"

"Well, Glory. I want to tell you, but then I ... ah, don't hit me like that. It jolts my shoulder."

"Then stop screwing around and answer my question."

"You're sure cute when you get angry."

"Unless you want me to slug your sore shoulder, honey, you better start talking."

"It was the way Ahmad smelled. He acted all scared when we broke in and then had him call the guards, but he didn't smell like fear."

"You know what fear smells like?"

"Sure, we all do. It's just that modern man hasn't needed the sense of smell to survive, so we have let that sense atrophy, mostly."

"So how did you smell his fear or lack thereof?"

"I had a hunch about scents the other day, so I started focusing on what I could smell throughout the day. As we use our senses, they become stronger. Then I meditated on scents, trying to get my senses as sensitive as possible. We live in a world where we smell the cooking in restaurants or the perfume some old lady slathers on, like putting mayonnaise on a BLT. We seldom tune into the subtle scents, say, in a forest. Scents like the decaying leaves underfoot, the smell of moss on a tree, or the smell of a rabbit hiding under a bush."

"You can really smell a rabbit in a bush?"

"Sure, how do you think Shila finds most of his food. I know; I'm no wolf. Well, maybe just a little," Hokee had to smile despite his pain, "But if you try, you find that furry scent mixed in with all the rest of the smells in the forest. The trick is to learn to separate the scents, just like you do with sounds. Now, there can be many sounds, but a mother will hear her baby cry over the television, people talking, and the dishwasher banging away."

"So, that was what you were doing when you had us all sitting in silence, and you sat with your eyes closed. You were sorting out scents?" Glory seemed pleased to have figured this out on her own.

"Exactly. That's about it. I knew something was off with the way Ahmad was acting. He just seemed a little too smug, with a gun stuck in his face. Even after we called in and disarmed his guards, he still did not reek of fear. I had to find out why. Finally, in probing his mind, I saw a picture of a woman coming into his office. I focused until I could pick up her scent in the office. It was there but extremely faint, so I knew she had not been there recently. I couldn't get the woman's image out of my mind, and so I kept looking into Ahmad's brain until I saw a picture of her holding a gun. At that point, I felt smug and pleased with myself for scoping out his backup plan. Unfortunately, my hubris inserted itself into the equation, and I only saw the one woman."

They rode in silence for a while before Hokee asked, "Are you okay with killing those women?"

"Not really, but I can't process that right now. We need to get that bullet out of your shoulder before you get blood poisoning."

"Yes. I can tell it's in there pretty deep. Fortunately, she shot me with a smaller caliber gun. I wonder if the shooting in Ahmad's will get reported? If it makes national news, we may not get a doctor to treat me."

"Oh shoot, I hadn't even thought about that," Glory suddenly got even more worried.

"Hassan Construction is, no, cancel that; it was one of the biggest contractors in the world. What happens to an organization like that is sure to make the news." Hokee was thinking out loud. "I guess the question is whether they report me being shot? What does it do to their narrative? How are they going to spin the stories? I shot Ahmad and gave him a busted face. Two of his ladies are dead. Will they spin some story about a big native American and his girlfriend? It would be nice to hear the news."

"Assuming Ahmad does report the shootings to his local police. It will take them some time to respond, gather facts, and decide on a course of action. That could well take several hours before the media gets alerted." Glory was hoping this was the truth as she responded to Hokee's bleak suggestion.

"We need to find some kind of emergency clinic. They must have those here in Egypt. Certainly in a developed city like Aswan." These were Glory's thoughts, talking herself into a better mood.

Hokee was feeling the pain and exercised his mind control to keep the pain in check. Knowing she was right, they would need to find an emergency clinic; he informed Glory about what he knew of Egyptian medicine. "The caduceus is an ancient Egyptian symbol representing balance and strength. They use it throughout Egypt for many religious and meditation practices and the medical profession. We need to look for that symbol beside a door frame or entrance to a building. I think we can tell from the outside if they offer medical help or the spiritual kind."

"How are you doing, Hokee? You will not pass out on me, will you?" She was half-kidding, which she tried to sell with a weak smile, but the concern also came through.

"I'm okay, honey. The shoulder hurts, but nothing that I can't control. I've got the bleeding stopped for now. I won't pass out. This wound is nothing compared to previous experiences. Listen. I have a technique for dealing with pain. It's what I do when I sit in the cold river bed. Briefly, I focus all of my attention on one particular thing, like my breathing. If my focus is intense, I no longer feel my physical body. So if I seem to zone out, I may only be focusing my mind, and I don't want you to panic."

The drive seemed unduly long for both the driver, feeling the tension and her patient struggling with pain. Finally, Aswan outskirts began showing up, and the loading docks along the river near the Aswan dam became more plentiful. There was a lot more river traffic as they neared the dam. Approaching the city, Glory turned off the highway they had been traveling on, onto a road that looked like it went into a business district. Both passenger and driver studied the buildings they passed, looking for a caduceus. Finally, they both spotted the familiar double snake and rod symbol outside a new rock-faced building after driving nearly three miles. There was a convenient parking lot next to the building Glory turned into before shutting off the engine.

"Do you think you can check out their services before I go in, or do I need to go in with you?" Hokee didn't want to expose his gunshot wound to anyone outside of the medical profession, but he didn't want to make Glory feel it was all up to her.

"Listen, lover boy. I'm a highly trained investigative reporter from New York City, the Big Apple. I'm pretty sure I can find out what they do inside of that building."

"Sorry, Glory. You're right. I should have shown more faith in your abilities. It must be the bullet in my shoulder making me senile."

"That's okay, sweetheart. I'll forgive you. I'll see you later," she said as she left the vehicle. Hokee watched her enter the building before losing sight of her inside.

Glory disappeared for about five minutes before returning with a young Egyptian man about thirty-five years old, wearing a white lab coat. The man was slender, with a full beard and smiling black eyes. Glory introduced the man to Hokee as Doctor Salah, who spoke perfect English.

"Miss Bingham informs me you have a bullet in your shoulder which you would like me to remove. Is that correct?"

"Yes, Doctor Salah, if you would be so kind," Hokee responded with a smile.

"I won't ask how you came to be carrying this piece of lead in your body as most people in your circumstance just tell me some wild story, but come on in, and I'll see what we can do for you."

Getting out of the car and walking with Glory and the doctor back to the building, Hokee couldn't help himself, "Doctor, I'll tell you the truth. A beautiful woman shot me."

"No doubt you had it coming," the doctor responded with a smile. "With a pretty lady like this at your side, you shouldn't be fooling around with some other woman, especially if she has a gun."

"Yes, doctor. I've learned my lesson." It seemed best not to say anymore, and besides, they were inside the clinic, and the doctor motioned for Hokee to remove his coat and shirt.

It is customary for foreigners to pay for medical services before receiving attention, and Glory gave the doctor five hundred dollars before Hokee removed his shirt. Then, giving Hokee a local injection to deaden the pain, Doctor Salah had the bullet out, and Hokee patched up in less than thirty minutes.

Doctor Salah gave Hokee a small bottle of pain pills to help in the coming days, plus a bottle of antibiotics with instructions to take all ten pills, one a day, to avoid getting an infection. Glory drove them to a nearby hotel, which turned out to be Sofitel, where they crashed until the following day. After a hearty American breakfast in the main dining room, they found an airport and purchased first-class tickets to Boise, Idaho. They found flights, but there were four plane changes. In twenty-six hours, they would be in Boise and a few hours later at home with Shila, nature's perfect healer.

About the Author

Clark has three previous books of fiction with heroes who challenge the status quo.

As a farm boy from Idaho, where he sets most of his stories, Clark often fought for a place among professional engineers.

Twenty years of black-ops work with the CIA provides the background for his novels.

Note from the Author

Word-of-mouth is crucial for any author to succeed. If you enjoyed *Hokee Wolf II: Satanic Rituals*, please leave a review online—anywhere you are able. Even if it's just a sentence or two. It would make all the difference and would be very much appreciated.

Thanks!
Clark Viehweg

We hope you enjoyed reading this title from:

www.blackrosewriting.com

Subscribe to our mailing list – *The Rosevine* – and receive **FREE** books, daily deals, and stay current with news about upcoming releases and our hottest authors.
Scan the QR code below to sign up.

Already a subscriber? Please accept a sincere thank you for being a fan of Black Rose Writing authors.

View other Black Rose Writing titles at
www.blackrosewriting.com/books and use promo code
PRINT to receive a **20% discount** when purchasing.

www.ingramcontent.com/pod-product-compliance
Lightning Source LLC
Chambersburg PA
CBHW010732100726
47899CB00009B/3017